Praise for the no

"A Perfect Ten! ... Debu with *Falling Star*, a powerful, moving, riveting tale of greed and betrayal, love and self-discovery ... Excellent characterization, great dialogue, and non-stop action make the book almost impossible to put down ... Fast-paced, engaging, witty, and fun to read, *Falling Star* will grab you on the first page and hold you enthralled until the last. I highly recommend this fabulous book!"

– Susan Lantz, *Romance Reviews Today*

"Dishy and fun – in other words, perfect summer fare."

– *Booklist*

"You'll never watch your local TV news program the same way after reading *Falling Star*. Diana Dempsey has poured her experience as a news anchor into a fast-paced novel about television, big business, and the reality of growing old in a youth-obsessed culture. A fun and feisty debut."

– *New York Times* bestselling author Jane Heller

"(In *To Catch the Moon*) Alicia Maldonado, Deputy D.A. of Monterey County, CA, may have landed the case that could make her career: the murder of golden boy Daniel Gaines, who recently announced his candidacy for governor. Tough and self-assured, Alicia is a likable protagonist who achieved success through grit and determination ... Dempsey's low-on-glamour depiction of the D.A.'s office is on the mark, lending much credibility to this suspenseful novel. The romantic sparring between Alicia and Milo sparkles with wit and adds sensuality to this sizzling, tension-filled mystery."

– Romantic Times

"Skillfully plotted and filled with realistic detail ... (*To Catch the Moon*) deftly interweaves romance, murder, and ambition with issues of social status and trust."

– Kristin Ramsdell, Library Journal

"Diana Dempsey creates realistic and memorable characters, complete with flaws, that you can really root for; then she puts them into trouble so terrible you can't figure out how they'll ever triumph ... This is an author to watch."

– Books for a Buck

"Spicy, sexy, and sultry: (in *Too Close to the Sun*) popular Dempsey has another hit on her hands."

– Booklist

"*Too Close to the Sun* is the romance of Gabby and Will, who fall in love almost immediately. Kept apart by their extreme differences, their road is rocky and sometimes seems an impossible journey, but one that comes to a wonderfully satisfying conclusion ... This is a book that will long live in my memory, and it's a story that begs for a sequel, even a series ... *Too Close to the Sun* is an absolute must-buy for everyone, and I highly recommend it."

– Diana Risso, Romance Reviews Today

"How can you not like a character named Happy Pennington, the daughter of a retired cop and the current reigning Ms. America? Well, I liked her! And her sidekicks in crime-solving, fellow beauty queens Shanelle and Trixie, and a hunk named Mario Suave (yes!) and you have a fast-paced, funny, roller coaster ride through Vegas … I love that Ms. Dempsey nails her locations so you really feel as if you're there. When reading *Ms America and the Offing on Oahu*, I was craving a Mai Tai by the beach. In this second installment of the Beauty Queen Mysteries, I wanted an all-night buffet and a glitzy show … The Beauty Queen mysteries are on my must-read list, and I can't wait for the next installment."

– Jacqueline Vick, *A Writer's Jumble*

"*Ms America and the Offing on Oahu* is excellent summer reading material … The plot and characterization are solid, the main character is interesting and witty, and she drops just enough beauty pageant background information to tell the reader that he/she is in good hands … The writing is first class."

– *The Mystery Site*

Available from Diana Dempsey
in print and digital editions

Falling Star

To Catch the Moon

Too Close to the Sun

Chasing Venus

Ms America and the Offing on Oahu

Ms America and the Villainy in Vegas

Ms America and the Mayhem in Miami

Ms America and the Whoopsie in Winona

Ms America and the Brouhaha on Broadway

Ms America and the Naughtiness in New Orleans

A Diva Wears the Ring (novella)

Ring of Truth (featuring the novella *A Diva Wears the Ring*)

Social Media

www.DianaDempsey.com

www.Facebook.com/DianaDempseyBooks

www.Twitter.com/Diana_Dempsey

MS
AMERICA
and the
OFFING
ON OAHU

Diana Dempsey

BRAMERTON
PRESS

Dear Reader,

This is my debut mystery, the first story I ever wrote in first person, and the first book in which I totally let loose with high jinks and zany humor. I don't know if I ever had as much fun writing a book!—and so I am delighted that *Ms America and the Offing on Oahu* launches a series. I hope you enjoy it as much as I do.

Let me thank Rhonda Freshwater of Freshwater Design for her marvelous cover. I love the art Rhonda designed for my women's fiction and she has come through again in creating a unique look for the Beauty Queen Mysteries. Thank you, Rhonda!

I love to hear from readers, so drop me an e-mail at **www.DianaDempsey.com** and be sure to sign up for my mailing list while you're there so you hear first about my new releases. Also join me on **Facebook** at **Diana Dempsey Books** and follow me on **Twitter** at **Diana_Dempsey**.

All best to you! Keep reading.

Diana Dempsey

CHAPTER ONE

I know it's hard to imagine a woman getting offed by a tube of lipstick, but I'm here to tell you, it can be done.

I wouldn't have believed it until the night I saw it myself. It was the same night I won the coveted crown of Ms. America, or should I say, was given the crown, since the woman who was poised to emerge triumphant got iced instead.

Seriously bad luck for her, I won't quibble about that, but it just goes to show that what's unfortunate for one beauty queen can really open up doors for another ...

Don't let me get ahead of myself. Allow me to set the scene.

Oahu. Early September. A balmy evening. (Aren't they all in Honolulu?) The Royal Hibiscus Hotel, an oasis of splendor on an island whose entire land mass is pretty oasis-like as far as this Midwesterner is concerned.

The pageant finale, complete with live audience and television crews beaming the proceedings to millions of homes across the nation. Fifty-one contestants primped, pinned and poured into evening gowns with more sequins per square inch than a *Dancing With the Stars* contender. All of us wearing massive quantities of glittering jewelry, most of it faux, and sashes displaying the names of our home states. Our hair is held in place by so much hairspray that the CFCs we spewed into the atmosphere getting ready probably caused a measurable retrenchment of the ozone layer over the middle Pacific. On a stage as wide as my suburban block back home, we're arrayed on tiers like brides on the wedding cakes we stuffed into our husbands' mouths in years past, since this particular pageant is geared toward married women, who, as we all know, rule.

In another fifteen minutes, though, one of us will rule more than the rest. We're down to the short strokes now, past the parade of states and the swimsuit, talent, and evening gown competitions. We're not far from that exhilarating moment when the host announces the winner.

But before he does, it'll get truly tough. Because a handful of us will be named to the Top Five and they will have to open their mouths to do more than just smile. They'll actually have to *speak*.

The interviews have been known to trip up the best of us.

Host Mario Suave, who is more beautiful than anyone else on stage and knows it, parts his luscious Latin lips. "For the last two weeks, as these stunning ladies have graced this gorgeous island, we here at the Ms. America pageant have been searching for that one special woman who embodies the best qualities of the American wife. Beauty, charm, kindness, poise, and determination!"

Mario pauses to let the crowd holler and clap. He basks in the glow, then waves his buff, tuxedoed arm to indicate us lesser luminaries, trapped on our tiers. "And these ladies behind me have risen to the challenge. Do you know why?" He leans forward and cups his hand to his ear, as if expecting a brilliant answer to burst from the crowd.

"I'll tell you why!" he shouts a second later. He straightens and points his finger at the audience. "Because the last four letters in American spell I CAN!"

The crowd goes wild. Clearly there is no observation too corny for a beauty pageant. This I've known all the years I've competed, which is basically my entire life.

To my left I hear a barely contained wince. I glance at Ms. Arizona, the brunette and statuesque Misty Delgado, who that very afternoon became the *infamous* Misty Delgado of YouTube fame. Or should I say, notoriety.

"Cut the crap, Mario," she mutters. To her credit, her smile hasn't wavered. She is hissing through teeth a Disney heroine would envy. "Name the top five. These effing stilettos are killing me."

Mario seems to pick up the cue. "With no further ado, I will now name the outstanding married ladies who will be our top five finalists. One of them"—pause for effect—"will take home the crown of Ms. America."

With that portentous segue, a drum roll begins. Mario flourishes a white index card. The crowd holds its breath. We queens do, too. "Ms. Wyoming, Sherry Phillips!"

Redheaded, very pretty, a threat from head to toe. She sashays down to stage level. I relax briefly, then tense again for the second card.

"Ms. Rhode Island, Liz Beth Wong!"

Darn! Extremely perky Asian girl. And again, not me.

"Ms. North Carolina, Trixie Barnett!"

Her I have to be happy for. She's a real gem. But *shoot*! Only two more names.

"Ms. California, Tiffany Amber!"

Argh! I nearly stomp my foot. Awful creature. Her type rhymes with witch. Tall, blonde, flawless, fake. Absolutely drop-dead gorgeous.

Oops. Forget I said that.

"Ms. Ohio, Happy Pennington!"

I don't recognize it at first. Then Misty pinches my thigh, with more vigor than is strictly necessary.

I squeal. Me! I can't believe it. One of the top five! The last one to make it in! My hands fly to my face in that *I can't believe it!* gesture that's as natural to successful pageant contenders as taping our boobs for extra lift and separation.

I get a hold of myself and begin the treacherous descent from my tier, clutching the arms of my fellow contestants for support so I won't topple to certain, ignominious defeat. I encounter barely veiled glares as I progress but by that point am too delirious with rhinestone ambition to much care.

By the way, don't ask about the origin of my first name. Not now, anyway. My mother came up with it, and believe me, there's a story there.

I keep a smile plastered to my face, never forgetting the cardinal rule of pageantry: *Sparkle! Sparkle! Sparkle!* I wink playfully at Mario, who flashes his dimples in return, then cross the stage to assume the position, my eyes trained on the judges in the first row. Of course, what with the glare of the stage lights, I can't actually see them, but still I nod in their direction with what I hope passes as confidence. No one measuring my heart rate would be fooled.

Ms. North Carolina trips over to grab my hand in what after two weeks of acquaintance I know to be a genuine display of happiness for me. Earlier that evening she won Ms. Congeniality and I guarantee you that vote wasn't rigged. Some beauty queens might be vipers in spandex and silicone but this one is truly nice. I squeeze her hand back, she giggles in shared glee, then returns to her mark a few feet away.

I take a deep breath and try not to think what winning this thing would mean to me. Of course I've claimed a few crowns—after all, I had to win Ohio to get here—but I've limped away defeated far more often than I've taken that thrilling victory walk down the runway. And I've never come close to winning a national competition before.

I already know where I want the prize money to go. Straight from the Ms. America coffers to my daughter's college fund. With a little something left over for my husband. Then we could all advance our lives from this.

Oh boy, how excited Jason must be for me right now. And my mom …

For a moment I'm forced to squeeze my eyes shut. I can't imagine what this would mean to her. All those rinky-dink pageants she put me through … Of course, to her they were swank events that could catapult her daughter to a socioeconomic level she herself could never achieve. Not so different from what I want for Rachel, is it? Ironic, let me assure you. And let's not forget, if I did manage to grab a national crown, it might make up a little, just a little, for Pop leaving.

I know they're out there in the audience right now, Mom and Jason, sitting next to each other in forced comradeship. No doubt Pop is home watching on the tube and cheering me on. Rachel? Not so much. I'm sure she's on-line bemoaning how her mom is embarrassing her.

Mario's voice cuts through my thoughts. And none too soon, for I realize that we top five are about to make our way to the isolation booth. It's been wheeled onstage by two of the buffer male dancers, who are holding onto the thing so it doesn't slip around as we step inside. Great: another way to fall over.

En route Mario waylays Ms. Wyoming, who'll be first to do the final interview. The rest of us slither inside the booth. Buff Dancer #1 closes the door. Profound silence descends.

"Wow." That in a tone of awe from Liz Beth. She's one of a half-dozen Asian girls in the competition. "This thing is, like, really sound-proof."

"Did you, like, just fall off the turnip truck? Or in your case should I say the bok choy truck?"

My head snaps right in Ms. California's direction.

"Of course it's sound-proof," Ms. California Tiffany Amber goes on, wiping invisible lint from her glittery silver gown. "Otherwise why would they stick us in here? You'd better smarten up for your interview question, Rhode Island, or you're toast."

Liz Beth wilts. The walls of the isolation booth seem to close in a few more inches. I swear it's a hundred fifty degrees in there. I lick my lips, my mouth like sandpaper. I smell nervousness all around me and believe me, it's not pretty.

All of a sudden Trixie from North Carolina laughs. "Well, y'all, I'm just glad they don't do headphones anymore." She's a girl-next-door type and invariably cheery. "Remember that? Making the girls listen to that cheesy elevator music so they didn't hear the question instead of putting them in one of these isolation contraptions?"

"It was hell on hair," Tiffany says as she smooths her perfect blond coif. "But that would hardly matter for you."

Trixie's eyes widen as her hand flies to her chin-length copper-red hair. "Is there … is there something …"

The booth door opens. Buff Dancer #2 motions out Liz Beth, who by now looks as freaked out as a nun at a peep show. Tiffany chortles as she leaves.

A second later I clear my throat. "Don't listen to Tiffany, Trixie." I reach out to rub her arm. "Your hair looks terrific."

"As if," Tiffany opines. "Anyway, Congeniality never wins."

"Stop being a bitch, Tiffany." My voice is getting stronger by the second. "Trixie, there's always a first time. And I think the judges are really high on you."

"Really?"

The door opens again and this time Trixie's in the firing line. I give her a thumb's up right before she steps out.

"Smart, Ohio." Tiffany shakes her head, disgust twisting her perfectly symmetrical features. "Make the competition feel fabulous."

"Maybe we don't all need to cut everybody else down to feel good about ourselves."

"Right. Tell that to yourself when you lose."

I'm concocting a pithy riposte when Tiffany shuts me up by lifting her gown to reveal a lipstick and compact taped to her right thigh.

She rips off the tape. "Never thought of this, did you?" She sneers. "I do it every time. For a last-minute touchup to guarantee I'm even more exquisite for my close-up."

"Too bad it won't be close enough to reveal your rotten soul," I mutter. Then the door opens and this time I find Buff Dancer #1 signaling me.

"Don't trip on those clodhoppers of yours," she singsongs as I take his arm.

I hoist a pound or two of fuchsia satin gown in my free hand and throw back my shoulders. Jousting with Tiffany has made me a zillion times fiercer than when I stepped into the isolation booth. Now I want to blow that blonde barracuda into oblivion.

We head toward Mario. I'm blinded by the stage lights as I remember the timeless advice of Miss America 1972 Lauren Schaefer—of Bexley, Ohio, mind you—who said that when you walk in your evening gown, you should glide as if you were on rollers being pulled by a string. With applause ringing in my ears, I float across the stage, my smile beatific. I'm no Tiffany Amber in the looks department, I will confess, but I am slender and brunette and the appearance gods have been kind. Buff Dancer #1 deposits me at Mario's side. The audience settles. I take a sustaining breath.

Mario glances at his index card. I guess he can't remember the question he's just asked three times. "Ms. Ohio, if a genie offered you one special power, what would you like it to be?"

I laugh. "Oh, that's easy." To my mind rises other pageant winners' advice: *Use a dash of humor!* "I'd like to be able to guess the winning lottery number before it's announced!"

Laughter and clapping burst from the crowd.

I giggle and go on. "But seriously, folks. As a wife and mother, the special power I'd most like to have is the ability to do ten different things at the same time. Then maybe I'd finally catch up with all the To Do's on my list!"

Both of Mario's dimples flash. Now I know for sure I done good. He motions me to go stand beside my fellow Top Fivers, then grins at the camera and says, "Very cleverly answered by Ms. Ohio, Happy Pennington. Now for our final contestant, Ms. California, Tiffany Amber!"

Cheers and applause rise to the rafters. Apparently Tiffany has scads of people fooled. As for me, I feel like booing.

Buff Dancer #2 opens the door to the isolation booth,

then steps back. I steel myself for Her Supreme Bitchiness to flounce across the stage.

Instead Tiffany pitches forward and crash lands face first onto the stage floor. Twitching ensues. In fact, what with the silver gown, she looks like a marlin gasping for breath on the deck of a fishing boat. Then, after one particularly impressive series of flops, she shudders and goes still.

The crowd's cheers give way to an audience-wide intake of breath. The orchestra screeches to an awkward halt. Mario calls for a cut to commercial. I can't often describe myself as flabbergasted but I sure can now. All we contestants are as frozen as marionettes who've lost their puppeteer. Except for North Carolina, who grabs my arm. "Good Lord!" Trixie squeals in my ear. "What in the world's happened to that girl?"

Buff Dancer #2 attempts to find out. He hurries over to Tiffany, still lying face down, then bends toward her and shakes her shoulder. He starts to turn her over. A second later horror crosses his face and he lets her go, tripping backward as if he can't get away fast enough.

By this point the air is electric. All the judges and half the audience are out of their seats. Uniformed security guards are making their way onto the stage. The crowd is beyond murmuring; we've heard a scream or two. Mario races over to Tiffany, kneels beside her, and takes her limp arm by the wrist.

A second later he raises his head toward one of the guards and with his free hand covers the microphone on his tuxedo lapel. I don't so much hear him say it as I watch his lips form the words. "She's dead."

CHAPTER TWO

Honestly, I don't think even Bert Parks would know how to handle this. As it is, Mario Suave does himself credit.

With great care, he lays Tiffany's arm back on the stage floor. Then he straightens and steps away from the inert silver mound no one can stop eyeballing. "Ladies and gentlemen, a tragedy has befallen us here at the Ms. America pageant." Not a quaver in his voice or a tremble of his lips. He even reins in his dimples. "Please return to your seats and remain calm. The authorities will instruct us how to proceed."

I can guess what Tiffany would say if she were still alive: *As if.* The crowd is having none of either seats or calmness. People are making a frenzied break for the exits as if Tiffany succumbed to something that might bump them off in short order. I guess the idea isn't crazy. None of us has a clue what did Tiffany in.

And it couldn't have happened to a nicer gal.

As you might imagine, I'm keeping that observation to myself. Trixie squeaks again in my ear. "This makes the Misty Delgado YouTube thing look like *nothing.*"

"You're not kidding." I turn around. The six-foot-tall Ms. Arizona hasn't budged from her tier. Actually, no one has. Instructions have not yet come down from on high.

But it appears they're about to. Mario steps in front of us finalists and motions the rest of the girls down to stage level. "We're off the air. We've gone to billboard."

"What does that mean?" Sherry from Wyoming might be a pretty redhead but she's a few diamonds short of a tiara.

Trixie pitches in. "It means they put the sign thingie up on the TV that says Ms. America Pageant, stay tuned or whatever."

"Stay tuned for what?" Liz Beth Wong wants to know. "Are they gonna announce who won?"

I shake my head. Sometimes. "Liz Beth, now is not the time to bring that up."

"Well, can we go back to our rooms then?" This pearl, too, from Sherry.

"I don't think so," I say. "This is a crime scene now. The cops won't let anyone go anywhere. Look." I point at the exits, all now blocked by security guards but still mobbed by audience members who won't take no for an answer. I wonder if my mom and Jason are in that pulsing horde. Probably. For the sake of the guards' heads, I hope my mom isn't sporting one of her double-wide handbags this evening.

"You're exactly right, Happy." Mario nods gravely in my direction. I feel like preening, even in the face of disaster.

Or semi-disaster, given my low opinion of one Tiffany Amber.

Then something else occurs to me, which I make the mistake of voicing aloud. "I hope nothing else happens.

What if there's a psycho out there targeting beauty queens?"

"Oh my God." The color drains from Liz Beth's face.

Mario hustles over to prop her up because she looks like she's about to hit the deck. "Let's not worry too much about that. But we should be super prudent from now on." He raises his voice to address all the girls. "That means, ladies, when the authorities release you, go straight back to your rooms, don't let anybody in that you don't know, and don't talk to strangers."

Those were pretty much the pre-homicide pageant rules, and now I don't think anybody will offer much argument.

We remain in huddle mode for some time while cops traipse hither and yon across the stage, strewing yellow crime tape around everything that won't move and one thing that will. Not surprisingly, the isolation booth commands a great deal of their attention.

I find it all deeply compelling. I don't know if it's because I'm the daughter of Lou Przybyszewski, retired from Lakewood PD, but I have long harbored a certain fascination with matters homicidal.

It is creepy, though, watching the medical team come in to collect Tiffany. Even after they lift her onto the gurney and pull a sheet over her blonde head, I half expect her to sit up and cackle, *Fooled you!*—or some such crazy thing. But it doesn't happen. For once Ms. California is silent. I think that's when I know she is really, truly dead. We all draw back a few inches when she's rolled past us to points unknown.

By this point the cops are letting the judges and most audience members go, after jotting down information about them. The auditorium is emptying even of the reporters who descended en masse when they heard a contestant snuffed. We watch as one cop disentangles himself from the posse near the isolation booth and heads in our direction. Clearly this is the homicide investigator, because he's in plainclothes. In fact, he's wearing a Hawaiian shirt, which passes in these parts for business attire.

He and his paunch stop directly in front of me. He looks like Don Ho's chubby cousin. He flashes his badge and eyes my Ms. Ohio sash. "Are you Happy Pennington?" he asks.

I feel many eyes settle on my face. Usually I'm enough of a ham to enjoy being the center of attention. Not this time. "I am."

"You were the last contestant to exit the isolation booth before Ms. Amber, is that correct?"

Not much in that I can deny, either. "It is." I realize I'm answering as if I'm already on the witness stand but I can't seem to help myself.

"Then follow me," he directs, and after one desperate sideways glance at Trixie, I find myself being separated from my fellow contenders and led across the stage to a distant locale whose advantage is, I gather, that no one can overhear us. Except for the female cop who joins our duo.

The cop who found me flips to a new page in his little notebook. "I'm Detective Momoa and this is Detective Jenkins."

Jenkins is a heavyset blonde woman. I nod at her. She says nothing. Maybe she specializes in peering intently as I feel her eyes bore into me like nobody's business.

Detective Momoa speaks again, his pen poised over a clean page. "Would you spell your name for me, please?"

"Do you mean Happy Pennington or my legal name?"

"What is your legal name?"

"Happy Przybyszewski."

That gets his attention. He looks up from the notebook. "Excuse me?"

"Przybyszewski." It sounds like shih-buh-CHEF-ski. I've always been inordinately proud of the fact that it has only two vowels and you have to get nine letters in to hit the first one. "It's Polish," I explain, though I think he might have already gotten that part. I spell it out. "Years ago, when my mom started entering me into pageants, she decided I needed a simpler name so she came up with Pennington. I think she thought it sounded" —I hesitate, suddenly embarrassed— "upscale."

"And the name Happy?" Jenkins pipes up. "Is that real?"

I don't appreciate the snideness I detect in her tone. "Yes."

She snickers. "Did your mother think that sounded upscale, too?"

By now I'm feeling a tad huffy. "She named me that because it's cheerful." I let it go at that. If the woman needed a little joy in her life at that point in time, that's her business.

Momoa moves on to dull particulars like my vital stats and what we contestants did during the two weeks of preliminary competition, that sort of thing. Then he homes in on the final moments of tonight's festivities. "What transpired in the isolation booth?"

Transpired is one of those verbs that stops you short. "Well," I say, "I guess what surprised me was how mean Tiffany was. Usually the girls don't talk much but when they do they say nice things. To encourage one another."

"But that wasn't true tonight?" Momoa prods.

"No. Tiffany was snarky. You know, derogatory. Making insulting comments."

The cops exchange a glance. I can't put my finger on quite why but I get the impression they think trash talk is standard beauty-pageant fare.

"Did anybody respond in kind?" Momoa asks.

"Well …" This is mildly tricky. "Not really."

"Everybody just took it?"

I remain silent and shift my weight to my other stiletto.

"Even in the heat of competition, everybody remained silent?"

All right, he wore me down. "I suppose I told her off a little."

Momoa narrows his eyes at me. "So you and she had a pointed altercation?"

Another big word. "I would call it more of a spat. I just don't think it's right that somebody should deliberately try and unnerve their fellow contestants right before the scariest part of the competition." I glance at Jenkins, though why I think she'll be supportive I have no idea. "Lots of girls think the swimsuit competition is the scariest, because you have to parade around in front of millions of people wearing nothing but an eighth of an inch of Lycra, but personally I've always thought it was the final interview."

They appear to digest this snippet of pageant wisdom. Then Momoa resumes his line of questioning, which I must say is putting me rather on the defensive. "Ms. Pennington, did you bear animosity toward Ms. Amber?"

That five-syllable behemoth blares CAUTION! in my brain. "I would describe it more as disappointment that Tiffany chose not to adhere to the highest standards of pageant competition."

He harrumphs. I feel like I dodged a trap. Though his next question makes me worry I'm about to stumble into another one. "Did anything unusual happen while you and Ms. Amber were alone in the isolation booth?"

"Not really," I say, then, "though I suppose there was one thing."

"What's that?"

"She had a lipstick and a compact taped to her thigh. Under her gown."

Momoa's pen stops moving. "You saw them?"

"She lifted her skirt and there they were. She told me she always did a last-minute touchup to, and I quote, look more exquisite for her close-up." I add that detail to highlight Tiffany's arrogance but that's not what Momoa seizes on.

"Did you see her apply the lipstick?"

"No. I just saw her rip off the tape to get it loose."

Jenkins pipes up. "Isn't it strange for her to have had tape in her possession?"

"Not at all," I say, before I realize this might require a semi-humiliating explanation. You see, as I may have mentioned previously, we queens all want to make the most of our assets on pageant night. The favored technique is like a poor girl's boob job: cut precisely fourteen inches of tape, bend forward at the waist, and tape from one side to the other. A finer lift you'll never see without going under a scalpel.

Jenkins continues to look perplexed.

I feel obliged to expound. "If a beauty contestant wants to, shall we say, enhance her looks, she uses tape. Post office tape. Like to seal boxes for shipping."

I watch her eyes drop to my boobs. Her stare is more penetrating than ever. She is clearly trying to assess whether my own perkiness springs from natural causes.

"Never, never duct tape," I add. Many a queen has learned that lesson the hard way.

Momoa caps his pen. "That's all for now, Ms. Pennington. Be aware that until further notice, you and your fellow contestants will be required to remain on the island."

I know why. We're all under suspicion. No one's mouthed it but one word is hanging in the air. It has only two syllables but it's extremely potent nonetheless.

Since it's the end of the interrogation, I feel emboldened to pose a question of my own. "Are you working on the assumption that Tiffany Amber was murdered?"

Momoa and his sidekick have started to walk away but he halts to glance back at me. "We're not at liberty to discuss that." Then he turns and keeps going.

I don't have to be a cop's daughter to know that's an affirmative.

CHAPTER THREE

"Were those policemen mean to you?" Trixie wants to know. She raced across the stage in my direction when she saw that I'd been sprung by Momoa and Company.

"Except for the part where they half accused me of murdering Tiffany, not really."

Beneath her bangs, her auburn eyes widen. "Did they really?"

"Well, they kind of fixated on the fact that I argued with her in the isolation booth." By this point it has occurred to me that I'm the last person to have seen Tiffany Amber alive, apart from the center stage twitching sequence witnessed by millions. That makes me, I know only too well, a "person of interest."

Trixie and I amble toward the abandoned tiers. Mario's disappeared along with the judges, the audience, and most of the girls. Only cops are still around in any number. "What's been going on out here?" I ask Trixie.

"The policemen had to give smelling salts to the dancer who tried to turn Tiffany over. When they were talking to him, he fainted."

"Wow. I wonder what spooked him so bad. I mean, apart from her being dead and all."

Trixie edges closer. "I think there was something really awful about how her face looked. I mean *really* awful."

"Like, grotesque?" I imagine being dead is never a good look but apparently there was more to it than that.

Trixie turns around to face the emptying auditorium. "They wouldn't let her husband see her. He asked to. He said he wanted to say goodbye."

I turn to follow Trixie's gaze. Hunched over in the empty front row is a dark-haired man in a pinstripe suit. I take that to be him.

"They have two daughters," Trixie says. "Three and five."

"Oh, no."

"Ava and Madison. They're not here, thank the Lord."

"Such little girls. That is so sad."

Trixie's eyes haven't budged from the tableau before us. "Rex has been trying to comfort Tiffany's husband but he keeps shooing him away."

Rex Rexford is pacing the narrow space between the stage and the front row. In his customary white suit and pastel shirt, with his bouffant blond hair teased especially high for tonight's festivities, he cuts quite a figure.

"He must be pretty broken up," I observe.

"I wonder how long he was Tiffany's pageant consultant?"

"I didn't know till I saw him here with her that he'd gotten back in the business."

"Speaking of being in the business ..."

Trixie's voice trails off but I know who she's eyeing now. Sally Anne Gibbons is cruising the aisles, purveyor of pageant wear and sometime consultant herself. Maybe she's gone native in the last two weeks because she's outfitted in a muumuu. In fact, she's filling it nearly to bursting. Like Rex, her coppery red hair has been arranged into a high-rise helmet-like coif for the occasion.

Trixie speaks again. "Do you think the policemen know how mad Sally Anne was with Tiffany about that gown mix-up?"

"I don't know. I'm sure not going to be the one to tell them." I've had quite enough of their piercing stares and probing inquiries, thank you very much.

Trixie leans closer. "Are you sure you don't want to? It might deflect suspicion from you."

I'm taken aback by that. "I don't know that any deflection is necessary."

"Oh, probably not, you're right." Trixie immediately backs off but I'm left a trifle alarmed. "Anyhoo," she goes on, clearly trying to change the subject, "I'd love a beer and a burger but I don't know if I dare risk it. What if we have to get back in our swimsuits tomorrow?"

"God, I hope not." And so much for making the top five. I can't imagine I'd pull that off again in a re-do. "What do you say we call it a night?"

Trixie needs no further encouragement to head backstage, where all us girls did our quick changes during the competition. Each of us has a little area, complete with lighted mirror, where we stash our outfits and cosmetics.

Trixie lowers her voice. "I have to admit I'm having an uncharitable thought."

"It can't be worse than any of mine."

Her tone gets even more confiding. "Even after all this, I still kind of care who wins this thing. Isn't that awful?"

"No. So do I." Sure, having a corpse on stage put a damper on my competitive spunk, but it didn't erase it entirely. Particularly since the stiff was Tiffany Amber.

"It makes me feel so selfish. Somebody's dead, a mother of two no less, and I'm thinking about myself."

We're backstage now and pause to watch the cops huddled in Tiffany's area. I can see they've already dusted for prints and bagged her items in clear plastic.

Trixie shudders. "This gives me the willies. I think I'll go get my stuff."

I nod, too distracted to answer. I can't tear my eyes from what the cops are doing.

The show ends in short order, though, as they disperse and take Tiffany's belongings with them. I gather my own things. Trixie calls goodbye to me from across the way and toddles out with the last few girls. I realize I'm alone backstage.

I'm not aware of deciding to go there but before long I find myself standing in what had been Tiffany's area. It's kind of a sty now, what with the dusting for prints. I see myself reflected in her mirror, all done up in my halter-style fuchsia gown with beaded bodice, my Ms. Ohio sash cutting across my body, every strand of my long brunette hair lacquered into place. Just hours before, Tiffany stood in that exact same spot, scanning herself for any imperfection. Yet in mere minutes she'd be dead. It gives me an eerie feeling to realize she had no idea.

Or did she? Who knows what was going on with her? Something had to be, something big, because tonight somebody killed her. I know it's possible there's some beauty-queen stalker out there who just happened to pick Tiffany as his first victim but somehow I don't think that's the case. I do know one thing for absolutely sure: Tiffany didn't kill herself. If a girl like that got really depressed and wanted to end it all, she'd never do it like this. She'd wash her hair and polish her nails and get all dressed up and write a heartrending note on scented stationery and then down a bottle of pills, all in the privacy of her own bedroom. She'd never submit herself to that humiliating exhibition. And I am sure that Tiffany Amber wanted to win the Ms. America title tonight, and in that isolation booth she was doing her damnedest to make it happen. But something, someone, got in the way.

That undeniable truth gives *me* a sudden attack of the willies. I back away fast from Tiffany's area and crash smack dab into a rolling clothes rack that hours before had been laden with evening gowns, no doubt one of them Tiffany's silver number.

"Shoot." I bend down to rub my foot, which slammed right into one of the rack's low bars. That's the last thing my stilettoed foot needed after hours of being stood on. I'm wincing and rubbing, rubbing and wincing, when I notice a hotel room card key lying on the floor next to the rack.

It's not mine, I know that. Mine's in my cosmetics bag; I just checked. I don't know whose this one is. I wonder about that. And then I pick it up.

From backstage I wend my way out of the auditorium toward the main hotel building. It's some distance away, along winding paths lined by hibiscus and birds of paradise and illuminated by a waxing moon and the tiki torches that are lit aflame every evening at dusk by a Hawaiian hunk wearing only a loincloth. He makes for a good show, too, I can tell you. The air is warm and sweet and I hear the surf pounding. It's so late nobody is out. I pass only one couple, honeymooners by the looks of them, who are feeding bits of bread to the fat white and gold and orange koi in the stone-edged pond.

They look really happy. The couple, not the fish, I mean, though the latter appear reasonably cheerful, too.

Then a sound like a macaw shrieking pierces the night air.

Oh God. Here we go.

"Happy! Happy Pennington!"

I've barely turned around when my mother grabs me in a hug. She's a tiny bird-like woman, Hazel Przybyszewski, but when she's inspired she can lay on quite a grip. "That damn husband of yours told me you were all right but I didn't believe him." She pulls back a few inches and peers up at my face so intently that I'm thinking she could teach Detective Jenkins a thing or two. "I guess for once he was right."

"I am fine, Mom, really I am."

She lets me go, then fishes for a tissue up the sleeve of her floral dress. She's a petite redhead, her hair so thin on top I can see her skull. Watching her, I realize she's trembling. And for all her bravado, there's a tear in her pale blue eyes. That's when it hits me: tonight was hell for her. A mysterious death, a panicked crowd, her only child inches from mortal danger—it must have brought home to her in one agonizing rush all she suffered those long years as a cop's wife.

I seize her in a hug of my own. She clutches me briefly then pulls away. "I'm okay, I'm okay." A deep breath and a swipe of the nose later and she's more composed.

In fact, I note with some regret that she's totally back to normal.

She throws out her arms. "I thought you were going to wear the strapless white chiffon gown! What's with the hot pink? You know I don't like those neon colors, even for the so-called" —she draws quotation marks in the air—" 'sexy' pageants."

"This gown is fuchsia, not hot pink. And it did get me in the top five."

She raises her index finger in the air. "Maybe so, young lady, but did it get you to number one? I ask you that."

"Nobody got to number one! They haven't named a winner yet."

She harrumphs. "Because of the spectacle that California girl put on."

"Mom …" I lower my voice. "She's dead."

My mother rolls her eyes as if the smart money

knows the whole thing had been a ploy for attention. "If you'd worn that white gown it wouldn't matter if she was dead or alive. You'd have won."

"Happy!" That comes from a distance. It's Jason's voice, calling from ahead.

When he joins us, I'm reminded that the man I married seventeen years ago—exactly half my lifetime— is still a hot guy. Dark curly hair, worn a little long just like when he played football in high school, with a slight olive tone to his skin and full sexy lips ...

True, he's not at his playing weight anymore. Too many hours watching the game on TV instead of being out on the gridiron himself. Still, in a suit and tie with the mechanic's grease gone from his fingernails, he can turn a female head or two.

"Congratulations!" He grabs me in a lip lock. I can just imagine my mom rolling her eyes. "Top five!" he says when he finally lets me go. "Good stuff. Rachel's stoked, too."

"Really?" I wipe a lipstick smear from his mouth. "You talked to her?"

"She called me when she saw a news flash on the web about the California contestant."

I hear that and the green-eyed monster pays a visit. Backstage I checked my cell for messages. None from Rachel. Why didn't my daughter call *me*?

Part of me knows why.

"By the way, everybody thinks she was poisoned," he adds.

"Poisoned, eh?" My mother clucks her tongue. "I wonder what she did to provoke that."

Jason winks at me over my mother's head. Sometimes my mom's insights drive us both crazy, but clearly tonight he'll let it all slide.

"Let's head back," I suggest, taking my mom's elbow to lead her along the path.

Jason falls in step behind us. "Anyway, you did really great, Happy. You should totally win. Do you know how they're gonna decide now who did win?"

"No. And I didn't really feel I could ask."

My mom moves ahead and Jason comes close to whisper in my ear. "I wish I could stay with you tonight."

I smile at him. "I do, too. But the competition's not really over."

"I could protect you." His dark eyes grow serious. "We don't know who killed that girl. I don't like the idea of you being here alone."

"I'm not alone. I've got Shanelle." My roommate, Ms. Mississippi. I've only known her two weeks but already I love her.

"Shanelle's great, but ..."

"Don't worry." I cock my chin at my mom, up ahead. "And don't say anything to make her worry."

He makes a zipping motion across his lips as we arrive at the main hotel building. The open-air lobby with its central court of palm trees and tropical flowers is deserted save for the macaw who sounds just like my mother.

I catch up to her. My mother, I mean. "Do you want me to ride in the cab with you back to the Lotus Blossom?" The Royal Hibiscus is where all the pageant people are lodged but it's a bit rich for most of the families, including mine.

"We don't need a cab," Jason says. "We brought the rental." He limits himself to a sedate peck on my cheek then glances at my mom. "I'll go get the wheels," he tells her and sets off.

My mother watches Jason go.

"How did you two get along tonight?" I ask her.

She sighs heavily. "I suppose he was all right."

From my mom, with regard to my husband, that's high praise. I wait with her till Jason returns with the car then kiss her soft powdery cheek. "Sweet dreams."

A minute later, in the carpeted elevator, the night catches up with me. I kick off my stilettos and seriously consider sitting down for the ride to the ninth floor. Outside 915, I slip the key card into the slot. A tiny red light flares and the lock refuses to budge. I take the card out, make sure I have it pointed in the right direction, then slide it in again. Again the little red light.

"Why?" I ask the door. "Why?" I lay my forehead against its unyielding surface before I realize there is a reason this key card isn't working. This one isn't mine.

CHAPTER FOUR

I'm a tad distracted remembering the *other* key card I have in my possession when the door is flung open.

"Girl, *again* you can't make that thing work?" Standing there in a long Bob Marley tee shirt, her hair held back by a headband and her face slathered with a cream mask, is my roommate, Ms. Mississippi, Shanelle Walker.

She grabs the key card from my hand and shoves it in the slot. Not surprisingly, she too gets the little red light. Her eyebrows, devoid of cream, fly skyward. She hands me back the card. "Guess the magnetic strip died. Just like Tiffany Amber." She gives me a wicked smile, then slams the door shut behind me, probably waking half the floor. She touches my arm with her index finger and makes a sizzling sound. "Oooh, you hot, girl!" She cackles and claps her hands. "You Ms. America now!"

"I am not." I throw my stuff on my double bed.

"Yes, you are! With Tiffany cold as ice, it's just a formality at this point. Since those dang judges didn't have the good sense to put me in the top five, the only other one in that group with half a chance is Trixie Barnett and we all know Congeniality never takes the big prize." She sets her hands on her hips. "I expect I know what the answer will be but I'll ask anyhow. You didn't poison Tiffany in that isolation booth, did you?"

"Of course I didn't poison Tiffany! Is that what people are saying?"

"Not you per se but the poison part, yes, ma'am." I see then that Shanelle's been on her laptop scanning the same headlines Rachel is probably reading back home. "It's only speculation but the experts all agree. Something like *cyanide*." She hisses the word.

I take in that detail as I whip the Ohio sash off over my head. I can certainly see how cyanide might mess with a girl's appearance. That could explain why Tiffany looked particularly nasty to the dancer who turned her over and ended up fainting.

"And how will they ever figure out whodunit?" Shanelle goes on. "That girl had more enemies than Tupac Shakur. And any one of us could've slipped something vile into her makeup bag while it was backstage. That's what everybody's speculating, too. And that's why the cops won't let us go home. Not that I'm in any rush."

Given my last-to-see-alive status with regard to Tiffany Amber, I'm pleased to hear I have lots of company on the suspect list. I reach behind my back and start trying to unzip my gown. Shanelle gets behind me to help. Another thought comes to me. "Didn't Misty Delgado room with Tiffany?"

"Till she couldn't take it no more and moved out." Shanelle harrumphs. "Now that's somebody I'd examine very closely if I was Oahu PD."

"It is suspicious how the two of them couldn't get along and then that video of Misty shows up on

YouTube."

"Right before the finale! And then during the finale Tiffany winds up dead." Shanelle backs away, the zipper undone. "You wanna use some of my tea tree face mask? I'll leave the jar out for you. Does wonders for your pores, girl."

At the moment it's not my pores I'm focused on. With Shanelle in the bathroom and my gown only half on, I dig out the paperwork the pageant people gave us when we arrived. There it is, the sheet I was looking for. I lay it on the bedspread and run my finger down the list of names and numbers.

Shanelle comes back into the bedroom. "I'd get some shuteye if I was you. You need to be fresh for tomorrow when they make the announcement."

I'm still hunched over the sheet. "What announcement?"

"That you won!" She clucks and gets into her bed, the one nearer the sliding glass doors that lead to the balcony, then rolls away from me. "You're the least enthusiastic beauty pageant winner I've ever met."

"That's because I haven't won any beauty pageants lately." Although I have been lucky now in one regard. I've found exactly the information I was looking for.

I disassemble the pageant version of myself—gown, helmet hair, pancake makeup—and dutifully get into bed, but end up passing the next hours in an agony of waiting. I know it is highly unwise to embark on my mission until the wee hours. And despite how exhausted I am, I can't bring myself to get a wink of shuteye in the meanwhile. I toss and turn so much I yank the sheet off the mattress.

Finally, at 3:48 AM, I allow myself to get up. Shanelle is either the best fake snorer in the western world or she truly is asleep. As quietly as I know how, I dress in my lime green Juicy Couture tracksuit and coordinating floral-print Keds and creep across our darkened bedroom, illuminated by only a slit of light between the pulled drapes, to grab both the key cards I have in my possession. One goes in one pocket, one in the other, so their magnetic strips don't conk out right when I need them.

I encounter no one on the elevator trip down to the third floor and no one in the corridor leading to number 328. No security guard is hulking outside the door, which I half expected. I walk past to suss out the situation. I don't know what I think I'll see. Yellow crime tape crisscrossing the door? None of that. But sure as day there is the telltale dust of fingerprinting all over the door handle.

That will not faze your plucky heroine, who has planned ahead.

I pull from my pocket both the relevant card key and a Kleenex tissue. I deploy the latter carefully across the door handle so it will be ready should I need it.

Will I?

The key card slips into the slot. A moment later a green light flashes and the lock releases. I twist the Kleenexed handle and presto!—I am inside the private lair of the late, unlamented Tiffany Amber.

Now, lest you think I am a scofflaw or an idiot, allow me to disabuse you of both notions. Not only do I consider myself an upstanding citizen, I am one. As a cop's daughter, I have the utmost respect for the law. What I've decided in this case is that I'm not breaking any laws. I am simply taking advantage of the opportunity presented by my auspicious discovery of the key card. Until it opened Tiffany's door, I didn't know for certain that it had been hers. True, given where I found it, I had my suspicions. And that's why I'm taking this risk: should I need to deflect suspicion from myself, as Trixie put it, maybe a little preparatory sleuthing will yield a clue I can use to point the cops in another, more profitable direction.

Not to mention that I'm damn curious, which is harder to rationalize.

I stand in the dark and ponder how to proceed. Of course, I haven't the slightest idea what I'm looking for. I guess the closest I can pinpoint it is: something weird. As I ruminate on what that might constitute, I notice an odd smell. It's subtle but it's there. I move forward a few inches, my nostrils working as furiously as any beagle's. What is that? I've smelled it before but never in hotel rooms. More like in back yards. Is it … citronella? Like those candles people burn to keep mosquitoes away? Why in the world would Tiffany's room smell of citronella?

Okay. That qualifies as weird.

Buoyed by that discovery, I move further into the room. I realize as my eyes adjust that this room is exactly like Shanelle's and mine, no surprise. The drapes to the balcony have been left open and I'm not touching them. I'm leaving everything just the way I find it. So no lamps can go on. As it is, I'm getting some illumination from the moonlight through the sliding glass doors.

One thing I ascertain immediately: Tiffany Amber was a pig. Clothes, makeup, magazines are strewn everywhere. Some of the mess can no doubt be blamed on the cops but I don't think all of it can. For example, the bedclothes are totally rumpled, as if she had some hell of an afternoon nap.

I glance at the items dispersed on the credenza near the flat-screen TV: empty water bottles, a tabloid or two, a few wilted leis, squeezed tubes of sunscreen, Oahu tourist brochures, newspapers. I see one newspaper has been folded open and something circled. I peer at it. It's the foreign-exchange rates and Tiffany, or somebody, circled the Japanese yen. I wonder if she and her husband were planning to continue on to Japan from here. Makes sense; they're already partway across the Pacific.

Further on I come across a few items I expect all the contestants imported to Oahu: Firm Grip and B-vitamin complex. Firm Grip is like hair spray for the derriere. You spray it on your behind and it makes your swimsuit cling to your skin so you can avoid the embarrassing spectacle of spandex creeping up your butt cheeks during competition. No doubt Tiffany had one can in her makeup bag and a spare left here. And as for the vitamins, it's been drummed into all of us that B complex with added B6 counteracts bloating, the bane of swimsuit competition.

Yet … what is that I see in the trash bin underneath the desk? *Potato chips?* A ginormous bag of them, bigger than would even fit in the minibar? I reel backward. I find it impossible to believe that Tiffany Amber was downing potato chips. Given the calorie count and how sodium contributes to water retention? No way.

So how did those get in here?

I turn again toward the bed, its bedclothes so tumbled the comforter is dragging on the carpet. Who makes a mess with a bed and also eats potato chips? Sometimes at one and the same time?

A man, that's who.

I wonder. Maybe Tiffany broke the no-man-in-the-room pageant prohibition. Maybe she was mattress dancing with her hubby this very afternoon, just prior to the finale. Somehow the notion that Tiffany flouted the rules does not shock me. She seems the type—arrogant, uber confident, snotty.

I edge closer to the desk. Anything of interest? No sirree. A memo pad near the phone with nothing written on it. But my beady little eyes detect that it has the imprint of writing. My morals being in a weakened state at the moment, I slip it into the waistband of my sweatpants.

The rest of my investigation yields nothing. I also note that by now it's 4:49 AM. Type A's will be out in force soon, getting in their jogs before dawn, right next to jetlagged travelers in search of java.

It's time to skedaddle.

I redeploy the Kleenex to exit Tiffany's room in case the cops get the urge for another bout of fingerprinting, then sprint away from her doorway the moment I'm in the empty corridor and slow to a respectable pace as I point toward the elevator bank. My heart is jumping like a drop of water on a hot skillet but I must say I am proud of my amateur sleuthing, despite the fact that it hasn't exactly provided clarity on who sent Tiffany to the great beyond. I am basking in the glow of my flawless performance when I turn a corner in the corridor and sideswipe ... Trixie Barnett.

She's in a tracksuit, too, and her chin-length copper-colored hair is held back by a headband.

"What are you doing here?" I manage.

"What are you doing here?" she parrots.

We stare at one another.

She caves first. "This is my floor. I'm in 351."

I deliver my prepared line, though I feel like a real schmuck lying to Trixie. "I'm on my way to the gym."

Trixie giggles. "You are not. You're going back and forth past the door to Tiffany's room. I've done it a bunch of times myself. Am I right?"

Yes, I could lie to Trixie again. But somehow it feels wrong. Plus I'd really love to talk to somebody about the tidbits I've gleaned. And Trixie is the most trustworthy soul among my island acquaintance.

It comes out in a gush. "Well, I admit, I did go past. A few times. And then"—brief hesitation—"I went in."

She shrieks. "You *what*? How did you get in?"

"Ssshh!" I drag her behind a potted palm and explain while Trixie oohs and aahs, exhibiting not a scintilla of disapproval of what some people might consider breaking and entering. Indeed she appears awestruck at my investigative prowess.

That's why she's Ms. Congeniality, I decide. She

makes everyone around her feel fabulous regardless of the transgressions they recently committed.

"My Lord, you're like Nancy Drew!" she says when I pause to take a breath. "I adore Nancy Drew. That's why I couldn't sleep and walked past Tiffany's room a gazillion times. Well, go on, tell me what you found in there."

By this point I'm spilling all, like a repentant sinner. Trixie's eyes bulge when I get to my theory about Tiffany and her chip-eating husband doing the nasty pre-pageant.

"But it couldn't have been him," she says. "He didn't get here till after the pageant started. He even missed the parade of states."

"How do you know?"

"I overheard the policemen talking about it after they interviewed him."

We stare at one another. No words are necessary. We both know the implications that follow this revelation: Tiffany had a chip-eating man who wasn't her husband in her hotel room with her. And not just in her room, either. In her *bed*.

Even more damning. And bedeviling.

"What about her laptop?" Trixie asks.

I shake my head. "What laptop?"

"She was on it constantly. That's partly what made Misty Delgado move out. She said the clicking of the keys got on her last nerve. Truthfully, I think there was more to it than that."

"There wasn't a laptop in there. The cops probably confiscated it. There could be tons of valuable information on her hard drive."

"Clues," Trixie breathes.

Exactly, I'm thinking. Which is why I am most peeved that the laptop is beyond my reach.

At least at present.

A couple walks past, the first people we've encountered since my corridor confessional. Their appearance brings me back to reality. "We look suspicious out here," I say.

Trixie nods. "And I suppose I should try to grab an hour of sleep. You, too." She grabs my arm. "But I don't know how I'll be able to! It's so exciting now that you're on the case."

I demur but she'll have none of it.

"You are! You're going to solve Tiffany's murder, I just know it. And then you'll be the heroine of the Ms. America pageant and even if you haven't already been awarded the title, which you probably will have been, you'll win then."

I'm breathless listening to her, not to mention wildly daunted by the task she describes. Part of me does wonder, too, if she was being totally on the up and up when she explained why she was out in the hallway like I was, also breaking the stay-in-your-room rule. But I'm too stupefied to deal with that right now. I get back to my room, which I reenter without incident, armed now with the correct key card. Inside it's as if I never left. Shanelle continues to produce the same low rhythmic snore she was generating an hour earlier but snorts suddenly when there's a knock on our door.

"I'll get it," I chirp, hoping she's too dazed to notice

that I'm dressed and vertical. I pull it open. "Trixie, you should be—"

The admonition catches in my throat as I see that it's not Ms. North Carolina darkening my doorstep.

CHAPTER FIVE

Indeed, this personage is the cosmic opposite of Ms. Congeniality.

"Detective Momoa," I stammer.

"Ms. Pennington," he intones.

I am at this point speechless.

He is not. His eyes run down and then up my lime green velour tracksuit without a flicker of appreciation. "I see you're up and about early."

"I am." In desperation I've again resorted to Witness Stand mode.

"Why is that?" he asks.

"I couldn't sleep?" I clear my throat. "I couldn't sleep," I repeat more definitively. "The events of last night were most disturbing."

"Have you left your room since you reentered it last night?"

I'm glad I got the lying out of my system when I told Trixie I was on my way to the gym because my intuition tells me that would be unwise now. "As a matter of fact, yes. That's why I'm dressed. I've just come back from a walk." He might have seen me in the hallway, after all. Oh God, I hope he didn't see me in Tiffany's hallway.

He narrows his eyes. "You disregarded the

instruction to stay in your room?"

"Well, I knew I couldn't sleep. And that I'd be careful."

He doesn't look convinced. "Where did you go?"

"Up and down the corridors. It's the hotel version of mall walking. You know, indoor exercise." I hold up my right foot, hoping the floral-print Ked in which it's encased will serve as convincing proof of my aerobic intentions.

"Were you walking with Ms. Barnett?"

I'm thinking he has phenomenal intuitive powers until I remember that I answered the door saying her name. "Part of the way," I respond.

He performs the minutest nod I've ever seen in my life. Then, "Have a good day," he says, but somehow I get the feeling he doesn't really mean it.

I close the door and lean my forehead against it. Oh God. I don't know what he knows except that now he knows that I know that he's watching me. Oh God.

"Who the hell was that?" asks Shanelle. She sounds aggrieved, and justifiably so, since it's like 5:18 AM.

I don't have to produce an answer because the room phone rings. "I'll get it," I announce and race to the nightstand. "Hello?" I say into the receiver.

"Happy Pennington?"

On the other end of the line is a snarky female voice immediately recognizable to all of us involved in the Ms. America pageant. It's really too bad the bigwigs let her come to Oahu. She's the receptionist at headquarters in Atlanta and the crankiest individual ever to man a phone bank.

"It's Magnolia Flatt," she drones, without waiting for me to confirm my identity. "Mr. Cantwell wants to see you in his suite here at the Royal Hibiscus. Pronto."

"Mr. Cantwell?" The owner of the pageant, the chairman of the board. Hope rises in me, jostling for space alongside terror and the aforementioned stupefaction. In the last few hours I have heard two people ascertain that I will win the Ms. America title now that Tiffany Amber's final interview is being conducted at the pearly gates. Maybe this is it, my moment.

Or maybe not.

"He's not exactly in a good mood," Magnolia adds. I hear something crash behind her. "I wouldn't make him wait."

Sadly, it does not sound as if he's in the frame of mind to be dispensing tiaras. I groan as I hang up the receiver.

Shanelle is sitting up in bed, looking grumpy. "What is up, girl? We got more nocturnal activity than a whorehouse in Biloxi."

"Oh, Shanelle, I have no idea what is going on." I slip the memo pad I pilfered from Tiffany's room out of my waistband and put it and her key card into my makeup bag. "I have to go out and I don't know when I'll be back." The way this morning is proceeding, I'm likely to find myself breakfasting in the Honolulu pokey.

Minutes later I discover that you can't ride the regular elevator up to the penthouse suite at the Royal Hibiscus. You must be accompanied by a hotel minion who escorts you to a private elevator which whisks you up untold stories until the double doors open onto a sky-high tropical Shangri La.

Floor to ceiling windows abound in every direction, offering a panoramic view of glittering Oahu below. The furnishings are beyond luxurious; they look like they were purloined from the island's most splendiferous sugar plantation. There's a grand piano in one corner, a giant palm tree in another, and exotic flowering plants throughout. I don't know much about Ming vases but I suspect there are a few here, among silk-shaded lamps in the shape of dragons and gold-flecked paintings that depict Chinese men waging ancient battles and water lilies floating lazily on murky water.

I clamp my jaw shut before it can drop open. But I needn't have worried, for nothing dashes an awestruck mood quite like the sudden heaving into view of one Magnolia Flatt.

Every time I see that girl, I get an overwhelming compulsion to offer beauty advice. Fortunately I've never acted on it, because I'm sure she'd slug me. But the fact remains that Magnolia would be a much more attractive female if she recognized two irrefutable truths: that the latest fads do not suit pear-shaped body types, and that when it comes to makeup, less is almost always more. Especially at the crack of dawn. As it is, only Cleopatra had a heavier hand with eyeliner and I don't think even the Queen of the Nile slathered on pink eye shadow.

Not to mention that Magnolia never can grasp that snarling at her fellow humans lessens her appeal. "So you decided to show up," she snaps. "He's this way."

Sebastian Cantwell, I will tell you, is a bit of a legend

around Ms. America parts. He's richer than God for one thing, very good at running through rail-thin Asian wives for another, and kind of a daredevil—crashing racing boats and sinking yachts and once burning down a wing of one of his mansions in England because of a science experiment gone tragically awry. He's not the youngest stud on the farm but nevertheless persists in wearing a blond ponytail. I suspect he thinks it makes him look rakish. In the corporate-titan world, it probably does. We contestants love him because not only did he buy the Ms. America pageant when it was foundering like one of his ill-fated boats, he put his own money into the cash prize, making it the biggest haul a beauty queen can win.

The penthouse suite has a library, believe it or not, and that's where Sebastian Cantwell is ensconced. He rises from behind a desk as big as a helipad and I see that despite the early hour he's decked out in a suit and tie. He takes one look at me and barks an order at Magnolia. "Coffee." To me he says, "How long will it take you to become presentable?"

"Uh ... half an hour?"

"Acceptable." He signals that I should sit in the chair in front of his desk. "Damnable business about California," he observes as I comply.

Unless the west coast has been hit by a massive seismic shock, I assume he's referring to Tiffany Amber by her state association. "You can certainly say that."

"I had an idea she was trouble." He steeples his fingers and cocks an eyebrow. "You didn't kill her, did you, Ohio? Because if you did, all bets are off."

"I did not kill her, sir." I start to get excited. What bet could he be talking about but one?

He observes me while tapping his index finger on a crimson leather blotter. "I told those bloody detectives they won't find the murderer in our lot. Look outside the pageant, I told them. That's where you'll find your man."

I nod. I heartily approve of his viewpoint even if I don't entirely agree with it.

"So you've won," he tells me.

It's so abrupt, I don't get it. "Excuse me?"

"You need me to spell it out for you. Fine. You won the final interview. You might not have if California had a chance to answer but she didn't, did she?

"So you won, Ohio. You're Ms. America. Title, prize money, year of service, roses, tiara ..." He waves his hand. "The whole kit and caboodle."

I'm going to start hyperventilating, I just know it. "I'm thrilled and honored, sir. That's incredible. Thank you."

"Don't thank me. But don't let me find out you're lying about this murder business, either."

I can see how that would be a dealbreaker. "I won't. And I'm not." I try to catch my breath. I wish this victory sounded more set in stone but I guess this is as definite as it's going to get. I sure hope Detective Momoa starts sniffing around elsewhere. What if he keeps pestering me and Cantwell decides it's not worth the brain damage having his new Ms. America be suspected of murder most foul in the isolation booth?

Magnolia interrupts these distressing thoughts by

reappearing with a porcelain coffee set.

"Too late now," Cantwell informs her. He rises from his chair and to me says, "Chop, chop. The press conference is downstairs in half an hour. It's already past eleven on the east coast and I want a new headline for the noon broadcasts."

I bow and scrape a few more times and then bolt from the suite. Ms. America cannot accept her crown and scepter wearing a Juicy Couture tracksuit, regardless of its timeless appeal.

I have one thought as I race to my room. Fighting with Tiffany in that isolation booth turns out to have been the best thing I ever did. I was never fiercer or more determined than when I exited that booth and look what it got me? My first national title.

I know Tiffany's not in her grave yet. But if she were, she'd be rolling over.

CHAPTER SIX

I am happy to report that my first press conference as a national beauty pageant winner comes and goes without a single disaster. I think that's pretty impressive given that I hadn't slept all night and was still in kind of a daze over the fact that I'd won.

Jason waylays me the second my stilletoed feet step off the dais. "Hey, Ms. America." His smile is as bright as neon. He gives me a soft kiss on the lips, about the most we can swing given that reporters and pageant people are still milling around the banquet room. "I told you you'd win! Congratulations."

"Thanks." I grin. I've been grinning a lot in the last few hours.

"You look pretty darn hot, too."

I must agree. I'm wearing a "ladies who lunch" suit, a bright pink Jackie O affair with a sweet little collar and three-quarter-length sleeves and big cloth-covered buttons and a slim knee-length skirt. Unlike Jackie's, mine is accessorized with a rhinestone tiara. I bought the suit for the preliminary interviews with the judges, which calls for a classier look than other competition events. Like swimsuit, for example, which demands skin and spray tan and little else.

"So." He lowers his voice. "Now that the

competition's officially over, think we can celebrate in private?"

I give him a sly wink. "I don't see why not."

His smile gets wider.

"But it has to be later." The grin fades. "Mr. Cantwell says I have paperwork to sign. The contract, I think."

"You sign that baby fast. The quicker you do—"

"The quicker I get the prize money. I know." I can't believe it. A quarter of a million dollars. It's a mind-boggling amount of cash. It's more than our house is worth. That makes something occur to me. "You know what? Maybe you can go after *your* dream now."

"You're right!" He rubs his hands together. "Flat-screen TV, baby. HD, 47-inch widescreen—"

"That's not what I meant, Jason."

He looks confused.

"Pit school! You've been talking about it for years."

"Well ... sort of." He frowns. "It's a lot of time away from home."

"The point is, now we can afford it. And the timing's good because I'll be away sometimes traveling for the pageant."

He shrugs. "I don't know. Most people who do the training don't get a NASCAR job anyway. So it's kind of a waste of time."

I slap him playfully on the arm. "Since when is bettering yourself a waste of time?"

He narrows his eyes. "You're not trying to get rid of me, are you? I saw that Mario Suave guy giving you the eye."

"He was not!" Was he? Kind of a flattering idea. "Anyway, remember when I researched pit school on the web?" I'm the one in our family who does the legwork. "If I recall, there was a program in North Carolina that lasted for twelve weeks or so. And it cost something like twelve grand."

"Which is a ton of money. We could get six flat-screens for that."

"We only need *one* flat-screen." Actually, we don't even need that. "I was just thinking that with Rachel giving me guff now about applying to private universities, we have more than enough to cover pit school, too." Not that I'm happy about Rachel's attitude. And she knows it. Which is why she's not calling me much.

But if I've learned one thing from how my mother pushed me into pageants, it's not to make your child do what you couldn't yourself. That's a recipe for resentment.

Jason gives me another soft kiss. "Let's talk about it later."

"Okay. It's just that I'm so excited. This prize money means that everyone in this family can take a few steps forward."

"Right now the only steps I want to take are into Best Buy, to see what's up with flat-screens." He kisses my forehead. "See you later."

I watch him go. I guess my husband isn't the most ambitious guy I ever met. But he's just such a darn good mechanic! He could make something more of himself, I know it. I bet that if he pushed through pit school, he could get a job with NASCAR.

I turn to exit the banquet hall and end up barreling into Trixie. Like me, she's showered and dressed and looks a lot better than she did at 4 AM.

She grabs me and squeals loud enough to wake the dead. "Happy, Happy, Happy, I just heard and I am so happy for you! Whoops, I knocked off your tiara."

I sense the thing sliding leftward. It feels like the Titanic on my head. "Now I know why Queen Elizabeth practices wearing hers before big occasions."

Trixie continues to talk with a bobby pin between her teeth and both her hands righting my crown. "I should get a job doing horoscopes. I predicted you'd win and what do you do? Go and win." She steps back, beaming. "You're on straight now. I'm so happy for you. Let's celebrate by eating real food."

"I could stand getting my breakfast drink but after that I have to see Mr. Cantwell and sign the paperwork."

"Ooh!" she squeals again. "Well, I'm going to eat like a pig and then be a saint after ten AM."

We head for the hotel's casual café, where Trixie selects a lemon poppyseed muffin the size of a newborn's head. The girl behind the counter looks at me and asks, "The usual?"

"Please."

Trixie and I sit at the counter to watch my morning concoction being concocted. Pineapple juice, strawberries, a banana, a dash of vanilla extract ... Then, "Is wheat germ good for anything but fiber?" Trixie asks me.

"I think it's good for PMS."

She regards the brew with heightened appreciation then lets out a yelp. "Oh my Lord, I cannot believe I almost forgot to tell you. There's news about Tiffany Amber. A rumor the police took some man in."

"They arrested somebody already? Are you kidding me?"

"I'm not sure they arrested him. They may have just brought him in for questioning."

"Does anybody know who the guy is?"

Trixie shakes her head, pops some muffin in her mouth. In silent rumination she munches and I gulp. I wonder if this man the cops took in killed Tiffany. If he did, wow. We queens have been on Oahu only two weeks. In that short a time, how could somebody get a man mad enough to snuff her? Somehow, knowing her as I do, I think Tiffany Amber is capable of that achievement.

My appreciation for Oahu PD grows with this revelation. And once someone does get arrested for murdering Tiffany, I'm off the hook. The tiara will rest safely on my head, even minus a few bobby pins.

Trixie whispers in my ear. "There's Tiffany's husband again. Tony Postagino."

So like me, Tiffany Amber had a stage surname. "Him?" I didn't get a very good look at him the prior night. I give the once-over to a thirty-something dark-haired man walking through the lobby. He's slightly heavyset but not bad-looking. He's wearing a bright Hawaiian shirt not so different from Detective Momoa's. "Those aren't exactly widow's weeds," I mutter.

"No. But what do people in Hawaii wear when

they're sad?"

That is a true imponderable. I set my empty concoction glass back on the counter. "All right, on to the paperwork. Then I'm going to try to get away with sleeping all day."

An hour later, when I make it back to my room, Shanelle is there wearing a bright yellow sundress, which looks gorgeous against her mocha-colored skin.

Her hands fly to her hips. "What did I tell you, sister?" Then I find myself being hugged even more vigorously than I was by Trixie. "I was about to lay a bet on you but you didn't even give me time." She pulls back and eyes my ensemble from bow to stern. "And who says rhinestones don't go with a linen/cotton blend? You look sweeter than pie in summer."

"Thank you kindly." I often get a little southern when I chat with Shanelle. I start taking off the suit. "I am whipped, though. Do you mind if I pull the drapes and have a long snooze?"

She narrows her eyes at me. "You were awfully rambunctious last night. What was up with that?"

"Well ..." My addled brain tries to think fast. "Magnolia Flatt called me really early to come up to Cantwell's penthouse suite."

"That must be a sight to see."

"It sure is." I glance at the desk near the sliding glass doors. "Your laptop's booted up, right?" Back home in Mississippi, Shanelle is some kind of computer geek. She's on her laptop constantly, just like Tiffany was reputed to be. "Do you mind if I check out the news about Tiffany Amber before I take my nap?"

"Be my guest." She moves toward the laptop, clicks a few keys. "Our gal is a top story. Nothing like a beauty queen cut off in her first bloom. Or in the case of our pageant, maybe her third or fourth."

She chuckles and moves aside to let me sit in the desk chair. I'm now wearing the hotel's fuzzy robe. With the tiara. For some mysterious reason I can't bring myself to take it off. My eyes run down the first story. "So Tiffany sold real estate for a living. I didn't know that."

"In Riverside County, California." Shanelle moves away toward the bathroom. "Foreclosure central, from what I understand."

"It says here her husband's a lawyer. So he must haul in the bucks."

The rest of the article tells me things I already know. I google Tiffany's name, which brings up a bunch more stories with no fresh information. Then I google Tony Postagino. I don't admit it to myself but I'm sort of investigating. One thing Pop often says: in a murder, always look first at the spouse.

Tony Postagino didn't have opportunity, though, because none of the husbands were allowed backstage. Almost no men were, because it was where we contestants changed clothes between competitions. It was like a women's locker room.

"The husband has a website," I tell Shanelle, clicking on the link.

She returns from the bathroom, mascara wand in hand, just in time to see a slick-looking website fill the screen. "Fine-looking graphics," she remarks.

Which spell out 1-216-GOT-TONY? NO RECOVERY, NO FEE. And *Hablamos Español.* "He does personal injury," I say.

"In other words, he chases ambulances." Shanelle clucks her tongue. "Nice."

"And lucrative, probably. Although in the photo he's wearing the exact same Hawaiian shirt I saw him in this morning."

Shanelle waves her wand in the air. "You cannot get a man to shop. Unless he's gay."

"I feel really bad for him." I turn from the screen. "His wife dies all of a sudden, in this really bizarre public way. And he's got two little girls at home, both younger than five. Did you hear that some local guy got called in for questioning?"

"Mark my words." Shanelle points the mascara wand at me. "That girl had some nasty ghosts in her closet." She sashays away. "And they'll all slither out now, like worms after a rain."

CHAPTER SEVEN

I hear pounding on my door. I pull the pillow over my head but amazingly that does not make it stop. As dreamland slowly recedes, it occurs to me that I really should answer. After all, my status has changed in the last twelve hours. I'm Ms. America now. Maybe there's an emergency in the pageant ranks to which I am called upon to respond!

I leap out of bed yelling "I'll be right there!" Thanks to the blackout drapes the hotel room is pitch dark, though the digital clock on the bedside table informs me it's 4:37. I assume that's PM. Shanelle is really a trooper if it's four in the morning.

Seconds later, encased in the fuzzy robe, I pull open the door to see a gigantic bouquet of yellow roses in the arms of a very short Hawaiian man. He holds them out toward me. "For you, Ms. Pennington."

"Thank you."

He smiles and nods and sets off down the corridor.

I'm so in awe I forgot to give him a tip. There have got to be two dozen roses in yellow, my absolute favorite rose color. I push my nose into their sweet fragrance, set the vase on the desk, switch on the lamp, and extract the gift card.

*Congratulations, Happy! The pageant is honored to have
you wear its crown.*

*Since circumstances prevented you from receiving the
traditional bouquet at the finale, hope you'll enjoy these as a
substitute.*

Mario Suave

Wow. I stare at the roses. They look good in the
glow of the lamp and even better when I pull the drapes
and the rays of the sun make the blossoms appear even
more golden.

That is really nice of him. Extremely considerate.
The comment Jason made flits through my mind. *I saw
that Mario Suave guy giving you the eye.* I don't really
believe that's the case, but if it is, it's flattering. After all,
I'm married but I'm not dead.

Eventually I force myself off my duff and into the
shower. It's only after I'm dressed and admiring the cut
of my orange and white geometric pattern halter dress
that I run across, in my makeup bag, the pad of paper I
pilfered from Tiffany's hotel room.

I carry it to the balcony. No question: there is
definitely the imprint of writing on the top sheet.

I remember a trick Pop taught me, and cut off a
length of post-office shipping tape, whose presence
among my possessions is not a mystery to you, dear
reader. Then I lay the tape over the imprint.

Yup, when I return to the balcony and hold the
paper in the sunshine just right, the imprint becomes
legible. 3-8-2-6-3-7.

I don't know the importance of that series of

numbers to Tiffany. In fact, they could have been written by an earlier guest in her room. But I decide to hold on to the pad just in case.

I make it outside for what I like to consider *Showtime!*—when the sun is about to set and the Royal Hibiscus celebrates with the ritualistic lighting of the tiki torches on the property. It seems to me that this is the hotel's daily gift to its female guests, almost better than the twin mint chocolates it leaves on the pillows with the turndown service.

The person doing the lighting is a man, a young man, a young tanned Hawaiian man with an Adonis-like body clothed only by a loincloth-type thingie that sort of flips open and shut as he runs, his torch aloft. I'm always half hoping those famous Kona winds will whip up as he performs this rite, making his loincloth swish open even more productively, if you get my meaning.

At any rate, I always watch him with a fair amount of attention and enjoyment, and I know from the sudden silence that descends upon every other female in the vicinity that I'm not alone in my appreciation.

Tonight he has the usual line of giggling kids running after him as he bounds from one torch to the next. As I walk in my strappy white sandals along the curving path toward the beach, I'm seeing him from the rear, which isn't an A-1 viewing position for the reason cited above but still isn't bad.

I'm thinking a little stroll on the sand, then maybe a Mai Tai, some dinner, an hour of TV, and back to bed. I'll call Shanelle's cell, see what she's up to. Probably Trixie's out and about. I spoke to my mom and Jason earlier and begged off getting together, saying I needed sleep. Which is true, but still I feel guilty leaving my mom so much in Jason's company. He is not exactly her favorite person. I'll make it up to both of them tomorrow.

It's in that Scarlett O'Hara-like frame-of-mind that I pass Torch Man standing next to a palm tree. He's at a standstill, the kids are dispersing, and his torch is no longer held high. His duties must be concluded for the night.

I'm a bit further along the path when I stop short, a scent I just picked up finally registering in my brain. I turn around to retrace my steps and there right in front of me I see the source of the unusual aroma I've encountered twice recently. Once at 4 AM in Tiffany Amber's hotel room. And again out here as the tiki torches are lit.

The scent is citronella.

And the source is Torch Man.

CHAPTER EIGHT

He's alone now, leaning his forehead against a palm tree. He straightens and swipes his hand across his nose. He's more Torch Boy than Torch Man now. For one thing I see that he's really young, like 22. And for another, he's crying. A few tears are running down the cheeks of a truly sculpted face, which I'm noticing for the first time is just as finely made as his body.

I approach him. "Are you okay?"

He jumps and moves a few steps away. "I'm fine."

"You look upset to me. Maybe you need somebody to talk to." I'm winging it here. I have no idea what I'm doing.

He shakes his head.

"My name's Happy. What's yours?"

He hesitates, then, "Keola."

"Did you know the woman who died? Tiffany Amber? Is that why you're upset?" When in doubt, plunge in with both feet.

His dark eyes widen. "How did you know? Are you a cop?"

Bingo. "I was a friend of Tiffany's," I lie. "I was also in the beauty pageant."

He eyes me more closely. "Aren't you the one who won? I think I saw you on TV this morning."

It's fun, hearing that. Refreshing and new. "Yes, I'm proud to say I did win."

"Tiffany would've beat you if she hadn't died," he says. I get the feeling he's not being snarky, just matter-of-fact.

I can't say I disagree with him. "She was a strong contender. Were you really close with her?"

He looks away. For a second I expect the waterworks to resume. Then, "Do you know I'm famous, too?"

"Uh … really?"

"My family. The Kalakauas. We're descended from royalty."

I'm starting to wonder if Keola is a few orchids short of a lei when he confirms that suspicion by reopening his mouth.

"King Kalakaua was the last reigning king of Hawaii. People called him the Merry Monarch because he really enjoyed life. He revived the hula." He chuckles. "I hula'ed for Tiffany once. She loved it."

I take in the pecs, the hips, the abs. I just bet she did. "Do the cops know that you and she knew each other really well?"

"We talked about it."

"This morning? When they took you in?"

"Yeah."

I'm starting to feel like a pro at this whole investigating thing. Then again, this is like taking candy from a baby. Keola Kalakaua seems so unguarded.

I wonder if it was the scent of citronella that put Oahu PD on to him. There may have been other evidence in Tiffany's room that led them to him that was gone by the time I got there.

Keola pipes up. "I told the cops I didn't kill her. If I knew who did, I might kill them. But Tiffany? No way. Never." He looks away from me toward the ocean. He seems to drift into a kind of reverie, like he's remembering their time together. I'm thinking a high percentage of it was spent horizontally.

I stare at him. Boy, is it a blessing being a man. No woman could eat potato chips like this guy does and maintain that physique. For I have no doubt that he's the one who was in Tiffany's hotel room the prior afternoon, before the finale. Surely he's the one who helped Tiffany unmake her bed, something fierce.

I wonder why Tiffany had an affair with him. Was something wrong in her marriage? Or was she just letting loose while she was away from home, kind of a Hawaiian When-In-Vegas thing?

Whatever, it was a crappy way to treat her husband. And her daughters.

"Okay, bye then," I say to Keola.

He doesn't acknowledge me. His head is hanging and I watch his hand reach again toward his eyes. His grief seems real. He doesn't strike me as smart enough to fake it.

Nor does he seem smart enough to have murdered Tiffany. It had to be someone pretty cunning who did her in. It can't be that easy to get your hands on poison, then know exactly how to use it. If that is how it was done.

I realize the sun has dipped into the sea and decide

that it's too dark now to walk on the beach. I head back toward my room, thinking of Keola.

I hate when beautiful people are on the dumb side. Not to be snotty but it gives us all a bad name. It bothers me that everybody assumes we beauty queens are empty in the attic. Just once I'd like it if somebody appreciated me for my brains, too.

The evening and night pass as I hoped they would. Quietly, with room service and TV and sleep. The next morning I'm down in the lobby sipping my breakfast drink and waiting for Trixie when I see Detective Jenkins, Momoa's female sidekick, locked in conversation with Tiffany's husband. Still flush with victory from my verbal probing of His Highness Keola Kalakaua, I pretend to be interested in the brochures by the concierge desk and sidle closer.

Jenkins is speaking. I try to listen in. I feel kind of bad for her. From my dad I know how hard it is to be a cop: not enough pay for the hours and the danger. I imagine it's even tougher for a woman, because it would be next to impossible to find a man who'd put up with the lifestyle. I notice she's minus a rock on the left hand ring finger. Something about the straggly blond hair with the two inches of brown roots tells me she goes through life a trifle dispirited. The cop uniform doesn't help. It was not designed to flatter the female form.

"Let me make sure I understand," she says to Tiffany's husband. "You don't want the items returned to you?"

He mumbles something. I'm thinking that maybe he said he can't look at them. His head is hanging like

Keola's was last night and he's rubbing his forehead.

"I understand," Jenkins says. She seems flummoxed. Then, "Would you like me to ask the hotel to box everything and ship it to your home in California?"

At that he raises his head. His eyes are so bloodshot it looks like he hasn't slept in a week. "That's where I want to go," he announces, very clearly. "I want to get back to my daughters."

"I understand. But I'm afraid that's not possible at the moment."

"Why the hell not? When will it be possible?" He's pretty agitated. I can see that people other than me are listening, all while pretending to do something else. "Do you know how difficult this is for me? My little girls are asking a million questions that I can't begin to answer." His voice catches. Again he drops his head and shades his eyes with his hand.

Jenkins says nothing. All us eavesdroppers shuffle around.

He pipes up again. "I'm sorry for that. Pardon me. I'm not myself."

"I understand," Jenkins says. "I'll relay your concerns to Detective Momoa. In the meantime I'll arrange to get those items shipped. Her laptop as well?"

"All of it." He walks away.

I wonder if he knows about Keola. I hope not. I hope the cops are sensitive enough to keep that salacious tidbit to themselves until such time as they must divulge it.

I get a little edgy when I see Jenkins approaching the

concierge desk. She looks at me, then glances at the shark-cage-diving brochure in my hand. I had no idea I was even "reading" it. "Are you planning an underwater adventure?"

"Possibly." I return the brochure to its slot. "We all have a lot of time on our hands."

"Not all of us."

Touche.

She engages the concierge in a somber conversation about shipping to California the belongings of "the deceased." One word Jenkins uttered earlier is lodged in my brain: laptop. That's one of the items to be returned to the Postagino home. It's also one of the items I'd love to get my hands on. Tiffany's computer could be bursting with clues.

I see Trixie across the lobby and wave to her. She's dressed like I am, in a bikini underneath a cover-up, though her spandex is pastel orchid and mine is neon purple. We're both carrying wide-brimmed hats with coordinating beach bags, and wearing beaded flip flops and sunglasses. Neither has been shy with pool-appropriate gold jewelry, since I'm sure that Trixie, like me, hasn't the slightest intention of actually entering the water. Chlorine is hell on hair.

"You're not wearing your tiara." She sounds disappointed.

"That would be too nutty. And it wouldn't fit under the sun hat." Then I tell her the real reason. "Plus I was afraid I'd fall asleep and somebody would snatch it."

Her eyes widen. "You're right! We know there's a criminal element around here."

More like a homicidal element.

I notice Jenkins eyeing us as Trixie and I amble toward the pool. I'm embarrassed, to be truthful. Here I am, about to sip tropical drinks and bask in the sun and there she is crime-busting.

Though I'm hatching a plan of my own, investigation-wise.

CHAPTER NINE

First order of business: choosing lounge chairs.

There is strategy involved.

You want sun but a way to get out of the sun. You want a wide viewing area to be able to appraise a large fraction of your fellow sunbathers. You don't want to be too close to the bar, because there's too high a chance some sunbaked reveler will drop his Singapore Sling on you. Nor do you want to be too near the rental hut, because then you'll spend the day listening to parents tell their kids what's too expensive to get. And you don't want proximity to the deep end, because then you'll get soaked fifteen times an hour by boys doing cannonballs into the pool.

Given those parameters and how many prime lounges are already crammed full of oil-slicked bodies, there are remarkably few good options left, even at 9:12 AM.

Trixie and I claim our spots and pull out our dogeared paperbacks. Mine has a pink and green striped cover with a picture of a woman's tanned, toned legs in cute tangerine-colored sandals. Trixie's cover is mostly gray and features a stormy ocean with a woman in a baggy sweater walking alone on the beach looking forlorn.

"Book club?" I ask.

She nods. "Maybe I can finish it this morning."

"How many characters have died so far?"

"Only one."

"You're getting off easy."

So am I, truth be told. Magnolia gave me a 3-ring binder filled with info I need to digest now that I'm Ms. America. I should be reading that but I don't feel like it. I'm rationalizing my laziness by pretending I won't risk smudging the binder with sunblock.

I glance at Trixie, whose nose is buried in her book. I wonder if her background is at all like mine. Probably not. No doubt she was smarter than me. I got pregnant at 17 and then Jason and I got married. Only when Rachel was a year old did I get my high-school equivalency. And only when she was in first grade did I go back at night to study toward my bachelor's. Since I have to work full-time, it's taking me forever to finish it. But I'm determined to graduate some day, regardless how long it takes.

I suck down the last of my breakfast drink and eye the crowd. I must say, the male guests at the Royal Hibiscus should be paying extra this month. The presence of us queens at the hotel has considerably improved the poolside eye candy for them. For us gals, not so much. As usual, there are a few delusional men who think they look good in Speedos. Others sport so much body hair they could double as Sasquatch. There are some handsome forty-somethings, though, with a little gray at the temples, and a few buff young studs who look like they work out twice a day.

They remind me of Keola. I tell Trixie what I learned the prior evening.

Her eyes bug out as I relay the final details. "Even if he were smart enough to pull off killing Tiffany, though," she says, "he couldn't have done it because there's no way he would've been allowed backstage."

"I was thinking that, too." My cell phone rings. I look at the display and my heart lightens. "It's my daughter," I tell Trixie. "I haven't spoken to her yet today. Do you mind if I take the call?"

"Don't be silly!"

I flip open the phone. "Hey, Rach!"

"Hey, mom. You still jazzed to be, like, a total celebrity?"

"I am if you're still psyched to be the daughter of a total celebrity."

It takes her a second too long to answer. Then, "Sure. I mean, it's cool."

Not exactly a ringing endorsement. "You're not getting grief about it at school, are you?" That happened when I won Ms. Ohio. Mean boys asking how did it feel to have your mom be cuter than you. Mean girls saying it must be hard to have your mom be a throwback to the dark ages.

"Well," Rachel says, "it's not like you're saving the world or anything but it's cool."

That is what my daughter would rather I do. The truth is I'm not up to it. "That's going to have to be your job, Rach. For when you're done with college," I specify.

"Can we talk about college another time, mom? I mean, we don't have to talk about it *constantly*."

"I didn't think we did."

"You bring it up, like, *incessantly*. Anyway, I gotta go. I have class."

"Okay. We'll talk later."

"Bye." She's gone.

Trixie sets down her book. "How's she doing?"

"Great," I lie. I am saved from further discussion of my angst-filled relationship with my teenage daughter by the arrival of a girl bearing skewers of cut-up strawberries and pineapple. Trixie and I both partake.

"Look," Trixie says. "Right across from us."

I follow her line of sight to the other side of the pool. Ms. Arizona Misty Delgado. "I like her suit." A tankini in a burnt sienna color, with lots of ring detailing.

"Goes with her olive skin tone really well. That must be her husband."

A buff blond guy is on the lounge next to her. They're clearly together but they seem awkward. They've pushed their loungers together but their bodies are facing opposite directions.

"He's hot," Trixie opines, and I agree. "So why was *she* having an affair? Uh oh," Trixie adds.

Uh oh, indeed. A kid is approaching them passing out brochures that I can read from here: VENTURA AERIAL TOURS. He hands one to Misty's husband, who takes one look, then rises from his lounger and calmly tears the brochure into about ten pieces, which he dumps into his wife's lap. He then walks away. Meanwhile Misty's eyes have not left her magazine. She's doing a good job of pretending that nothing in the least untoward has just occurred.

"I don't think they're going to be taking the aerial tour," Trixie observes.

"Well, Misty's already been flying with Dirk Ventura, if you take my meaning."

We know that, and every YouTube aficionado knows that, thanks to the video which appeared hours before the pageant finale showing Misty and chopper pilot Dirk Ventura not exactly *in flagrante delicto*, but damn close.

"If it hadn't been for that video," Trixie says, "Misty would've been in the top five. She probably would've knocked me out."

This is a pageant for married women, after all. Cavorting with men who are not your husband is verboten if you want to place, or win.

Then again, Tiffany appeared to get away with it.

"Misty wouldn't have knocked you out," I tell Trixie, "but she would've been in, I agree. So who shot that video? And uploaded it?"

Trixie is silent. It was the big mystery of the pageant until an even bigger one loomed: Who killed Tiffany Amber?

Maybe the two episodes are linked. After all, Tiffany and Misty were roommates until Misty moved out. How weird is it that the two of them were embroiled in the two big bizarro things that happened in this pageant?

"You were on that first aerial tour, right?" Trixie asks me.

I nod. I'm chewing pineapple.

"With Misty," she prods.

I swallow. "And Ms. Alaska and Ms. New York."

"What did you have to do to win that again?"

"Answer a math question."

"Oh, that's right."

The Ms. America pageant's two weeks of preliminary competition involve a variety of skill tests for us queens. Who can pitch a golf ball closest to the hole? Who makes the best brownies? Who can diaper a baby doll the fastest? Sometimes the winner earns points that count toward the pageant finale; other times she wins some perk. In this case, the first contestants to answer a math question correctly won an aerial tour of Oahu provided by none other than the strapping Dirk Ventura.

"What did you think of Ventura?" Trixie asks.

I ponder for a moment. Then, "I thought he was cocky. He's a good-looking guy but he struts around. It's like all of Oahu is a campus and he thinks he's the Big Man On."

"A lot of women like that."

"Misty must. She made sure to ride shotgun during the tour and the two of them talked a lot over the headsets. I don't think she even looked out the window. The rest of us were in the back seat and didn't say a word."

"You got to concentrate on the scenery."

"Which was amazing. Diamond Head, Waikiki, Hanauma Bay ..." I've seen things on this trip I'll never forget. Above and beyond Tiffany Amber tumbling dead out of the isolation booth.

Trixie leans closer. "So who are you going to investigate next?"

It's more *what* am I going to investigate next. "I don't want to tell you because I don't want to jinx it. Plus"—I hesitate—"it's kind of risky."

"So was going in Tiffany's room! But look what that got you. You never would have known about Keola if you hadn't smelled that citronella in there."

"True."

"Nancy Drew wouldn't have solved a single mystery if she hadn't taken risks."

"Nancy Drew didn't have Detective Momoa on her tail."

"She had other impediments," Trixie pronounces.

Somehow Trixie has a way of firing me up. I rise and drop my cover-up over my bikini. "All right, I'll put my plan into action." I grab my things and slip into my flip flops. "I may or may not be back."

"Whichever. I'll be waiting for a full report."

"Just make sure to answer if I call from the jailhouse."

CHAPTER TEN

I return to the concierge desk and am relieved to see a different woman on duty than was there earlier. She, too, is wearing the hotel uniform for female employees: bright floral sundress and hibiscus tucked behind the ear.

"Excuse me," I say. "I've bought so many souvenirs here on Oahu that I need to ship some things home to Ohio. Is there any chance the mail room has boxes and shipping tape that the hotel guests can use?" Not that any beauty queen is ever out of shipping tape but she doesn't know that. Of course I don't really need a box, either. "Naturally I'd be happy to pay for it."

"Well ..." She eyes me. "You're the one who won the pageant, right? I saw your picture in the paper this morning."

"Really?" I'm liking this winning thing. "I'll have to look for a copy."

"Tell me your room number and I'll get you a *few* copies." She smiles at me. "And while we usually send people to the mailboxes place around the corner, I'll give the mail room a call for you."

"Thank you so much." I feel kind of guilty as she picks up the phone. She wouldn't provide this perk if she knew what I intend to do with it.

I glance around. This would not be a good time for

Detective Jenkins to put in a return appearance. But there's no sign of her. Only the usual assortment of happy-looking travelers, pasty ones fresh from the airport with welcome leis around their necks, and sunburned ones without.

A bit later the concierge hangs up. She smiles at me again. "Someone from the mail room is on his way up with a box and some tape for you."

"Terrific. Thank you again." Darn. I wait, my mind working. Then a middle-aged Hawaiian man shows up carrying what I claim I need. I take it and engage him in conversation as I lead him back the way he came. "When I'm done packaging everything, why don't I bring it down to the mail room?"

"Oh, no, leave it with the concierge and I'll come get it."

"No, really, that's all right." I lean close and whisper to him. "I don't want to bother her with this again. They're always so busy at the concierge desk."

"I understand but we don't like guests going down into that part of the hotel."

"The basement?"

He laughs. "It's not our best feature."

"I don't mind." We're at the staff elevator now. In fact, it's just arriving. I step inside. I see I've sort of boxed him in—ha ha. He looks a bit reluctant but gets in, too. "This isn't so bad," I say as the doors open onto the basement floor. It's what you'd expect, with beige walls, fluorescent lights, linoleum floors, and mysterious pipes suspended from the ceiling. Down here the air conditioning can't quite combat the warmth and humidity. I hear the hum of mysterious generators, and the rumble of industrial laundry equipment.

We turn one corner and at the end of the next corridor is the mail room, identified by a sign. The gray metal door is open.

That makes me happy, and so does the fact that I spy numerous mailing boxes that appear ready to ship. My guide turns to me. "I guess it'd be okay if you brought your box back down here when it's ready to go. If nobody's here when you come back, just leave it in the hallway. I'm never gone long. 'Course you can always leave it with the concierge, too, and she'll call me to come get it."

I nod. It occurs to me that I really should ship something home so all this doesn't seem suspicious. "Your shift must start pretty early in the morning."

"Six to three," he says cheerfully.

"That's early. Well, thank you. I'll be back."

"Aloha," he calls as I retrace my steps.

I feel bad again. I hope this nice man doesn't get into trouble from what I'm about to do. I hope I don't, either.

I flip-flop my way back to the elevator, where I press the UP button. I then remove my flip flops, whose slapping sound is pretty loud, and dart around the next corner. The elevator comes and goes with me still on the basement level plastered against a wall.

I'm barely breathing. How am I going to explain this if somebody sees me? The elevator's right around the corner but somehow I couldn't find it? Sadly, many people would believe that of a beauty queen.

I put my new shipping tape in my beach bag along with my flip flops, and set it on the floor next to the collapsed shipping box. I'll need my hands free.

It seems to take forever but eventually I hear footsteps coming from the direction of the mail room. I plaster myself back against the wall, as if that would help. Someone—the mail room man, I hope—stops at the elevator bank. I hear an elevator arrive, then sneak a peak around the corner. It's him all right, stepping inside.

Once he's gone, I run to the mail room. God, I hope he left it open. And God, please don't let him come back fast. I know it's perverse to involve the Almighty in activities of dubious legality, but I hope He understands this is in service of a good cause.

The mail room is open. Prayer one answered. I head for the stacking boxes that appear ready to go out. Tiffany's is neither the top one, nor the second from the top.

The mail room man's words ring in my ears. *I'm never gone long.*

Not the third from the top, either.

But with the fourth I hit pay dirt. This one is addressed to Mr. Tony Postagino in Riverside, California. I lift it and set it aside. It's fairly heavy but not too bad. None of the other boxes are going to him.

Only one box? Yes, I realize, looking around. Because there are two suitcases as well, with tags instructing the mail room to box and ship them to Tony Postagino.

The thing I really want is Tiffany's laptop. Would

that be in a suitcase or a box?

Box, I decide. Because she probably carried it to Oahu in a computer bag and that would be too bulky to go in a suitcase. I restack the other boxes, lift hers, and run.

I am so bad, I think to myself as I race away from the mail room carrying my booty. *I am so hosed if anybody sees me.*

I'm not far from the elevator bank when I hear my cell phone ringing, loud and clear, from my beach bag. The basement corridor is suddenly filled with a Muzak version of Gloria Gaynor's "I Will Survive." To make matters worse, I then hear the elevator begin its downward swoosh to the basement floor.

I am about to be discovered. Thief, '80s-music fan, marauder.

I sprint, fling myself around the corner, drop the box, then dive for my beach bag and the cell phone inside. I shut the damn thing up just as the elevator doors whoosh open. Footsteps again. I try desperately to hold my breath. I'm on all fours in the middle of the corridor, which really is no different from being plastered against the wall, though I feel strangely more vulnerable.

The footsteps are receding. Apparently God is heeding the prayers of his new Ms. America, though I suspect that if I keep this up, I won't have His forbearance for long.

I gather my and Tiffany's belongings, which is quite a load, and within seconds am in the elevator riding to the main floor. I wish I could go higher but that is not an option. When the doors open, I exit as nonchalantly as my thieving self can manage and sashay toward the elevator bank that'll take me to the ninth floor.

It is only when I am outside my own door that it occurs to me that if my roomie is in, I'll have some explaining to do.

CHAPTER ELEVEN

Of course Shanelle is in, because my good karma can't last indefinitely.

She's on her bed wearing a black camisole and pink shorts and painting her toenails a metallic white. She's let her hair dry into a natural Afro and tied it back with a black headband. She glances at the box in my arms and her expression grows quizzical. "What you got there?" she asks me.

"Uh ... just some stuff." I set the box down in the narrow space between my bed and the wall. I then throw my beach bag on top of it, aiming for the shipping label that spells out in big block letters MR. TONY POSTAGINO.

She rises from the bed and hobbles closer, undeterred by her fresh pedicure and the toe-separating thingie that's protecting it. She's looking at me the way mothers look at their children when they know said children are up to something of which the mother will not approve. Unless I want to wrestle her to the floor and thereby ruin her new polish, I cannot stop her from doing what she does next: picking up my beach bag and reading the label on the box.

Her eyes move slowly to my face. "I will ask you again. What you got there?"

"How much time do you have?"

She sits on my bed. "Start from the top."

The story does sound fairly preposterous when I hear it aloud. When I finish, Shanelle has this to say. "You're in deep, girl."

I don't like how serious that sounds.

She goes on. "Have you lost your mind? You just won the title of Ms. America and a quarter million dollars. That would all go bye-bye if anybody found out about this. And the cops do have some idea how to do their job. Even if they don't, it's not your business. Tiffany was no friend of yours." Somewhere in there she rises to her feet and puts her hands on her hips. "So what is this really all about?"

That is a good question, given everything that's on the line. "Part of it," I say, "is that I've kind of got this in the blood. Investigation, I mean. My dad's a cop."

"So he's a pro."

The phrase *unlike you* hangs in the air. "There's something else, too. I'm under suspicion myself since I was the last one in the isolation booth with Tiffany." I tell her about Momoa questioning me, and that it was he who showed up at our door at 5 the morning after the finale. "It's better for me if I can figure out who killed Tiffany. If Momoa keeps sniffing around me, it might make Cantwell decide I shouldn't wear the crown. He might give it to somebody else in the top five." I'm suddenly inspired. "Like Sherry Phillips." I know Shanelle's opinion of Ms. Wyoming.

Sure enough, Shanelle scrunches up her face as if a foul odor were pervading our room. "He wouldn't dare.

Half the synapses on that girl don't fire."

"But she could be in third position." I've had another inspiring idea since we've been talking. "You know what? You could help me investigate. You work in information technology, right?"

"I manage the I.T. department at a bank." Her eyes narrow. "Why do you ask?"

"Guess what I might have in that box. Tiffany's laptop."

"Are you telling me we could read her email?"

"If you can figure out how to get into her computer."

I have never seen Shanelle move faster. She pushes past me and hoists the box on my bed, using her manicure scissors to slice through the shipping tape. In seconds we're inside. And soon we're fist-bumping each other.

"There's her laptop bag!" I singsong. I was right that it wouldn't be in one of Tiffany's suitcases.

I'm lifting the bag out when Shanelle grabs my arm. "This is unchristian."

"There is nothing wrong with doing our level best to bring a homicidal maniac to justice."

"Well, when you put it that way."

We relocate to the desk, where we push the vase of yellow roses out of the way. Shanelle, by the way, was highly entertained hearing who they came from. She begins to boot up the laptop. Soon we're asked for a password.

"I was afraid this would happen," I say.

Shanelle's fingers hover over the keys. "Usually it's

a telephone number or a birth date or a kid's name or a wedding date."

"Hmmm. I use my daughter's birth date."

Shanelle glances at me. "Don't we have a list of the contestants and their contact information?"

"That has home addresses and phone numbers. And email addresses." I go in search of the paperwork, meanwhile trying to remember what Trixie told me Tiffany's daughters' names are. I read off Tiffany's phone number.

Shanelle types it in. "Nope."

"Try the work number." That gets us nowhere. "How about her street address?"

Shanelle tries a couple variations. "Nope."

"Try Ava." The name of one daughter.

She shakes her head.

"Madison."

"No go. I'm glad this isn't configured to lock down after a lot of mistakes."

"No kidding. Hey, wait a minute." A light has gone off in my head. I jog to the bathroom and dig into my makeup bag. Yup, it's still there, the pad of paper I lifted from Tiffany's hotel room, which has a series of numbers imprinted on the top sheet. "Write these down," I tell Shanelle. "3 – 8 – 2 – 6 – 3 – 7." I stare at the sequence. "You know what? I bet these are her measurements."

Shanelle harrumphs. "My ass."

"I'm serious." I watch Shanelle's hands drop into her lap. "Why aren't you typing them in?"

She shakes her head. "That girl was a thirty-eight

up top like I'm a thirty-four down below."

"Shanelle. Now is not the time to focus on whether or not Tiffany Amber was truthful about her bust size. Key them in."

"This is a travesty," she declares, and just as the last word leaves her lips, we pass to a new screen.

Our victory screams are short-lived as Shanelle's cell phone rings. Her ring tone is "Back to Black" by Amy Winehouse. She pops up from the desk chair while I remember that somebody called me while I was stealing Tiffany's shipment home. I pull my cell from my beach bag and turn it back on. I have two voicemails from reporters trying to score one-on-one interviews with me, which Cantwell told me were verboten until the investigation into Tiffany's death concluded. No talking to the press, he instructed after the presser.

Pop called, too, I see, and left a voicemail saying he was just checking in since we hadn't talked since yesterday.

I snap my cell shut. I am suddenly filled with humungous regret. My father would not approve of what I'm doing. No cop would. Nor would any evidence that I find in this manner be admissible in court. This misguided mail theft of mine would just back up what I know my father already thinks: that his daughter should stick to girly things and leave all the serious brain work to others.

And the danger isn't over, even if Shanelle and I don't spend another second probing Tiffany's computer. I still have to get the shipping box back into the mail room with no one seeing me. Otherwise its absence will be noted and the cops will be onto investigating that, too.

I flop onto my bed. Shanelle glances at me but continues her conversation with her husband. Lamar did not come to Oahu like so many of the husbands because he couldn't get off work.

I am pondering my idiocy on the crime-busting front when Shanelle finishes her call and races back to the desk. "You ready?" she calls over her shoulder. "Lamar says hi, by the way."

"I'm having doubts," I tell her.

"I got no time for doubts." She's squinting at the screen. "We are about to read Tiffany Amber's email and I am hoping to be entertained."

"I'm serious, Shanelle." I sit up. "I'm now thinking it was a ginormous mistake to take that box."

"Well, it'd be even stupider to have the thing here and booted up and not peruse its contents. Let's check it out for fifteen minutes and then you can box it back up. Besides, you got me into this, girl, and now I want a payoff." Her voice trails away. Clearly she's intent on reading something. She lets out a cackle.

"Something good?" I ask her.

"Nothing that gives any clues who snuffed her."

That draws me up and to my former position behind Shanelle, reading over her shoulder. I don't know that my roommate, savvy as she is, shares my instincts when it comes to criminal behavior. There could be something of value hidden in those emails that she's not seeing.

A while later, I conclude there isn't. "I think we should see what programs she has installed," I tell Shanelle.

She closes Tiffany's email, clucking her tongue. "I was expecting more from that girl. For somebody who probably got murdered, her email was deadly dull." We're back to Tiffany's desktop. "Now this," Shanelle murmurs, "is bizarre." She points to an icon.

"FX Trader? Maybe it has something to do with real estate. It doesn't sound like it, though."

Shanelle opens the program.

I frown. "Foreign-exchange trading?"

"Should we log in?" Shanelle asks.

"Let's try. We probably know the password."

Indeed we do. And within seconds it becomes clear that Tiffany Amber has quite an impressive history of currency-trading transactions with FX Trader. Impressive in all respects but one.

"She lost a buttload of money," I say.

"She had a lot to lose." Shanelle points at the screen. "Look at the size of that deposit."

"Fifty grand. Wow."

"Foreclosures or not, I guess the real-estate business wasn't all bad."

"Maybe her husband won some big court case and they invested the proceeds in this."

"Bad idea."

We trace Tiffany's trading history. She started small, made money, put in more money, made more, and then her luck changed.

"She should've stopped when she was ahead," I say.

Shanelle turns to me. "I saw something about this on the *Today* show. About Japanese housewives speculating in currencies to make cash on the side. It's called arbitrage, I think."

Shanelle's mention of Japanese housewives reminds me of the newspaper in Tiffany's hotel room that had the yen/dollar exchange rate circled. Now I know Tiffany wasn't keen on currencies because she and her husband were planning to travel abroad.

I haven't confessed the hotel-room break-in to Shanelle, though, and I don't intend to, so this tidbit will remain my secret. "This is a pretty high-risk way to make extra money," I say. "Because you could lose it all, too. Why would Tiffany do that?"

"Since she had the rich lawyer husband, you mean."

I look over Shanelle's shoulder at the columns of numbers on the screen, all representing actual cash dollars. Up, down, up, down. "You know what? I think this is like gambling. Maybe Tiffany had a gambling problem."

"An addiction. Coulda been her fix." Shanelle arches her brows. "And maybe when she lost too much, it caught up with her."

CHAPTER TWELVE

"Enough of being a spy." Shanelle shuts down Tiffany's laptop. "I'm ready for a drink."

I glance at my watch. "It's getting to be that time."

On Oahu, things go from wonderful to magnificent as the sun descends each evening into the sea. The Royal Hibiscus does it up in style, what with His Highness Keola Kalakaua making his half-naked torch-lighting run while guests gather at the lobby lounge to nurse a cold one and watch the sky turn glorious shades of purple, orange and pink.

"I need to shower," I tell Shanelle. I'm still in my bikini cover-up and my skin is tacky from my 30 SPF sunblock.

"Make it quick."

I dutifully run to the bathroom. "By the way, my mom is coming over."

"She's a card, your mom. What about Jason?"

"He met some other guy who's into NASCAR and they're going out for a beer."

In twenty minutes I'm showered and wearing a tropical print strapless dress with a sweetheart neckline and an Empire waist with a sparkly row of sequin trim. My feet slide into my best strappy sandals and I tie my hair into a damp chignon. I do a ten-minute makeup and

I'm good to go. Since by beauty-queen standards I've been fast, Shanelle's happy. She's wearing an adorable cocoa-colored halter-style tiered dress with a deep V neck and a low-cut back.

By the time my mom appears, we've repacked Tiffany's laptop and hidden the shipping box. My mom is wearing white polyester pants and a daisy-print blouse. Her earrings are two porcelain clip-on daisies. And as always, she is in what she calls comfortable shoes, code for ugly. I dread the day my aging feet demand I give up heels.

We hug. "It's nice to see you," she says. "It's hard to believe we've been on the same island these last few days."

"Hello, Mrs. Przybyszewski!" Shanelle whips off those four syllables as if they were her own. She pushes past me to hug my mom. "And don't you go making Happy feel bad for being busy. You know what it's gonna be like now that she's Ms. America."

Judging from the last few days, it will involve breaking the law, downing cocktails, and soaking up the sun. No wonder so many women enter this pageant.

"I suppose so." My mom's tone is grudging. She's just inside the room when she spies the yellow roses on the desk. She makes a beeline, then gives the bouquet a thorough inspection. I suspect she's trying to locate the note card. "Gorgeous," she pronounces, then she glances at Shanelle. "From your husband?"

"No, they're Happy's."

My mother's glance drifts toward me. "Sure as the day is long, these did not come from *your* husband."

I start to protest but Shanelle interrupts. "They're from Mario Suave." She has a mischievous glint in her eye.

My mother arches her brows. "He's a little dark-skinned but he's a good-looking Latin man."

Shanelle whoops.

"And he's done very well for himself," my mother goes on. "He came from poor beginnings but pulled himself up by his bootstraps. More of those immigrants who come to this country should take a page from his book."

I grab my white envelope clutch with its faux tortoiseshell details. "Since when did you become an expert on Mario Suave?"

"I read," she says smugly. I note she doesn't specify *what* she reads. She's not exactly a *New Yorker* subscriber. More like *People* and *In Touch Weekly*. "He did have a child out of wedlock but I suppose we've all had to deal with that problem at one time or another."

Shanelle and I exchange a glance. I remain silent until I process what my mom said. "Really? Mario's a dad?"

"He has a daughter named Mariela who lives with her mother Consuela in Miami."

"How old is his daughter?" Shanelle asks.

"Sixteen," my mother answers.

A teenager like Rachel. "Are he and Consuela married?" I try to sound casual but I'm not sure I succeed.

"Not to my knowledge," my mother says.

I'm trying to picture Mario's ring finger on his left

hand. I'm not seeing a gold band there. That doesn't necessarily mean anything, though.

Nor does it mean anything that he sent me roses, I'm sure. I bet he considered it part of his duties as emcee.

"If he's not married, he's ripe for the picking," Shanelle says.

"Not for me," I say primly. "I'm married."

"That can be easily remedied," my mother points out.

Shanelle claps her hands. "You're full of piss and vinegar today! Let's go put a cocktail in you."

I make a move for the door. "I hope we can still get seats."

My mother grimaces. "Will it be crowded down there? You know how crowds give me headaches."

"It'll be just enough people to be interesting," Shanelle opines, and she turns out to be right.

There isn't so much of a horde that we can't get seated, and at the Royal Hibiscus the service is mainland quick. I get a Bing Cherry Daiquiri, Shanelle a Banana Colada, and my mom a Bee's Knees. We order a coconut shrimp appetizer and settle into our overstuffed chairs to watch the sun go down and the sky get painted a myriad of colors.

"If I keep eating like this," Shanelle says, double-dipping in the tamarind ginger sauce, "my hips will be as wide as Pearl Harbor."

"It's okay, we're on vacation," I proclaim.

"Vacation?" My mother's expression darkens. "What about all that work you're doing for the pageant?"

"It's always vacation in Hawaii," Shanelle says, "whether you're working or not. Look who's coming." She raises a shrimp in the direction of the lobby. My mother and I peer over our shoulders to see.

"You remember Sally Anne Gibbons," I tell my mom. "She owns the Crowning Glory Pageant Shoppe in Las Vegas." Why Sally Anne needs an extra P and an extra E in her store name, I cannot tell you. Maybe it's in tribute to the extra E in Anne.

Shanelle mimics Sally Anne's cigarette-ravaged voice. "Crowning Glory is the only full-service pageant boutique west of the Mississippi."

We both giggle and watch Sally drop her heft into a wicker chaise positioned in front of the giant open windows that front the ocean.

"She's blocking my view of the sunset," my mother says.

Shanelle and I shush her in unison.

"I think Sally Anne's already had a few," Shanelle murmurs a few seconds later, sipping from her own adult beverage.

There is certainly evidence to that effect. For example, Sally Anne is not exactly sitting up straight. She's sprawled, and her face is red in a way that looks more booze-induced than sun-kissed. Her copper hair, which is usually arranged into a sort of hairsprayed dome, is slightly askew this evening. None of this, however, stops her from raising her finger to summon a server. A minute later a Mai Tai is in her hand. Another minute later, the glass is empty. Again her finger rises in the air.

"That woman drinks like a fish," my mother says.

"Mom, lower your voice."

"What, I can't call a spade a spade?"

"Just do it quietly."

By now Sally Anne has been served her second cocktail, at least by our count. It disappears down her gullet as fast as the first one did.

"She's not going to be able to walk out of here," my mother says. "She better be wearing sensible shoes."

She appears to be. Given Sally's recumbent state, we have a full view of her footgear.

"She's really taken to muumuus since she's been here," Shanelle observes.

"I don't think I've seen her in anything else the entire time." I analyze Sally Anne's black floral muumuu as my hand reaches for the coconut shrimp. My willpower here has gone to zilch.

Apparently so has Sally Anne's. I watch her finger go back up in the air.

"How is a muumuu different from a caftan?" Shanelle wants to know.

This is the sort of fashion question I love. "Isn't a muumuu always short-sleeved? And I think they almost always have a flounce."

"I've never seen a caftan with a flounce," my mother puts in.

"Then what's a tunic?" Shanelle asks.

"It's a butt-length caftan. Look." We watch as the young male server who gave Sally Anne her two drinks huddles with the older bar manager. "I bet they're going to cut Sally Anne off."

"They better. She's inebriated," my mother says.

"This should be good." I can't tear my eyes from the scene. The server takes a deep breath and approaches Sally Anne. He bends down to speak quietly to her.

"What?" she bellows. "I insist on speaking to your manager." It takes Sally Anne three attempts to pronounce manager correctly. Eventually she gets her wish and the manager does walk over. I'd say he appears reluctant to do so.

He has good instincts, because when he bends toward her, she slaps his face. The onlookers, of whom there are a goodly number, gasp.

My mother's next observation rings out over the hushed lounge. "She keeps this up, she'll find herself in the hoosegow."

That provokes a twitter or two. But not from Sally Anne, whose tormentors now include a third male hotel staffer. The men raise her from the chaise, which would be a crane-worthy task even if she weren't resisting, and begin to lead her away.

But the drama is not yet over. Sally Anne is halfway across the lounge when she halts, jerks her fleshy right arm away from the young server, and points toward the lobby. "You!" she cries.

Everyone in the lounge pivots to see the next object of her ire. It's Rex Rexford, Tiffany's pageant consultant, in blue madras walking shorts, a white linen campshirt, and brown leather sandals. His normally bouffant blond hair is slightly wilted, whether from humidity or grief over his deceased client, I cannot say. Like all of us, he seems mesmerized by Sally Anne's quivering index finger.

"Your client was a bitch!" Sally Anne screams. It comes out a little slurred but I think we all get the gist. "I know you're not supposed to speak ill of the dead. Well, I speak the truth about everybody, dead or alive. And Tiffany Amber was a lying, scheming bitch, pure and simple. I'm glad she's gone to the great beyond. So there!"

Rex's face blanches beneath his salon tan. I bet he regrets his innocent sunset amble across the lobby's central courtyard. Even the macaw is upset. It's shrieking loud enough to wake Tiffany, if she were in earshot.

My mother, however, is silenced by this diatribe. We all watch mutely as Sally Anne totters away, not quite under her own power.

"Wow." Trixie joins us, breathless. She's in turquoise cuff shorts and a cotton voile halter top. Her normally pale skin is a tad rosy, probably from the poolside sunbathing I cut short. "Can you believe that? Boy, Mrs. P, you really saw a show."

"We don't have to pay to see the luau after this," my mom says. "What's that woman's beef with the dead California contestant, anyway?"

Trixie looks at me, obviously aghast. "You didn't tell your mother the story? Mrs. P, it was the biggest scandal of the pageant before Tiffany Amber died. Two of the girls showed up on Oahu with the exact same gown, color and all, for the evening-gown competition. Can you believe that? And guess where they both bought their gowns? Crowning Glory."

My mother is enough of a pageant aficionado to understand immediately. "Did Sally Anne mess up the registration?"

Every pageant shop worth its salt participates in the national registry, designed to prevent exactly this disaster. When a gown or swimsuit is purchased for competition, the seller inputs the style and color into the database for that pageant, so no other contestant makes the mistake of purchasing the same outfit.

Trixie goes on. "Sally Anne claims that it was Tiffany Amber who messed up the registration, by changing the entries."

My mom looks confused. I take the story over. "Tiffany bought her gown at Crowning Glory, too, and Sally Anne says that when Tiffany was at the store, Sally Anne happened to be inputting data, and Tiffany expressed curiosity about how she did it, and then when Sally Anne went to wrap Tiffany's items, Tiffany changed the entries."

Shanelle and I glance at one another. We both know Tiffany had expertise with computers. And I believe she was both competitive and malevolent enough to have done exactly that of which she was accused.

Shanelle pipes up. "Then Sally Anne had to scramble to get new gowns to Oahu in time. Both girls wanted new gowns because they both felt tainted."

"I would have felt that way," Trixie says.

"And I bet," I say, "that Sally Anne had to eat the cost." Those gowns can be terribly expensive, too. I know.

"It's a huge blow to Crowning Glory," Shanelle adds. "Because now every contestant will wonder whether she can trust Sally Anne not to bollix up the registration."

"You should have heard the screaming fights those two had!" Trixie slaps her thigh. "Right here, in this very lobby."

"And there's no love lost between Sally Anne and Rex Rexford, either," I point out. "Even before this whole thing with Tiffany, the two of them were rivals, because they both do pageant consulting."

"I think Rex's girls do better than Sally Anne's," Shanelle says.

My mom pipes up. "That would only make Sally Anne hate him more."

So, so true. As the last drops of my daiquiri slide down my throat, I wonder if Sally Anne's anger morphed into revenge.

CHAPTER THIRTEEN

Shortly before 0600 hours, I'm out of bed. I will admit that I am feeling the effects of last night's daiquiri. That may be because it was followed up by a second.

By ten after the hour, I'm in my early morning snooping outfit, which you'll recall is comprised of a Juicy Couture tracksuit and floral Keds. This time I've eschewed my lime green velour for my black. It makes me feel more spy-like. Part of me also hopes that if I run into Detective Momoa, which I most sincerely hope does not occur, he won't immediately recognize me.

I know. I may be awake but I'm so dreaming.

I don't bother being quiet because Shanelle knows what I'm up to in this wee hour adventure. She's dozing, every once in a while emitting a light snort.

Careful to check the corridor before I step outside with Tiffany's box, I exit the room. I am so ready to be rid of this thing. Today my desire to unload it is as strong as my compulsion was yesterday to get my hands on it.

I encounter no one on my way down to the lobby and no one as I make my way to the service elevator. Before long I find myself once again on the basement level.

I listen. Save for the droning of the generators, it's

quiet. I set down the box and do a jaunt to the mail room to see if the door is open and the room is unoccupied. I score on both counts.

This is my moment.

Despite the encumbrance of the box, I break speed records getting back to the mail room. I throw some boxes aside to put Tiffany's on the bottom of the stack. Her two suitcases are no longer in evidence. All I can do is pray that somehow that nice man didn't notice that her box was missing and, if he did, that he didn't report it.

I restack the boxes. All systems are go. I enjoy a blissfully uneventful return to my room. Shanelle is still snoozing, which somehow I find amazing. Doesn't she pick up my agitation from my early morning mission? She snorts, rolls over. Apparently not.

I kick off my Keds and lie on top of my bed. After a while I begin to calm down. So much so that I actually fall back asleep. I am awakened some time later by the sound of a blow dryer. I conclude that Shanelle has embarked on her a.m. beauty ministrations.

She emerges from the bathroom wearing her fuzzy hotel robe. This morning she's straightening her hair, which is a process I don't envy. "Oh good, you're up." She goes to the TV and switches it on, then pulls the iron and ironing board out of the closet. "You put the box back in the mail room?"

"It's back there."

"Good. I'm hungry again, believe it or not. You want to do the breakfast buffet with me?"

Despite the fact that we both pigged out at dinner, I'm hungry, too. Maybe law-breaking requires extra calories, like pregnancy. "I'm game." I get myself vertical and head for the shower.

"I've got my flat iron heating up in there," Shanelle calls. "Don't burn yourself."

It's when we both have our laptops booted up, and the TV's on, and the iron, and Shanelle's flat iron, and the AC's on full blast, and we're both blow-drying our hair, that we hear a whiz and a pop and just like that, our electricity goes bye-bye.

"Darn." I look at my half-dried hair. Time for another damp chignon. I begin to loop my hair around my hand. "I'll go downstairs and alert housekeeping."

"We could just call."

"Remember we tried that when my blow dryer died? They don't pick up." This appears to be one area in which the Royal Hibiscus is a tad lax.

I'm in the lobby heading for the concierge, who clearly helps with all matters large and small, when I run into the young man who escorted me in the private elevator to Sebastian Cantwell's penthouse suite the morning after the finale. "Hi, Neil," I say. Not only do I remember his name but that he grew up in Michigan and a love of surfing brought him to Hawaii. I note that his pale skin has not taken well to the tropical sun.

"Hey, congrats!" His eyes light up. "Saw you won the pageant. Awesome."

"Thank you." Hearing that is not getting old. "You know, maybe you can help me. My roommate and I got an electrical short in our room and I know from before that it might take Housekeeping kind of a while to get to it."

"Hear you. Power's crucial." He winks at me. "Just lay your room number on me and I'm there."

In short order Shanelle and I have forgotten about the short and are on our way to the buffet, served at the lower-level restaurant that fronts the ocean, directly below the lobby lounge area. It's quite the spread every morning, and I usually have only my breakfast drink concoction and don't partake, but some mornings it gets me. We pull plates and begin loading.

"The only other time I was in Hawaii," I tell Shanelle, "when Jason and I went to Maui, I realized I ate bacon four meals in a row. At the breakfast buffet, like this, then in a BLT at lunch, spaghetti carbonara at dinner, and again the next morning in the buffet."

"And in the middle of all that you had to get into your bikini." She's a sausage girl, I can tell from her plate.

"I was younger then."

We see a few contestants clearing out from Trixie's table and take their places. I think Trixie might hold court in this location about two hours every morning, not eating so much as chatting. It's the Miss Congeniality thing.

"Your mom's fun," Trixie tells me.

"She's certainly"—I struggle to find an appropriate adjective—"outspoken."

Shanelle pops some kiwi into her mouth. It's not *all* fat on her plate. "She's going with you to the mani/pedi place later, right?"

I chipped the polish on my big toe. The imperfection is driving me crazy. "She wants a manicure. And she doesn't want to pay the hotel salon prices."

"It's like seventy-five dollars for a pedicure here," Trixie says.

"We're not in Kansas anymore," Shanelle singsongs. She looks at me. "You could do it yourself, you know."

"I always mess up the polish." This should be part of my beauty queen skill set, but sadly it is not.

Trixie moves over to sit next to me. "So I'm dying to know what happened yesterday!" she whispers. "I couldn't ask last night with your mom around. What did you do after you left me at the pool?"

"You don't have to whisper." I point my empty fork at Shanelle. "She knows all about it. In fact, she was an accomplice."

Trixie looks impressed. In low tones Shanelle and I report on my mail room escapade and what we learned from Tiffany's laptop. Trixie is as mystified by the currency trading as we are. "That girl had secrets. I bet that's what got her killed."

I freeze, my fork suspended in midair. Some distance away but in my line of sight is the hostess desk. And who do I see standing there but Detectives Momoa and Jenkins.

Trixie follows my gaze. "The policemen are back. I wonder what part of the investigation they're conducting now."

Pushing past them, none too gently, is Ms. Arizona Misty Delgado. She ignores the hostess and breaks into the buffet line, grabbing a plate out of turn and causing a minor commotion. Two older women ahead of her turn around to see what's up and she snaps at them. "What the hell are *you* looking at?" They raise their brows at each other and pivot back around.

"Somebody woke up on the wrong side of the lanai this morning," Shanelle says.

I watch Momoa, whose beady eyes are trained on Misty. "I wonder if she's in a lousy mood because she just got interrogated by the cops." I've never been that keen on Misty but in this case I feel her pain.

"Maybe they grilled her," Trixie says. "Because of her being Tiffany's roommate and all. *Ex* roommate."

Shanelle spears a piece of sausage. "So they know there was bad blood there. 'Course, there was bad blood between Tiffany and almost everybody she had any dealings with."

Except maybe Keola Kalakaua. His reaction to her death seemed pure grief.

Misty continues to behave like a buffet bully, darting in front of people to take what she wants without waiting. I wince when she slams a man's hand in the cover of a warming dish. He yelps but she sails right on.

Trixie shakes her head. "This is not going to convince the policemen that Misty's a nice person."

"Ain't no cop dumb enough to buy that charade anyhow," Shanelle observes.

"There's Magnolia," I point out, "behind Misty. Oh, dear."

Magnolia has decked herself out in yet another unfortunate ensemble. High-waisted short shorts, in hot pink no less. Her flesh is crammed inside the fabric with disastrous results. Every inch of her panty line is excruciatingly apparent. One finds oneself mesmerized by her buttocks, which I can say with confidence are not the feature she should be accentuating.

Shanelle pipes up. "That girl needs a thong something fierce."

"At least her camisole sort of fits," Trixie says.

I shake my head. Poor Magnolia. She labors under the delusion of so many women that if her clothes aren't tight enough to restrict blood flow, she won't look good.

All of a sudden Misty steps backward and spins around, right into Magnolia's plate. As if it's on tiny little wheels, Magnolia's Spanish omelet slides off her plate smack dab onto the pristine white skirt of Misty's sundress. It hangs on for a moment, then spills to the terrace floor, leaving an impressive splotch of egg and oil in its wake.

Like Mount Kilauea on the Big Island, Misty erupts. "Can't you do an effing thing right, you fat idiot? Not the videotaping, not anything! When I asked if you got the videotape you needed, I didn't mean of *me*, you moron!"

"Shut your mouth, you bitch!" Magnolia screams. We all watch as Magnolia pushes Misty's plate into her, causing Misty's eggs benedict to assume the center-skirt position briefly before tumbling to the terrace floor. Now the two crumpled egg dishes lay side by side, except for the bit that's landed on Misty's beaded sandal. Magnolia bursts into tears and runs from the scene, pushing past Detective Momoa, who hasn't budged this entire time.

I wouldn't be surprised if he's getting the impression that pageant people are a trifle moody.

Trixie squeals and grabs my arm. "Can you believe that? Misty Delgado was about to eat eggs benedict! Do you have any idea how many calories are in hollandaise sauce? Like *thousands*!"

I try to gather my thoughts. "What I can't believe is what Misty said to Magnolia. Misty made it sound like it was Magnolia who shot the videotape of her and Dirk Ventura that showed up on YouTube."

"But why would Magnolia shoot that tape?" Trixie seems deeply perplexed. I think she's still reeling from the high calorie count of Ms. Arizona's would-be breakfast.

"If Sebastian Cantwell knew, he would fire her for sure." My mind races. "She must've been trying to blackball Misty for some reason. She had to know Misty would never win once that video appeared."

"You know what's even weirder?" Shanelle leans her elbows on the table. "That part where Misty said something about asking Magnolia way back when if she got the videotape she needed. How do you explain that?"

I can't. But I can see clearly before me the next phase of my investigation.

CHAPTER FOURTEEN

I'm back in my room, alone. Shanelle has gone to the hotel fitness center to work off her sausage. As for me, I'm working on a game plan. Eventually I pick up the phone and dial Magnolia's room. She picks up. I greet her and say who's calling.

She produces her usual charm-filled reaction. "Great. Another contestant. What the hell do you want?"

I restrain myself from pointing out that She Who Wears the Tiara is no longer just 'another contestant.' "I wanted to know how you are. I saw what happened a while ago at the buffet."

"You and half the hotel."

"I was wondering if maybe you wanted somebody to talk to." I'm trying this tack since it sort of worked with King Keola. "I know Misty can be hard to deal with."

"And the rest of you pampered-ass beauty queens aren't?"

Don't hold back, Magnolia: tell me what you really think. "I'm just saying that I understand that whole thing had to be upsetting. And, you know, I'm Ms. America now and maybe I should try to patch things up between you two."

"Why bother? Once we leave Hawaii, I'm never going to see that bitch again."

"She might compete in the next Ms. America pageant." Some girls compete year after year in an effort to win. Good for them. But if Misty does, and succeeds next time, I'll be the one who has to pin the tiara on her arrogant head. Yuk.

"If I have to work with that pointy-chinned witch again, I'll quit," Magnolia declares. "If I still have a job *to* quit." She hangs up.

She's a tougher nut to crack than Keola. What a surprise.

I put down the in-room phone and pick up my cell. Time to make another call. A few seconds later this one gets answered, too. "Hi, Pop," I say.

"My beautiful girl!" he booms. "How are you?"

"Fine. It's kinda wild around here, you know, with details emerging about Tiffany Amber's life." Some of which I've ferreted out on my own, using, shall we say, unorthodox techniques.

"The girl who died? Well, that's how it goes."

"I guess so. Turns out she was into foreign-exchange trading. Isn't that weird? I wonder if maybe it was a money thing that got her killed?"

"Oh, sweetheart, you shouldn't be filling up your head with that. Think about what my beautiful girl just achieved! You're Ms. America now!"

"I know, but—"

"Don't you have appearances to plan?"

"Not really. Everything's kind of on hold until Tiffany Amber's death is explained." I should be reading the material in the 3-ring binder Magnolia gave me but I'm not even doing that.

"Everybody around here is asking me if this means you'll compete in an international pageant down the road."

"Ms. World, right, but—"

"That's what you should be focusing on, my beauty."

I sigh. He doesn't want me to investigate. I already knew that.

"You make me so proud, sweetheart."

"Thanks, Pop." I hear a knock on the door. "Mom's here. I gotta go."

The mere mention of his ex-wife is enough to clear my father off the line. I answer the door with my cell still in my hand.

My mom glances at it as she enters my room. She's in a cute shorts and top set we picked out at Chico's. "You'd rather make a phone call than talk to your mother who's here in the flesh?"

"I'm just finishing a call."

"With Rachel?"

"No, she and I talked this morning. Pop." My mother's face somehow manages both to crumple and light up at the same time. "He's fine," I tell her.

"Did you hear me ask how he was?" She looks away. "What he does, how he is, it's no longer any of my concern."

You may have gathered by now that their divorce is fairly fresh. It happened only four and a half months ago, after 49 years together. And no, it was not her choice.

"Mom." Maybe here, so far away from home, she'll be more willing to talk about it. I sit down on my bed and pat the coverlet. She settles beside me, with obvious reluctance. She knows what's coming. "You don't have to pretend with me," I say. "You can tell me how you really feel. I want you to."

She's staring out the sliding doors to the balcony as if there's something fascinating out there. Her lips set in a thin line. She's silent for a long time. Then, "I think enough has been said," she pushes out. "By everyone concerned."

"I really think you'll feel better if you talk about it." She seems to spring from the generation that believes it's not right to discuss these things. Even among family.

"What's to talk about?" She turns her head to look at me. It breaks my heart to see so much pain in those light blue eyes of hers. "You give a man your whole life, everything you've got, and he takes it as if it's his God-given right, and then one day he comes home and tells you he doesn't want you anymore. And what does he leave you with, after you've given him everything? Nothing, that's what."

I wish she appreciated the good years they had together. Maybe after a divorce that's too much to hope for. At least this soon. "It's not true that you have nothing." I pat her leg. "You've got me. And Rachel."

She's silent. Maybe she's wishing they'd adopted more children, that they'd be a bulwark against this heartache. I don't know whether they would or not. I do know there were many miscarriages before they adopted me. For all I know, there were some afterward.

She shocks me with her next question. "Is there some floozy sniffing around him? Has he told you anything about that?"

"No! Absolutely not. I really don't think there is." I watch her face relax a touch. I decide that's enough deep talk for one conversation. I pat her knee again and stand up. "Let's go get our mani/pedis. My treat."

She rises. "I'm not letting some stranger touch my feet."

"Just a manicure then? Sure." I grab my purse. "Do you want to buy polish beforehand so you'll have your own?"

She looks astounded at the concept. "Why would I pay extra to do that?"

We head out the door. "Some women do. They don't like getting the polish from the same bottle that's been used on other women."

We're in the corridor now. She's frowning in more earnest. "Is this place you're taking me to unsanitary?"

"No." At least I hope not. It didn't exactly come recommended; I just noticed it when the pageant bus drove past. I didn't feel right asking the hotel where to go because their own salon provides the service. I just don't want to pay those prices.

After a short walk through Waikiki, we arrive at Nail Palace. It's in a strip mall—even gorgeous Hawaii has those—and it's pretty much like every other establishment of its kind that I've ever patronized. It has a few nice accoutrements, though, mostly of a floral nature: some lovely exotic orchids, and bromeliads that are actually blooming.

After we check in, my mother sidles close to me, wearing yet another worried expression. "Everybody who works here is Oriental."

I'm glad this time she kept her voice down. "Mom, you should say Asian. And yes. I think they're Vietnamese."

She looks dubious. It doesn't help that several women choose that moment to look up from their clients to check us out and then make comments to one another that result in fits of laughter.

I spot an *In Touch Weekly* and press it into her hand. "Here. Why don't we pick colors and then you can catch up on the latest news."

I smile just looking at the racks of pretty bottles. I love this part. The array is truly dazzling. I was sort of forced into a pale pink for the pageant finale, as I had to match all my competition outfits, from my ladybug get-up for the parade of states—yes, you heard right—to my fuchsia evening gown to my turquoise swimsuit. Now I can be wilder. I throw caution to the wind and select a bright orange.

My mother reacts to my choice with an arch of her brows. I eventually prod her into a dusty rose.

We sit on the bench by the entry and wait to be summoned. Now that I think about it, I guess the ladybug did bring me good luck, as that fine beetle is reputed to do. The Ohio Ms. America brass demanded that I represent the state insect in the opening parade. I was not thrilled, I can tell you, especially by the antenna protruding from my shoulder straps, which thwacked me in the face every time I turned around. At least Ohioans from the deep dark past had the good sense not to pick the cockroach or some other truly repulsive bug as their state symbol. That I would have resisted with vigor.

My mother gets called before me. Her manicurist tries to engage her in conversation but I can tell even from across the room that doesn't go well. A short time later a spa chair frees up and I'm in. The woman who's doing me says in accented English that her name is Tia. She's mid-twenties and very pretty.

We get down to it, the mechanical massager in the spa chair working its magic. What with my nocturnal spying, I haven't been sleeping enough lately. I doze off until we get to the callous-removal phase of the operation.

Yes, I'm ticklish. I can't keep myself from jerking my foot away. "I'm sorry," I tell Tia. What I really don't want to do is kick the poor girl in the face.

"You sensitive," she says, and eyes me more closely. "You here for the pageant?"

"Yes."

"How you do?"

"Well, to tell you the truth, I won."

Tia's eyes fly open, then she squeals. She leaps off her stool and points at me, shrieking something that draws her coworkers like buzzards to a carcass. From the hand gestures and facial expressions I get an idea what they're saying even though I can't understand a word. *This one won? Can you believe it? Isn't she a little old? And wide in the rear? And look how those boobs sag!*

I see my mom looking over. All she knows is that the locals have discovered that her daughter won the pageant. Her face brightens with pride. She jabs her manicurist with her free hand and says something. Suddenly she's a conversationalist, because now she has an opportunity to brag. I'm going to have to give her manicurist a serious tip.

Tia sets her hands on her hips. "You know the girl who died?"

"Yes, I knew her."

That produces another animated round of conversation. "You know Keola, too?"

That's a surprise. "I do know Keola. How did you know?"

Tia translates for the group. They all roar. "Dirk, too, you know?"

I frown. "The chopper pilot? Yes, I know him a little."

This time the laughter is deafening. Tia points a warning finger at me. "Don't you talk to them," she says. "Unless you want ..." She makes an O with the thumb and index finger of her left hand and repeatedly pokes her right-hand finger into the circle created. This gesture appears to cross all national borders.

"No!" I shriek.

That denial seems to lessen my appeal as a source of entertainment. The other manicurists drift back to their clients. Tia resumes her position on the stool and shakes a bottle of clear polish. "We all know them. They bad. Keola go after that girl who died. Dirk even worse. He always go after the pretty ladies who come to the island.

I think he training Keola to do same thing."

I lean forward. "Are you kidding me? Dirk and Keola are friends?"

She nods placidly then bends over my toes to paint. "Sometimes they have bet."

"What? You mean a bet whether they can get a woman to sleep with them?"

"Stop move." Very lightly Tia slaps my calf. This revelation has gotten me so riled up that I can't sit still. "My boyfriend tell me that if they get her to do it, they get drunk and tell everybody. At the bar down there." She motions down the street.

I'm flabbergasted. There I was thinking that Keola, while not exactly a saint for sleeping with a married woman, was kind of a nice guy. He certainly seemed to grieve Tiffany. Now I find out that he and Dirk have some vile bromance where they seduce unsuspecting female tourists for sport. Disgusting.

Anger isn't the only emotion coursing through me. Pity's right alongside, for none other than Tiffany Amber. Like any woman, she would have been devastated to know she was the subject of this kind of revolting behavior.

CHAPTER FIFTEEN

I'm so agitated I can barely sit through my manicure. When that's dry enough for hightailing it from the salon, my mom and I embark on the walking tour of Waikiki I promised her. Then lunch. I'm beside myself by the time I finally drop her off at the Lotus Blossom and return to the Royal Hibiscus.

Despite my fairly fresh pedicure I boldly stride onto the sandy beach and make for the rental hut, where tourists in better moods than me are procuring equipment for playing around in the pool and the Pacific. Yes, holding court there for his day job is Keola Kalakaua, wearing a floral wreath on his head, perhaps in honor of the royal blood he claims flows through his veins. He's no prince in my book, I can tell you that.

"I've got a bone to pick with you," I say to him when a family renting boogie boards finally toddles away from the hut.

He looks at me. He seems cagier than he did during our last encounter. Of course, I'm not exactly laying on the charm this time. "What's up?" he inquires.

"I heard something about you that's not very flattering."

He shrugs.

"Don't you want to know what it is?"

"Somebody talking stink about me, you'll tell me soon enough what it is."

He does know something about women, at least those on the warpath. "I heard that you and Dirk Ventura are friends."

His brow arches. "That makes you mad?"

"That depends. Do you and he ever make bets?"

He can't stop a smile from curling his lips. There's my answer.

"That's lousy behavior," I tell him. "Really crappy. Did you two have a bet about Tiffany Amber?"

He doesn't say a word. He busies himself with rearranging some surfboards that are just fine the way they are.

"Aren't you going to defend yourself?" I ask him.

"Why should I?" His brown eyes drift to my face. "I didn't do nothing wrong."

"What?" My decibel level ratchets up a notch. "You don't think it's slimy as hell seducing a woman just so you can win a bet with some guy?"

"Not when she wants it."

I slap the beach hut counter. "You give men a bad name." I turn away, crossing my arms over my chest. My hostility against those bearing a Y chromosome must be radiating pretty well, because a cute little boy who was approaching the hut abruptly halts in the sand when he sees my face. He turns around and runs away.

I'm scaring small children. That takes the wind out of my sails.

I pivot back to face Keola, who's now wiping sand off goggles. "So that's what you're saying? That since

Tiffany was willing to sleep with you, you're off the hook?"

"She wasn't just willing, she wanted it, okay? She told me she wanted to get even with her husband. He was having an affair, she said."

"So that makes what you did A-OK?"

"Listen, I fell for her. I had feelings. Deep feelings."

"Here we go. Bring out the violins."

"I'm not kidding. I got hurt. Because I don't know if she cared for me like I cared for her."

"Yeah, right. I'm sure you're all torn up inside worrying about that."

"I am. Because now I'll go to *my* grave wondering if she cared. Because I only asked her for one thing, *one* thing, and she wouldn't give it to me."

"What'd you ask for? Her prize money if she won?"

His eyes fly open. He looks as stunned as if I'd announced that I'm the Madonna come to the Hawaiian islands.

I slap the hut counter a second time. "Are you kidding me? Is that seriously what you asked for?"

"My mom's sick, all right? My family could really use the money. And everybody staying at this hotel is loaded or they wouldn't be here."

"I'm not loaded and I'm here!"

He turns away. "It's none of your business anyway."

I can't believe I guessed what he asked for, my first try. I don't know if I believe his story about his mom. At any rate, I've had enough of His Highness for now.

I walk away trying to lighten my mood by assessing

what I learned. One: that Keola and Dirk are friends. Two: that Keola and Dirk had a bet about whether Keola could seduce Tiffany. Three: that Keola asked Tiffany for her prize money, which she said she wouldn't give him, since she may have been a bitch but she wasn't an airhead.

What else did I learn? That Tiffany thought her husband was having an affair. Then again, maybe she just told Keola that to justify her sexual wanderlust. Or maybe Keola made it up to justify his own behavior.

I step from the beach onto the oceanside walkway and stand in line to rinse the sand off my feet. After a few moments admiring my new bright orange pedicure, which survived this ill-advised foray, I head for the lobby.

I haven't considered Keola much of a suspect in Tiffany's murder because I just don't think he's smart enough to have pulled it off. Nothing he said today convinces me otherwise. And I haven't seen a motive.

Though now I have to wonder: could Keola have been so mad at Tiffany for refusing to give him her prize money that he offed her for spite? That doesn't seem likely but I shouldn't judge too quickly.

I enter the open-air lobby and sigh. This is all so confusing.

"Hey, Ms. Serious Babe-i-tude!" calls a male voice behind me.

I turn around to see the perennially sunburned hotel employee to whom I reported Shanelle and my electrical short this morning. "Hey, Neil, how you doing? Got any surfing in today?"

"Yeah, it was boss. Kamikaze waves, for sure." The man may be pink as a roast pig but he has a megawatt smile. "Power back on in your room?"

"Yes, thank you. My roommate and I appreciate it."

"Right on." All of a sudden his expression darkens. I follow the line of his eyes.

Sebastian Cantwell is crossing the lobby with Detective Momoa. They appear to be deep in conversation. Cantwell looks like he's about to set sail on the British version of *The Love Boat*. He's wearing white trousers, a white dress shirt, a navy blue jacket, and, yes, a red silk scarf around his throat. At least he hasn't tied it around his ponytail.

I lean closer to Neil, whose gaze is fixed on the pair. "Who is it you don't like? The cop or my new boss?"

"Got nothin' against the fuzz." Neil's eyes snap to mine. "Can you keep a secret?"

No, but I'm not going to tell him that. I lean closer. "Tell me."

It takes him only a second to start babbling. "I always kind of thought that pageant guy was a tool but I didn't remember this till yesterday. Then it came back to me, who else I took up to his suite. Besides you and that yuckbabe Magnolia."

"Who?"

"The girl who bit it. The one who died."

"You mean Tiffany Amber? Are you kidding me? When?"

"I don't know, about a week after you all got here."

"I can't believe it. Are you sure?"

"Totally."

That is an absolute no-no. Pageant rules stipulate no private contact between contestants and pageant officials, for obvious reasons: it might gain the girl an unfair advantage over her rivals. The only pageant person any queen should have one-on-one dealings with is Magnolia Flatt. "Did she go up there alone?" I ask Neil.

"Sure did."

"How long did she stay?"

"Long enough." He looks away. A clerk at Reception is calling him. "Sorry, gotta go. Catch you later."

I'm paralyzed in the middle of the lobby courtyard as Neil jogs away. The macaw and I stare at one another as I reflect on this latest bombshell. It's been one revelation after another today and none reflects too kindly on the people around me.

Did Tiffany sleep with Cantwell, too? Even if she didn't, they should not have had a private meeting. I'm dying to know what that was all about. But I can't exactly go up to my new boss, the man who controls my destiny as Ms. America – and my prize money – and demand answers.

I see Momoa part from Cantwell, glance at me, narrow his eyes meaningfully, and then move away. At the moment Momoa doesn't frighten me as much as usual. I'm wondering if for once I know something he doesn't.

CHAPTER SIXTEEN

I return to my room having reached one inescapable conclusion: Sebastian Cantwell must be flung into the same slime-filled man box already occupied by Dirk Ventura and Keola Kalakaua. For what reason besides sex would he have met privately with Tiffany Amber? I can't think of a single possibility.

I toss my handbag onto the bed and sink beside it seconds later. Am I the only person in this archipelago not conducting a clandestine affair? Apparently so.

I suppose I could separate these sexual transgressions into categories. There are the adulterers, like Tiffany and Misty. And possibly Tiffany's husband, Tony Postagino. Then there are the fornicators, like Keola and Dirk and Sebastian Cantwell. Maybe they should be considered less naughty. After all, none of them are married.

Then again, Dirk and Keola made those despicable bets. And Cantwell was forbidden by pageant rules even to *talk* to a contestant privately. Much less ... you know. So those factors elevate their waywardness, in my humble opinion.

Again I sigh. I'm discovering that much dirty linen is aired during this murder investigation business. It makes a person feel positively scummy. I'm sure that's part of the reason my father wouldn't want me getting involved. He puts me on a kind of pedestal, which is both good and bad.

I take a bracing shower, and after that again feel ready to face the world. Which is good, because it's barely 4:30 in the afternoon and this Ms. America has delving to do.

Wearing my blue paisley patio dress with spaghetti straps, I am so filled with resolve as I sit at the desk near the sliding glass doors that I barely glance at the yellow roses Mario Suave gave me. Since I've decided I must put off the Sebastian Cantwell matter until I can figure out how to handle it, there's another puzzlement I will address, one I haven't been able to get out of my mind. It's the accusation Misty Delgado hurled at Magnolia Flatt this morning in the buffet line. *When I asked if you got the videotape you needed, I didn't mean of me, you moron!*

I want to know what Misty meant. And I want to know *now.*

I scan my pageant paperwork and before long my fingers are punching in Misty's room number. A man answers. I presume it's her husband but given what she's been up to of late, I don't know why I should. "May I please speak with Misty?" I inquire.

"She's at the salon," the man growls, and hangs up.

Lousy mood; has to be the husband. Can't say I blame him, though. Time for my second salon visit of the day, though this time I don't anticipate being the recipient of any services. Especially not at Royal Hibiscus prices.

The salon here at the hotel is called a spa, which I

gather is what allows them to charge more. The brochure describing it makes liberal use of the nouns *retreat* and *escape*. As I enter, I conclude the designer must have been a real mosaic devotee, because it's everywhere. Somebody's also fixated on Buddha, whose sculpture seems to fill every nook and cranny. Tucked into one corner is a Spa Shop. I glimpse shelves groaning under the sort of brightly colored, beautifully shaped bottles that make my female heart sing. At the reception counter are sprays of orchids, and behind them women sporting the same lab coats as Clinique salesgirls. There's less makeup on these spa women but they seem possessed of the identical superior attitude, like they've achieved Internal Peace to a degree that your rattled self can only aspire to.

Somehow I feel like I should speak softly, though I might not be heard above the fountains and piped-in New Age music. "Good afternoon. I'm Happy Pennington, the new Ms. America. I understand our Ms. Arizona Misty Delgado is here and I must see her on urgent pageant business." I'm quite proud of that phrasing, which sounds both businesslike and pressing. It came to me as I rode the elevator down to the lobby.

The spa women look at one another. They're virtual twins, of identical height, build, and skin tone, and both with long black hair slicked back into buns. "We do not disturb our clients during their restorative treatments," one says.

"She could be in a transcendent state," says the other.

"I understand completely," I lie. "But I'm afraid I

must insist. This concerns the tragedy our pageant has suffered." I stole that phrasing from rose-giver Mario Suave's own lips.

The faces of both spa women contort. One gestures to me to follow her into the sanctum sanctorum. Nothing like the specter of death to pry open doors.

We walk down a corridor, passing many closed doors and a few open ones, which reveal darkened interiors and empty massage tables. At one door the spa woman halts, knocks lightly, and pokes her head inside the small room. A moment later she moves aside, motions for me to enter, then closes the door behind her as she exits.

Misty's Latina-goddess self is lying on her back on a massage table. I'm relieved to see she's clothed, at least sort of, in a simple black bikini. A mask shades her eyes. But there's no sunlamp shining on her, no nothing. She must be getting an invisible treatment because it looks to me like all she's doing is taking a nap. She could do that in her room for free. Then I notice something small and dark on her belly. I inch closer and peer down at her perfect abs. Then, "Ewww!"

"Oh, you bumpkin, shut up," Misty snarls.

"Is that a *leech*? Oh my God!"

"It's medicinal."

"It's medieval! You're letting it suck your blood?"

She whips off the mask. "No, I'm letting it sing me a serenade. Of course I'm letting it suck my blood! That's the point."

"How vile!"

She jolts upright. I see now that she has four leeches

on her and none of them has budged, despite her sudden movement. Of course not, I realize: they're attached. "Leech therapy has been performed since the time of Hippocrates," Misty informs me. "They're placed on reflexogenic points, like in acupuncture. For your information, I'm getting my blood detoxified."

"What, they suck it up and then they spit a better version back in?"

"No, you hillbilly, their saliva releases an enzyme into the bloodstream."

"How do you know they're not giving you something else besides that enzyme? Like, for example, bacteria?"

She screws up her face. "I don't think so. These are medically trained leeches."

So they have little MDs from Leech U? I'm not buying. Apparently my face reveals my skepticism.

Misty lies back down and replaces her mask. "There's no point explaining to you. You're incapable of understanding."

I am; it's so true. All I know is that Misty has leeches attached to her body that are growing more engorged by the second. One of them sloppily tumbles off, fat as a bumblebee. It reminds me of Sally Anne Gibbons after her third Mai Tai. "Okay." I take a deep breath. "I'll get to the point."

"I'll be amazed if you have one."

"You said something this morning in that fracas you caused in the buffet line—"

"That was no fracas. And none of it would have even happened if that fat-assed yokel Magnolia Flatt hadn't slammed into me with her overloaded breakfast plate."

My recollection of events is that Misty pitched into Magnolia, but my cause will not be served if I dispute the point. "Be that as it may, you said that Magnolia didn't get you the videotape you needed but instead got the videotape of you and Dirk Ventura. What did you mean by that?"

Misty lifts the mask off one eye. "*This* is urgent pageant business?"

"Yes, it is," I declare forcefully. "So what did you mean? What videotape did you need?"

She replaces the mask. "I plead the fifth."

"Come on, Misty. That tape of you and Dirk made YouTube's top ten. Everybody already knows the whole story. There's nothing to hide anymore."

"Top seven," she corrects.

"There you go. So just tell me. How did you even know that Magnolia was videotaping?"

"Because I saw her. During the preliminaries she was videotaping constantly. How is it possible you missed that?"

I have no idea. I think maybe I'm not always as observant as I should be. That will have to change if I hope to figure out who killed Tiffany Amber.

Misty goes on. "It just didn't make sense. There were professional cameramen shooting all the contestant events. There was no need for a know-nothing like Magnolia to videotape a single frame. Then one day I saw her in the hotel business office staring for hours at YouTube. I put two and two together."

"So what was the tape you told her you needed?" I watch Misty purse her lips. "Misty, what was it?"

For a while she says nothing, then all of a sudden she rips off the eye mask and bolts upright with such speed one of the leeches goes flying. I step aside just in time to avoid being slimed. The creature plops unceremoniously onto the floor.

But the real show is Misty and the diatribe into which she's launched. "Listen, you supposed Ms. America you, I don't have to tell you a damn thing. If it weren't for that effing videotape, I'd be holding the title." Her mouth twists. "You're a poser and nothing more. I wouldn't be surprised if Cantwell takes the crown out of your clumsy hands within the week. So don't get too comfy-cozy wearing it."

"Don't blame me you didn't win, lady. It's nobody's fault but your own that that videotape even exists. Nobody ordered you to sleep with Dirk Ventura."

"Tiffany was having an affair, too!"

"You know about that?" I ask before I realize it's no surprise that Misty knows. Misty was with Dirk Ventura. For all I know, Misty may not only have supported Dirk putting Keola up to seducing Tiffany, she might have come up with the idea. Because if Tiffany were found out, she'd be knocked out of the competition, and the way would be clearer for Misty to win the crown.

"It didn't hurt *her* to have an affair!" Misty hisses. "Look where she got!"

I eye her dubiously.

"I mean before she died, you imbecile. Her sleeping around didn't keep her from getting in the top five."

I cross my arms over my chest. "What's your problem with Tiffany, anyhow? You hate her when she's alive, you hate her when she's dead. What's up with that?"

Misty leaps up from the table and leans into me, jabbing her finger at my nose. I see the two remaining leeches clinging to her belly for dear life. "Tiffany Amber was a lying, scheming bitch, exactly like Sally Anne said. I hate having anything in common with that double-wide Sally Anne but in this case I have to agree with her. Tiffany thought she was better than everybody, better than you, better than me, better than all of us. Well, she wasn't. And just like Sally Anne, I'm glad she's dead."

Without further ado, Misty grabs the two leeches, one in each hand, plucks them from her skin, dumps them onto the floor, and wipes her bloody fingers down her naked belly. Then she stalks from the room, not even bothering to grab a robe.

I'm thinking that if she'd performed at that level in the talent competition, she might have made the top five, even with the Dirk Ventura videotape.

CHAPTER SEVENTEEN

I return to my room exhausted. Shanelle, though, is awake enough for both of us.

"Good, you're dressed." She is wearing white capris and a strapless plaid bustier with a sweetheart neckline. "Let's go get drinks."

I flop onto my bed. "Are we at it again?"

"Of course we are! Is it or is it not sunset?"

"It's sunset." I roll over. "That's why I want to go to sleep."

She slaps my bottom. "Up! We're on Oahu, we're not going to sleep the day away unless we're lying on the sand. Rise and shine, girl, we still got five or six hours of fun left."

I force myself into a vertical position. "All right, but I'm drinking only wine tonight. And only one glass."

"Fine."

But when we get to the lobby lounge, Shanelle points in my direction and declares that I'll have a Lava Flow. "And I'll take a Chi Chi and, oh, Trixie!" Shanelle motions Trixie over from the general area of the macaw. Ms. Congeniality appears only too happy to oblige. "What do you want?"

"The usual," Trixie says. "A Blue Hawaii. Hi, Happy. You look a tiny little wee bit tired. What have you been doing today?"

How do I explain?

"You'll feel better after you have your drink," Shanelle says. "Just relax and sin with the rest of us."

"I told you I was having only wine. What is in that thing you ordered me?"

"Oh ..." She looks away. "This and that."

I find out it has rum and coconut cream, disaster in the making for both brain cells and thighs.

"Will your mom be joining us?" Trixie asks.

"No. I begged off. I spent most of the day with her today." I did sneak in a little canoodling with Jason. It was sort of like being teenagers again. Of course, unlike years ago, this time foreplay involved reviewing six flat-screen TV brochures.

"How was the nail salon?" Shanelle asks me.

That questions launches us into a discussion of what I learned about Keola Kalakaua and Dirk Ventura. When that sordid tale has been told and dissected, we analyze the tidbit about Tiffany going to Sebastian Cantwell's penthouse suite. The trifecta is completed with a dialogue about how Misty found out about Magnolia's videotaping.

"Misty said another thing that I can't get out of my head." I set down my empty glass. "She said that if it weren't for the effing videotape, pardon my French"—I nod at Trixie—"she'd be holding the title. But what about Tiffany? I'm pretty sure that going into the finale all of us thought Tiffany was most likely to win."

"I sure did," Trixie says.

"The reason she said that is simple." Shanelle takes

a bite of the pineapple wedge from her Chi Chi. "She knew she'd murder Tiffany before the finale ended. And, arrogant you-know-what that she is, she figured that with Tiffany gone, she'd win."

"You've thought from the beginning that it was Misty who killed Tiffany," I say to Shanelle.

"You got that right, sister."

Trixie slaps her thighs. "Time to eat."

Clearly we've all gotten a lot more casual about this murder thing. We talk about it, then we go on about our business. "You know what?" I stand up. "Let's eat here at the hotel. It's expensive and not much of an adventure but I'm pooped."

"Fine with me," Trixie says. "I haven't used much of my per diem yet today so it's a good night for it."

Shanelle rises. "Let's do the casual place downstairs, though, not the fancy fish restaurant." Which has stratospheric prices, as if the seafood didn't come from a few feet away.

We're on the wide staircase that leads to the oceanfront café, scene of this morning's food fight, when something occurs to me, probably because I have Sebastian Cantwell on the brain. "He's got to be hating life," I say. "He has to keep paying for all the contestants to stay here on Oahu until the cops release us to go home. Hotel and food. It's already been two extra days and who knows how long it'll end up being?"

"He's so rich, though," Trixie points out. "Why would he care?"

"Phooey on Cantwell," Shanelle says. "I'm enjoying myself. Those cops should take their sweet time."

We arrive at the café's hostess stand. "The scene of the crime," Trixie whispers. "The second crime."

More of a misdemeanor, that one. I wonder if Misty will be able to get the egg stains off her white dress. Not that I care. Maybe Misty hates Tiffany so much because the two are so alike. Or maybe it's because both came to Oahu with a high chance of winning the pageant and both committed the same misdeed—having an affair—but only one got caught. Of course Tiffany ended up paying the ultimate price, but none of us knows why.

Actually, I suppose one of us does.

It's midweek and the hotel isn't full so we score a desirable table on the open-air terrace that fronts the ocean. For a time we sit silently, not even reading the menus, just feeling the sea breeze on our skin and listening to the surf create its timeless music.

"If it weren't for Lamar and Devon, I'd stay here forever," Shanelle says.

"I know, I feel the same way," Trixie says. "I wish Rhett were here."

I can't believe this. "Your husband's name is Rhett? As in Butler?"

She nods. "It's a southern thing. But my son's name is Tag, after Rhett's uncle. And my daughter's named Tessa."

"Why didn't Rhett come to Oahu?" Shanelle asks.

"A so-called emergency with his mother. Don't ask. Hey, look." Trixie points toward the ocean. "A wedding."

The aftermath, more like. A photographer is shooting pictures of the bride and groom, who are standing on the sand beaming into the lens. Various family members are off to the side watching, as are an astonishing number of bridesmaids in peach-colored satin and groomsmen with peach and white striped bow ties.

"I think the bride's wearing Vera Wang," Trixie says.

The gown is gorgeous. A strapless mermaid shape with an eyelet skirt.

"How do you know that's Vera Wang?" Shanelle asks.

"That's what I do," Trixie says. "I work in a bridal shop."

Off we go again, on another estrogen topic. It's when we're discussing how bridesmaid's dresses have changed over the years that I happen to see a few tables away another pageant person, dining alone.

I lean in and whisper. "Rex Rexford's over there. And he's crying. No—" I grab Shanelle's arm so she doesn't turn all the way around to look. "Don't be so obvious. I don't want him to see us watching."

Shanelle drops her napkin, then sneaks a peak as she bends down to retrieve it. She pops back up. "He loves to wear pink shirts, doesn't he? I think it's the wedding that's got him going."

"I think so, too," Trixie says. "I wonder if he's remembering Sonny." Sonny Roberts. Soft rock icon of the fifties and sixties. He whose pompadour rose even closer to heaven than Rex's. "They were together a long time," Trixie adds. "I wouldn't be surprised if Rex is still in mourning."

Sonny Roberts went to his reward several years ago. I remember seeing pictures of his funeral in *People*, the white casket topped with an enormous bouquet of calla lilies, Rex walking alongside with bowed head. And white hanky deployed in pretty much the same position I see right now.

"It's Sonny that got Rex into pageantry, isn't it?" Shanelle asks.

"I think so," I say. "Because Sonny was a judge so often, when he wasn't doing Vegas. Though I think Sonny wasn't getting gigs there so much anymore by the time Rex came along."

"That's because he was old as the hills by then," Shanelle says. "But not too old to be Rex's sugar daddy."

"Sonny must've left him a bundle," Trixie puts in. "Because he didn't have any kids or anything."

"I think Sonny remade Rex," I say. "Remember how Rex sort of got transformed over the years? He started out pretty geeky."

"He even had a different name," Trixie says. "What was it? Something not so slick as Rex Rexford."

It comes to me. "Ronald Bowser."

"Though I'm not sure the name Rex Rexford is all that slick," Shanelle sniffs. "Sounds like a soap opera name to me."

I'm a little sensitive on that topic. My mother was very close to choosing Carrington as my stage name, after Alexis Carrington, Joan Collins' character on *Dynasty*. To her that family represented the height of class. So there you have it.

"I think it's a very sophisticated name," Trixie says.

"I think there's a Rexford Drive in Beverly Hills."

The server clears away our entrees. We look at one another.

"We can't do dessert again," I say.

"What if we split it three ways?" Trixie asks.

"I'm in," Shanelle says, and in short order the dessert menus arrive. We pop for a chocolate and pecan parfait with a mango coulis and coconut ice cream. Shanelle leans her elbows on the table and lowers her voice. "We should consider the possibility that Rex isn't crying over Sonny but over somebody else."

"Tiffany?" Trixie breathes.

"The very same," Shanelle replies. "And I'll tell you why. I have it on good authority that if Tiffany had won, she would have had to give Rex twenty-five grand. That's his consultant fee. Ten percent. So maybe that's why he's crying."

The dessert arrives. We all dig in. I glance at Rex, who appears calmer. His nose and eyes are still red but his hanky is no longer in evidence. "Who's your source on that ten percent thing, Shanelle?" I whisper.

"That ninny Sherry Phillips." Ms. Wyoming. The first to be named to the top five. "Rex was her consultant, too, when she was competing on the state level."

Where she won, obviously, or she wouldn't be here. Rex's girls do well, there's no doubt about it. "You know," I say, "Rex is a man and he was cleared for backstage."

"That's because he's sort of a man and sort of like one of us girls," Trixie says.

"But he had no motive for murdering Tiffany," I go on, "if he stood to collect that much money if she won. This pageant has bigger cash prizes than any other."

"The mongo cash is why I entered," Shanelle puts in. "That and I'm too old to enter anything else."

"In another twenty-five years or so, we'll be able to compete in the pageants for seniors," Trixie says.

"Aren't those a little honky tonk?" I ask, then watch Trixie's face crumple. "Maybe not," I say.

"I can think of two other men who had clearance to go backstage," Shanelle says. She takes an itsy-bitsy bite of the ice cream. "Mario Suave and Sebastian Cantwell."

"Mario wasn't backstage once during the finale," I say. I like Mario, but my investigatory self replayed his actions in my mind. "As for Cantwell—"

"I never saw him back there," Trixie says.

"Neither did I," Shanelle adds.

"We could easily have missed him, though, in all the excitement." I glance again at Rex and remove the napkin from my lap. "I'm going over there to talk to him."

Trixie's eyes grow wide. "As part of the investigation?"

I nod and slip from my seat. I feel my companions' eyes on me as I approach my prey. "Rex? May I?" I indicate the other chair at his table.

"Be my guest, Happy." He nods politely. Poor guy; he's still sniffling. "Congratulations on your victory. I apologize for not congratulating you sooner. I'm not myself these days."

"I don't think anybody expects you to be. How are

you holding up?"

He swipes his mouth with his napkin. I note he's left most of the food on his plate. "As well as can be expected, I suppose."

"Have the police told you anything about how the investigation is going?"

"As a matter of fact, I heard something today." He lowers his voice. "Apparently the cause of death was cyanide poisoning."

"So Tiffany *was* murdered." A shiver runs through me, even though this news isn't really surprising.

"The police found the poison in her lipstick."

"Oh, God." Briefly I close my eyes. I'm remembering the moments before I exited the isolation booth, when Tiffany lifted her skirt and revealed the lipstick and compact taped to her thigh. While I was onstage doing the final interview, she was refreshing her lipstick. With a tube that had been laced with cyanide.

"I'll tell you who I blame," Rex says.

I open my eyes. "Who?"

"Sally Anne Gibbons."

"Why would she want to kill Tiffany?"

He snorts. "You have to ask?"

"Well, I saw those screaming matches, too, about the gown registry, but is that really enough to kill somebody over?"

"Absolutely. It cuts right at the heart of her business. Plus Sally's not right. In the head, I mean. You saw her go berserk at me last night in the lounge. And I'm grief-stricken. She's full of anger, that woman. I wouldn't put anything past her."

He has a point. Actually a few of them. And as a consultant, Sally Anne had access to the backstage area. I try to think. Tiffany's lipstick must have been poisoned during the finale when it was in her makeup bag backstage. Because she would have refreshed her face before each appearance onstage and everything was fine until that last fateful repair job in the isolation booth. I have no love lost for Tiffany Amber but the realization makes me shudder. "How do you know all this, Rex?"

He narrows his eyes at me. "Why do you ask?"

"Well, I guess I would call this inside information."

"And I'm an insider. I was closer to Tiffany than anybody else on this island."

I'm thinking: Maybe, maybe not. Does the name Keola Kalakaua ring a bell?

"Except Tony, of course," Rex adds. "Her husband."

"Did you hear all this from him?"

"As a matter of fact, I did." Rex angles around in his chair. He spies a server and raises a finger in the air, much like Sally Anne did when ordering her Mai Tais.

"How is he doing?"

Rex receives his check and signs off on it without even bothering to check the amount. Maybe Sonny Roberts did leave him a fortune, if he doesn't even need to review his bills. He throws his napkin aside and rises. "My heart goes out to Tony Postagino," he says. "The man does not deserve this anguish."

CHAPTER EIGHTEEN

Shanelle, Trixie and I are waiting by the elevator bank to go upstairs after dinner when who pops out of an arriving elevator but Mario Suave. All of us catch our breath. For Mario, who looks mighty fine in a tuxedo, is even more impressive shirtless in swim trunks with a towel slung over one naked shoulder. He is more than tall and buff and beautiful enough to give Keola Kalakaua a run for his torch-lighting money. Not to mention that he's a heck of a lot more successful than His Highness will ever be.

"Good evening, ladies," he says, and delivers one of his dimple-flashing smiles. For a second there I'm worried that Trixie might lose her balance. Mario's brown eyes home in on me. "Happy, glad I ran into you. I was going to call you later."

"You were?" I ask breathlessly. I guess I've been transported back to ninth grade.

"Pageant business," he says, and winks at Trixie and Shanelle.

Even Shanelle is affected. She seems a little agitated as she turns to me. "Pageant business. Okay then, see you later," and she grabs Trixie's arm to haul her into the elevator before its doors close.

I am now alone with Mario. Unlike most men I

know, he wears a fragrance. Must be the Latin thing. The scent is kind of heady and wonderful. He steps closer. I've got some height on me but I have to raise my head to look into his eyes.

Which I'm doing. Looking into his eyes, I mean.

They're brown, with little yellow flecks, and deep and soulful and ...

I clear my throat. "I never thanked you for the roses, Mario. They're really gorgeous. It was very kind of you."

It's a second or two before he speaks. "It was my pleasure."

We kind of stare at each other. It's like a moment in the movies. Then he clears his throat and this time his voice comes out more businesslike. "I wanted to let you know that we need to do a shoot with you in your evening gown exactly as you were the night of the finale. Video and stills. Of course this year we didn't get the usual shots of the winner but we still need them for promo and the web site."

"Sure. Sounds good." I try to match his businesslike tone but it's not easy since I'm half panting. "When's it scheduled for?"

"Tomorrow sometime. Here at the hotel, on the stage in the auditorium. Magnolia will get back to you with the specifics."

"Magnolia." I hesitate. "So she's still employed by the pageant?"

He smiles. I get another flash of dimple. "Barely. You heard about that?"

"I saw it. The scene with Misty Delgado. I was

having breakfast at the time."

He gives me a once-over. "I can't believe with that gorgeous figure of yours you're patronizing the buffet table."

He is a charmer. I heard he started out as a soap star on Spanish-language television and parlayed that into an American soap opera role. After that and one reality TV stint, he was golden. *People's* Top 50 Most Beautiful list and one hosting gig after the next. Now *this* man has ambition.

"A girl has to eat." I smile back. "So Sebastian Cantwell knows about Magnolia videotaping Misty Delgado with Dirk Ventura and uploading it to YouTube?"

"He told me Magnolia gave him a full confession. At least he hopes it's full and that another shoe won't drop."

"Did she tell him why she did it?"

"Jealousy, basically. At least that's what he thinks. She wanted to take the contestants down a peg, is what she told him."

"I'm a little surprised Mr. Cantwell didn't fire her."

He winks as if he understands the *Mr.* is for his benefit but totally unnecessary between us. "He still may. But there's so much going on right now, what with the investigation, that he doesn't want to add a search for a new employee to the mix."

"That's understandable."

He sidles still closer and jostles me playfully with his elbow. "So why don't you join me?"

"Join you for what?"

"A little Jacuzzi. A little relaxation."

I make the obvious mistake. "I don't have my swimsuit with me."

His eyes gleam. "I won't tell if you won't."

Ms. Prim takes over. I step backward to put some distance between us. "I need to get a good night's sleep so I'm fresh for the shoot tomorrow."

He nods. "Okay." He moves away, smiling as he goes. "Have a good night."

Then he's gone, though his fragrance lingers in the air. I'm feeling positively weak-kneed as I enter the elevator.

Was that a proposition? Kinda felt like one. What is it about Hawaii? It's one giant bacchanal here. Maybe even more so than Vegas. But it is kind of fun having gorgeous men around who say charming things and send roses and give smoldering looks. Doesn't happen in Cleveland with any regularity.

Just so you know, I am a happily married woman. But sometimes, I can't help it, I do wonder what my life would have been like if I hadn't gotten pregnant at seventeen and married Jason. I adore Rachel, don't get me wrong, and Jason is my first love, but who might I have met if I'd gone on to college? Played the field a bit?

I guess I'll never know.

The next morning I strap myself into my polyester and spandex workout gear. My goal is to reacquaint myself with something called exercise, with which I have not been familiar since the morning of the pageant finale.

I arrive at the hotel fitness center to find all the treadmills taken but one. I guess a lot of Type A's come to the islands. Maybe they're the only ones who can afford it. I've just upped my speed from a jog to a run when my cell phone rings. I figured I had to bring it with me because Magnolia might call to say that the shoot is shockingly early. In that case I'd have to cut my workout short. What a shame that would be.

But it's not Magnolia. It's my daughter. "What are you doing that you're breathing so heavy?" she asks me. "Oh, gross, you're not—"

"No, I'm not," I pant. "I am"—pant—"on the treadmill."

"It's kind of disgusting how you sound. You should do something more core-strengthening anyway, like Pilates. Or yoga. More cerebral."

When I work out, I don't care about my core or my cerebrum. I care about my butt and my thighs.

"Anyway," Rachel goes on, "that's not what I'm calling about. I'm calling about your prize money and my education and that whole thing."

"Rachel"—pant—"you know I told you that if you want to stay in state, if you're really sure about that, I'm okay with it." Okay is the operative word. My daughter has killer test scores and fantastic grades. I wish she wanted to try for a private university, especially now that I could actually pay for it. I bet she could get in.

"I know you told me that."

"I just want you to make the most of any educational opportunity you get." Pant. "Really push yourself."

"Mom, I totally get that you want me to have what you never had. And I'm glad you've given up the idea that I have to go to school with a bunch of privileged geeks."

"Well, I still think it's very valuable, the connections you make at the better universities. They'll last your entire life."

"Mom, do you ever listen to me? I mean, seriously. Connections don't mean diddly to me. I don't know what I want to do with my life but it's going to be something where I'm judged on my merit, not on who I know."

"Honestly, Rachel"—pant—"sometimes I wonder what planet you live on." That slips out before I can stop it.

"See? There you go again. Sometimes I think you never, ever listen to me."

Don't I? I'm hearing her now; I must be, because the words she's saying are making me crazy.

In my panting silence she speaks again. "Okay, I'm going to tell you something and I don't want you to freak."

That sentence alone makes me freak. I press the treadmill's big red emergency stop button and grasp the handlebars. "All right. I'm listening."

"Don't freak."

"Just tell me."

"I'm not sure I want to go to college next year."

"Oh God."

"I'm not saying I don't want to go at all, ever, but there's something else I think I want to do first. And it won't cost you a dime."

"Rachel—" I'm clutching the bars.

"I want to travel the world. And help people."

"What people?"

"People in developing nations who are downtrodden because of the West. I've found this group where you can go abroad and volunteer for a lot shorter time than the Peace Corps makes you do. Plus I couldn't get into the Peace Corps anyway because I'm too young."

"The Peace Corps?" I guess I shriek this into my cell. I notice people staring at me from adjoining pieces of fitness equipment.

"Not the Peace Corps. This is a different group. But it lets you go to all kinds of cool places, too, like Morocco or Tanzania or Guatemala—"

"Guatemala?"

"Oh, gotta go. AP Physics is about to start. Talk to you later." Click.

"Oh God." I try to catch my breath. Why can't this be easier? Why can't Rachel do what I want her to do? Go to a great college and get an impressive degree and embark on a fabulous career and marry a terrific guy and have a kid or two? In that order?

"Are you all right, miss?" It's the woman who keeps an eye on the patrons in the fitness center to make sure none of us has a heart attack on Royal Hibiscus property.

"I'm fine," I tell her. Lie, lie, lie.

My cell rings again. I flip it open. "Rachel—"

"It's not Rachel, it's your mother. What's wrong?"

"Oh, I don't know, I just had, not really a fight, but kind of a fight with Rachel on the phone."

"Did Jason say something to her?"

"No, mom! That's not it. Stop blaming Jason for everything."

"Stay put. I'm coming over."

I've barely gotten back to my room when my mother arrives, in high dudgeon. "What the hell did he say to her? He told me he didn't say anything but I didn't believe him."

"Let's go sit on the balcony." It's outfitted with two chaise lounges and a drop-dead view of the pool area. I pop open a soda water and hand my mom an orange juice. We're alone because Shanelle's souvenir shopping. She's convinced the cops will arrest Misty Delgado today and we'll all be forced off Oahu in short order. My mother and I make ourselves comfortable for a good, long grousing session. "Jason didn't say anything to her so get that out of your head. The bottom line is that she told me she may not want to go to college next year."

"Oh God." My mother's hand flies to her throat. "Why the hell not?"

"She wants to help people." I relay the rest of the sad tale.

My mother frowns as she listens. "Could it be some new boyfriend making her think like this?"

"I don't think so."

"You're sure she's not—" My mother arches her brows.

"God, no!" I say it automatically, and with force. Then I have to wonder how I can be so sure Rachel isn't pregnant. I can't, really, even though there's been no evidence of a serious boyfriend. True, there was the loser she took to the junior prom …

I must have screwed up my face remembering him. My mother pipes up. "You're thinking of that Ryan kid. I never liked him."

My mother and I agree on that. "I don't think it's Ryan, or anybody else. I think she wants adventure, something new. I don't know. All I know is that I want her to stay in school."

I feel my mother's eyes on me. This territory has got to feel so familiar to her. After the way my mom pushed me into pageant after pageant, I swore I'd never push Rachel into anything. Now here I am, breaking my own vow. And why? For the same reason my mother did what she did: for Rachel. For her own good, or at least my idea of what her own good is. How ironic.

Eventually my mother looks away. "I don't like it. What kind of boys will she meet in Guadalajara?"

"Guatemala."

"Same difference." She waves her hand dismissively.

I'm feeling like the bumpkin Misty Delgado accused me of being, because the truth is that's how I feel, too. I don't want my daughter traipsing off to some foreign country I don't know the first thing about, where she could catch some awful disease or get murdered in the dark and have her body thrown in a ravine or, as my mother clearly fears, fall in love with an exotic native who keeps her away from Ohio for the rest of her natural life.

For me it's just so simple. I want her to stay in school, here in America.

I feel tears rising. I hang my head but they keep

barreling forth just the same. A second later my mom's hand is on my spandexed leg.

"It's all right, Happy." Her voice sounds totally strong. She does tend to come through in the clutch. I choke out a sob. "She'll come around. And if she doesn't, you'll just have to cope. If you have to, you will."

Just like my mom did when I turned up pregnant at 17 and bullied her into giving me permission to marry someone she's never stopped resenting.

Increased sobbing ensues. I grab my mother's hand and hold on tight. I guess my winning the Ms. America crown isn't the only miracle to occur here on lovely Oahu.

CHAPTER NINETEEN

"Okay, so we have everything but the eye serum?" Trixie is standing beside my bed, holding a list. I'm lying on the bed, showered, wearing the hotel fuzzy robe. My mother is at the foot of the bed. "Washcloth," Trixie says.

My mother responds. "Check."

"Two cotton balls?"

"Check."

"Cold milk and a small bowl?"

"Yes on the milk. And for a bowl we've got a wineglass from the minibar. I hope they don't charge you for using it, Happy."

"They won't, mom," I say.

"You can complain if they do," Trixie says. "I just hope Shanelle is back by the time we need her. Mrs. P, please put the spoon in the freezer and wet the washcloth. With cold water."

My mother scurries to complete her assigned tasks.

"I hope this doesn't take long," I say.

"It will take as long as it takes," Trixie informs me. "And it's absolutely necessary, in my opinion, so don't fight it." A second later she's dabbing my eyes with the washcloth. "This will work," she tells me.

"It better." Because in the middle of my crying fit, which produced eye puffiness of epic proportions,

Magnolia called to inform me that the shoot was in precisely one hour. I think I detected satisfaction in her tone; knowing her as I do, I'm sure she quite enjoyed giving me short notice. Because when these sixty minutes are up, I am required to be in my evening gown, camera-ready, new Ms. America sash deployed, a perfect replica of myself on pageant night.

Circumstances clearly called for a Beauty 911. Trixie and Shanelle leaped into service and I soon realized that my pageant-loving mother was in seventh heaven, surrounded by a trio of real-life beauty queens facing an appearance emergency of the highest order.

"Mrs. P," Trixie says, "please place the cotton balls in the milk and bring me the spoon from the freezer." Seconds later Trixie lays the spoon over my right eye.

"That feels good," I say.

"Sshh. Mrs. P, tell me when it's one minute." At that mark, the spoon goes on the other eye.

Shanelle bursts into the room. "I got it. Thank the heavens there's an Ulta in Waikiki."

"Cotton balls," Trixie calls. Those replace the spoon.

Milk runs down the sides of my face. "This part is messy," I say.

"No comments from the peanut gallery," Trixie shoots back. "Please tell me when it's a minute, Mrs. P."

"Time," my mother says.

"Washcloth," Trixie says. She goes back to dabbing. Then she, Shanelle, and my mom hover over my face, their eyes narrowed and assessing.

"She looks better than she did before," my mother asserts.

Shanelle weighs in. "That's not a tough standard to beat."

"Ha ha." I try to rise from the bed but Shanelle pushes me back down. She has a small amber bottle in her hand.

"Final step," she intones, and drops a few beads of a mysterious liquid under each of my eyes.

"What's that?"

"Eye serum. With certified organic aloe leaf and natural antioxidants." Very lightly she pats the stuff in. "It also diminishes fine lines."

"I don't have any fine lines!"

Silence greets that dubious assertion. Then Shanelle straightens. "All right, I'm not too shy to ask. What got you started on this crying jag anyway?"

"Don't ask her that!" Trixie wails. "We just got her calmed down."

"No, I'm all right." I rise from the bed. "I'm not such a wuss that I'm going to go off again." I take a deep breath. "It's Rachel. She told me this morning that she might not want to go to college next year." The rest of the sorry tale spills out as I head into the bathroom and dump the contents of my makeup bag onto the counter. I start slathering on foundation as all three women follow me in. "I think what bothers me the most is that it seems like we're always at odds. We never agree on anything anymore."

"That's because she's a teenager!" Trixie perches on the side of the tub. "Don't let that worry you. As she gets older, you and she will agree on more and more. You'll get closer and closer, just like my mom and I did.

Isn't that right, Mrs. P?"

My mother is standing by the towel rack. She and I exchange a glance in the mirror. I see sadness in her eyes. Poor thing doesn't know how to respond. I pipe up. "Mom and I had a good heart to heart this morning, didn't we, Mom? Much better than we had when I was seventeen."

She looks relieved. "You can say that again."

Shanelle leans against the sink. "Well, one thing I know. Ain't no child of mine taking up residence in some Third World country. Devon wants to do good, he can do it right here in the good old US of A. We got plenty of need right here."

"I hear you, sister," Trixie says, nodding gravely.

"Amen," my mother says.

I feel like hollering *Hallelujah*! I restrain myself and move onto the shading phase of the makeup operation.

"Anyhoo," Trixie says, "I think when Tessa hits sixteen, I may ground her and commence home schooling."

A few minutes later, I've advanced to the three tones of eye shadow. "Home-schooling may not be a bad idea," I mutter. "How am I on time, by the way?"

"You have seventeen minutes," Shanelle informs me.

And after I finish my makeup, I still have to get dressed and deal with my hair. "Mom, will you make sure my gown isn't wrinkled?"

I don't have to ask twice.

"She's a dear," Trixie whispers to me.

I feel more tenderness for my mom today than I

have in a long time. "Uh oh." I feel the tears rising.

"No!" Shanelle grabs my arm. "Get a hold of yourself!"

I pull it together.

"If you're a few minutes late," Trixie says, "the world won't stop spinning."

Truer words have never been spoken. And in about nineteen minutes' time, with everyone's help, I've finished my makeup, fixed my hair, dressed, draped the Ms. America sash over my body, and bobby-pinned on the tiara. I'm checking the overall effect in the full-length mirror that hangs on the armoire's inside door when I realize for the umpteenth time that it's completely idiotic to think beauty queens are empty-headed nincompoops. In my experience they're competent and poised in any situation, even under pressure. As the new Ms. America, it might be my mission in life to dispel those inane stereotypes.

Done up as I am, I turn a few heads as I make my way to the Royal Hibiscus auditorium where the finale was held three nights ago. I arrive and discover that as is typical for these things, it's hurry up and wait. 45 minutes pass by the time the still and video photographers and their lighting teams have matters arranged to their satisfaction.

The shoot itself is uneventful. Having competed in pageants from age six, and done a little local modeling, too, I'm comfortable in front of a lens. The photographers eventually declare they have what they need, but it's not a wrap until Sebastian Cantwell signs off his approval.

And he's nowhere to be found.

"You'll have to hang out for a while," one of the photographers tells me. I drop into a chair in the front row.

It doesn't take long to realize that somebody is clomping around backstage. The footfalls are not exactly fast-moving. I have a suspicion who might be making them. And if I'm right, I might be able to make productive use of this down time.

CHAPTER TWENTY

Indeed I am right. It's Magnolia Flatt.

"Hey, Magnolia," I say.

She grunts. She's sweeping, and doesn't look happy about it. She's sporting plaid shorts that are two sizes too small and six inches too short. Her makeup has been applied with her usual bricklayer's finesse. Her eyeliner looks about as thick as the stripes painted on the expressways back home.

"How are you doing?" I ask her.

"How does it look like I'm doing?"

"Doesn't the hotel have people to do that?"

"Tell that to Cantwell."

"Ah." Now she's making a half-assed attempt to sweep the dirt into a dustpan. "Is he kind of mad at you right now?"

"What gave you that idea, Einstein?"

Not only is her ineptness painful to watch, I decide I have an opportunity here. I grab the dustpan. "Let me help you."

She eyes me and snickers. "In that get-up? I don't think so. Cantwell will only blame me if you get dirty."

"I won't get dirty. Plus we're done with the shoot anyway and this gown has to get dry cleaned when I get home." I bend down and hold the dustpan. "Come on."

We work in silence since I can't think of an opening gambit. Eventually I plunge right in. "You know, I spoke with Misty about the whole videotaping thing."

"So?"

"So there's one thing I still don't understand."

"That's your problem, queenie, not mine."

"Listen, Magnolia." I grab the broom and force her to look at me. "Do you or do you not want to keep your job with the Ms. America organization?"

She hems and haws a few times but finally answers. "Yeah, I want to keep it."

"Okay, then. Maybe I can help you. I'm the new title-holder and so I have some yank with Mr. Cantwell." If that's true, it's not because I'm the title-holder. It's because I know he surreptitiously entertained murder victim Tiffany Amber in his penthouse suite. "I could intercede with him on your behalf. But I'm not going to if you keep being snarky and unhelpful."

She rolls her eyes. "All right. Whaddaya wanna know?"

"I want to know what Misty meant when she said you didn't get her the videotape she needed. What videotape was that?"

"You really wanna know?" She puts her hand on her hip. "All right, I'll tell you. Videotape of Tiffany Amber and that torch guy Keola. Doing you know what. Or as close to them doing you know what as I could get."

"Why would you agree to get that for her?"

"Because she said that if I didn't, she'd go to Cantwell."

"And tell him that you were trying to get damning

video of one of the contestants to put up on YouTube."

"And for sure he'd can my ass."

"For sure he would." *He still may,* is what I'm thinking. "So Misty must have been pretty ticked off that you couldn't get the video of Tiffany and Keola."

"Oh, I got it," Magnolia says. "Only problem is, Tiffany saw me."

"You're kidding! What did she do?"

"She scared the bejesus out of me. I thought she was gonna rip me a new one."

Boy, I wish I'd been a lizard on the lanai wall for that confrontation. It gives me the willies to imagine how livid uber competitive Tiffany Amber must have been on seeing her chance of winning the pageant about to evaporate. "You can't be surprised she went ballistic."

"Let's just say she had no trouble prying out of me that Misty put me up to it."

Knowing that her chief rival was behind the plot would've made Tiffany even more enraged. "Did she smack you or something?" I for one would put my money behind Tiffany in a cat fight.

"She grabbed the camera out of my hand and ripped out the memory card."

I wonder what happened to the memory card. Maybe the cops found it in Tiffany's hotel room. Maybe that, and not the smell of citronella, led them to Keola the morning after the finale.

"Then that Keola guy laughed," Magnolia says, "and said Tiffany should do the exact same thing Misty did. Get me to videotape Misty and that chopper pilot guy and put that up on YouTube."

Turnabout is fair play. And of course Keola knew about Dirk and Misty. I note that the more I learn about Keola, the more conniving he appears.

"Keola even knew where I could catch the two of them," Magnolia says.

"Really? Where?"

"The chopper guy's sister owns a bed and breakfast. This funky joint about half an hour away. That one afternoon when you all had off, I went there with the camcorder. And I caught them."

"But I gather that unlike Tiffany, Misty didn't see you."

Magnolia smirks. "Let's just say she was otherwise engaged."

"I can guess why you agreed to videotape Misty and Dirk. Because otherwise Tiffany would go to Cantwell. Boy, you got it coming and going."

Magnolia rephrases in her own unique way. "Both those bitches blackmailed my ass."

But only one survived to tell the story.

I eye Magnolia, who's scuffing the floor with her shoe. She is one resentful character. "Why do you hate beauty queens so much?" I ask her.

She looks up. "You're all so fake. There's this whole pretense about how all-American and apple pie you are but half of you are skanky as hell."

"Hardly."

She shrugs. "I just think the world should know that it's a big giant fraud."

"I still don't get it. If you find the pageant world so disgusting, why do you want to keep the job?"

"What else am I gonna do?"

Magnolia Flatt is so negative. But even someone with a better attitude would be damn eager to get back at both Misty and Tiffany. Given all this, Magnolia has to be considered a suspect. She did have backstage access as well.

And does this ever explain Misty's outrage toward Tiffany! Misty's blackmailing scheme backfired big time, since it was Misty and not Tiffany who ended up on YouTube exposed as the philandering wife unworthy of the Ms. America crown.

Magnolia goes back to her desultory sweeping and I wander away. Is there someone else I should be considering as a possible suspect? Dirk Ventura comes to mind. If he cared for Misty, he might want to take Tiffany out. After all, Tiffany did wrong Misty, though much of it was Misty's own doing. But then again, maybe Ventura was in it only for the sex. That jibes better with the only other thing I know about him, that he lays bets with other guys about who he can seduce.

I'm about to go back to my front-row seat in the empty auditorium when I hear footsteps behind me in the backstage area. These are way too purposeful to be made by Magnolia. Then I hear voices. It's Cantwell and somebody else. I sidle up against the wall and listen.

"—before and I'll say it again. You're barmy if you think whoever killed that woman is part of the pageant! I tell you, man, look outside this organization."

Cantwell said the same thing to me the morning after the finale. It's his enduring refrain. Whoever he's talking to, a man apparently, mumbles something I can't make out. Is it Momoa?

Cantwell again. "And for God's sake, put some welly into the damn investigation! Keeping all these women here so you can trundle along at your snail's pace is costing me a bloody fortune. This goes on one day longer, I'll have my barristers draw up a suit."

If it's not Momoa he's talking to, it's somebody else from Oahu PD. And as it occurred to me last night, Cantwell does not like having to pay to keep us all here on the island, rich as he is.

The footsteps get closer. I realize I'd better reveal myself or it'll be clear I'm eavesdropping. I stride toward center stage as if to head down to the auditorium floor when Cantwell calls my name. I spin around. "Yes, sir?" I see then that it is Momoa with Cantwell.

Cantwell frowns at me. "The detective has something to discuss with you."

Fabulous. But especially in Cantwell's presence, I'm required to be gracious. "How can I help you, Detective?"

He holds something up. A videotape. Initially I get excited. The one of Misty and Dirk, I think? Or of Tiffany and Keola? Maybe Momoa wants to ask me about them, involve me in the investigation.

Then no, I realize, that can't be one of those videotapes. Magnolia's camcorder recorded via memory card. That's what she told me Tiffany ripped out of her camera.

Momoa solves the mystery for me soon enough. "This," he declares portentously, "is a recording drawn from one of this hotel's surveillance cameras.

Specifically, from one positioned on the basement level of this hotel."

My stomach drops. I half expect it to land on the stage floor beneath my billowing fuchsia satin.

"Ohio," Cantwell thunders, "what do you have to say for yourself?"

CHAPTER TWENTY-ONE

Things I learned as a kid from getting caught with my hand in the cookie jar come flying back to me. Tops on the list: Don't admit to anything you're not sure they know you did.

"Whatever could be on that tape that concerns me?" I ask. I'm trying to sound innocent even though I expect it to fly about as well as a one-winged canary.

"What concerns you, Ohio," Cantwell blares, "are segments of this videotape in which you're scurrying like a cockroach through the basement corridors of this hotel!"

Uh oh. Goodbye, crown. How in the world did I not see that there was a surveillance camera down there? I guess it's like me not noticing that Magnolia was videotaping constantly during the weeks of preliminary competition.

Then again, I should be glad of one thing. No one has yet mentioned a box. Maybe the camera caught me in the basement level but not pilfering US mail addressed to someone other than myself. In which case I really would be dodging a bullet.

Cantwell continues. "Do you care to explain your behavior?"

I face Momoa, who amazingly is less scary to me

right now than Cantwell. I trot out the same lie I told the concierge. "I went down to the basement to get a box from the mail room because I'm buying so many souvenirs here I won't be able to carry all of them home in my suitcases."

That won't do it for Momoa. "That does not explain your skulking in the corridors."

"I was just having a little fun, you know, a James Bond'y kind of thing." Lame, so lame. "I know it must look odd but I used to play spy games with my daughter when she was younger and I just kind of got into it while I was down there."

Momoa rocks on his heels. "Ms. Pennington, something strikes me. And that is that as I conduct this investigation into the tragic demise of Tiffany Amber, I repeatedly run into you."

I can only thank the heavens that it seems Momoa remains unaware of my nocturnal tour of Tiffany's hotel room. If he knew about that, too, I would surely be toast. "It is because I was one of the last people to see Tiffany alive that I'm so desperate to know what happened to her."

"I am sorely tempted to take you downtown," Momoa informs me.

That prospect sounds truly terrifying. Somehow I don't think Hawaiian police stations are any more cheerful than the ones we have back home. "There's no need to do that. Besides, I don't want to impede your investigation by forcing you to waste your time keeping tabs on me."

"I'm not at all sure that it is a waste of time,"

Momoa tells me pointedly.

"It is, Detective. I did not kill Tiffany Amber. Whoever did is still out there, perhaps ready to strike again." I'm not sure I believe that but I'll say anything to move Momoa's suspicious gaze away from me.

He steps closer. "Ms. Pennington, I am going to be keeping an even closer eye on you now than I have been before. Do we understand each other?"

I'm ready to cry with relief. He's not taking me downtown. Not yet. "Yes, sir."

"If I find out that you so much as jaywalked on Kalia Avenue, you will be arrested. Pronto. Do you understand me?"

"Yes, sir."

Momoa nods at Cantwell and walks away. He's barely gone when Cantwell gets about an inch from my face.

"Ohio, I am this close, *this* close," he hisses, his thumb and index finger half an inch apart, "to taking your crown from you and giving it to the third-place finisher."

"Don't do that, please, sir. I will do better, I promise."

"If you think for one second that that pitiful excuse for an investigator did not arrest you because he doesn't have the evidence to do so, you are wrong. Dead wrong."

"I'm innocent, Mr. Cantwell. Honestly, I am."

"So you keep saying. But I for one find your denials less and less persuasive. Moreover, your high jinks are keeping the investigation targeted on this pageant when we would all be much better served if the focus shifted elsewhere." He shakes his head. I hold my breath, watching a muscle in his jaw twitch. Then, "Give me one good reason, *one* good reason, why I should not take the title from you right now."

"I can give you two." The words spill from my mouth. "First, I have it on good authority that you entertained Tiffany Amber in your penthouse suite. Alone. During the preliminary competition. And second, while I have that information, I don't believe that Detective Momoa does."

Cantwell's blue eyes widen. "You ... little ... vixen."

"We all know that private meeting was verboten, Mr. Cantwell." My heart is pounding so mightily against my rib cage that I can barely speak. "Pageant rules forbid it. But what makes it even worse is that Tiffany Amber ended up dead."

"Are you suggesting," he's spitting out his words, "that I killed that woman?"

"No. I'm merely pointing out that your one-on-one with Tiffany would be of interest to the Oahu police department."

"You blackmailer, you!"

"Nothing of the sort," I lie. "I just think this is as good a time as any to bring up your clandestine interlude with the murder victim."

That shuts him up. He walks a short distance away across the stage.

I try to calm down, which is what I suspect he's trying to do, too. I don't know if it was brilliant or idiotic to say what I did but I really felt up against it. One thing is certain: Sebastian Cantwell recognizes that I have at least one card in my deck. True, now I've played it. But I can always play it again with Momoa if need be. I know that, and Cantwell does, too.

He walks back to me. "Listen, you diabolical female. Not that it is any of your concern but I met with California at her request. Curious what she wanted and all that. She had competitive spunk, I'll say that for her. She wanted me to intercede with the judges so they'd give her serious consideration, as she put it."

"Did you agree?"

"No, I did not agree! The only thing that makes these damn pageants remotely interesting is that they're genuine horse races."

I sail right past being compared to horseflesh in favor of wondering whether Cantwell decided not to pressure the judges before or after he slept with Tiffany. But I lack the cojones to ask that question.

He delivers his parting shot. "Ohio, California might have been a spitfire but she had nothing on you."

He strides away. I'm shaking, from terror, relief, exhaustion, I don't know what. But it appears I may have lived to wear my tiara another day.

CHAPTER TWENTY-TWO

Shanelle is not in our room when I get back. I don't know if that's good or bad. Part of me wants to vent. Another wants to crawl under the covers and wait until Momoa releases us queens to leave Oahu, though at this point I expect one notable name would be absent from the CLEARED TO GO list.

I choose a happy medium. I unlock the mini bar and crack open not only the little bottle of chardonnay but the bag of potato chips. The happy-go-lucky time when I cared about calories, sodium, and saturated fat is long past. At the moment I've got problems way more pressing than water retention and thunder thighs.

I stand on the balcony to consume my wicked repast. After a while I notice several sunbathers on the opposite side of the pool shading their eyes to witness me nine floors up in my fuchsia satin gown, rhinestone tiara, and Ms. America sash devouring potato chips and glugging white wine straight from the bottle.

Maybe it's the first time they've seen this behavior from a beauty queen. Let them stare. If by some act of God and Sebastian Cantwell I retain my crown, it won't be the last.

I can't even imagine how horrible it would be to lose my title, totally through my own doing. How could I hold my head up? I'd be an embarrassment to myself, Rachel, Jason, my parents ...

In short order the chips and the wine are but a memory. I emerge from a quick shower to find Shanelle back. "How did the shoot go?" she asks me.

"The shoot was fine. It's what happened afterward."

Wrapped in a towel, I tell the tale. Shanelle is aghast. She shrieks, screams *No!*, paces, slaps her hand upside her head—in short, she exhibits all the symptoms of deep upset. Eventually I realize that she may not be concerned only about me. "Don't worry," I tell her. "I really don't think they saw me with the box. So they have no idea you helped me hack Tiffany's computer."

She flops onto her bed. "I don't know why I care anyway. Hell, my pageant career is over. You got a lot more to lose than I do." She eyes me. "So what are you gonna do?"

I start to moisturize my face. "Be more careful."

"You're not going to stop investigating?"

"How can I? The only way I can get out from under this black cloud of suspicion is to figure out who killed Tiffany Amber."

She gets up and heads for the mini bar. She's disciplined enough to limit herself to a Diet Coke. "In that case, you up for the luau?"

"I completely forgot about that thing. Is it tonight?"

"Biggest draw on the island of Oahu."

I'm not sure about that but the Royal Hibiscus does do it up big one night a week. "What the hell. I may as well enjoy my freedom while I can."

Half an hour later I've got my face and hair done and am wearing a lime green chiffon babydoll dress with spaghetti straps and a twist of charmeuse at the bodice. Very on trend. Shanelle's in a strapless lightly beaded hankie hem dress with a dramatic floral print on a black background. Her hair's back to a natural Afro tonight.

"We look good, girl," Shanelle pronounces.

I agree. "No one would guess we narrowly avoided incarceration today."

And we're off. The lobby is mayhem what with the crush of people assembled for the luau.

"Nothing like roast pig to draw a crowd," I tell Shanelle.

Some people have taken the luau theme and run with it. I see one couple who are clearly ready to party. The woman is wearing a grass skirt, bikini top, lei and straw hat, and her other half is in boxer shorts and undershirt with a bright pink pool noodle around his waist and a snorkel mask over his face.

It's such a horde in the lobby's central courtyard that I can barely move. Shanelle is several people to my right, as immobilized as I am. The pulsing crowd is pushing me left into a palm tree and a stand of birds of paradise. One real live bird is only a few feet from my face. The blue and gold macaw, whose name I've learned is Cordelia, is perched on her tree just in front of me.

All of a sudden I feel hands in the middle of my naked back. They push, hard. I can't help myself; I pitch forward.

I see everything like it's unwinding before me in

slow motion. My hands flail in empty space. In front of me is Cordelia. She's looking right at me with astonishment written all over her narrow parroty face. I'm going straight at her; there's no denying it. She knows it and I know it. She squawks. I shriek. I fixate on her beady black eyes and quite sizable black beak, both getting closer by the nanosecond. There's nowhere to go but in one direction. My hands wave desperately in front of me. Then Cordelia's beak latches onto the index finger of my right hand. And bites down. Hard.

"Owwww!" I scream.

Cordelia lets go, then screams, too. She's terrified, I recognize that, but I will admit I'm more worried about myself. I lurch forward into the birds of paradise and end up sprawled on all fours in the exotic flora and fauna. All I know is one thing: my finger hurts like hell.

Actually I know a second thing. I'm bleeding like the poor stuck pig all we luau goers are preparing to devour for dinner.

It's pandemonium behind me. I hear Shanelle's shout cut through the noise. "What the hell happened to my roommate?"

Somebody pushed Shanelle's roommate, that's what happened. But what I care about now is the throbbing pain in my finger. I force myself into a kneeling position and look at my hand. It's like it belongs to another person. It's trembling and you'd think I could control it but I can't. And that blood I mentioned? Oh, yes. It's everywhere. Splotching my lime green dress and the birds of paradise like a crime scene.

Somebody rushes up behind me and takes me

gently by the shoulders. I turn my head to look. I expect it to be Shanelle but it's Mario. I'm happy to see him even though he's fully clothed.

"What in the world happened to you?" he asks me.

I cock my chin at the macaw. "Cordelia. She bit my finger."

"Come on," he says. "Let's find a doctor."

In short order he has me vertical. Then I have a Moses moment. In the face of my injury, the crowd parts before me as if they have all the room in the world. With his arm around me—believe me, I'm not complaining—Mario leads me across the lobby and down a short corridor to the hotel doctor's office. Clearly the Royal Hibiscus is equipped for anything.

Shanelle appears and she and Mario get me seated in the waiting area. I presume the on-duty doctor is in the examining room treating some other ill-fated tourist; that door is closed.

Meanwhile the blotch on my dress is getting more impressive by the second. Shanelle sits down next to me. "You're bleeding bad, girl. Did you trip on those heels and fall into that bird or what?"

"Somebody pushed me."

Mario halts his pacing to frown in my direction. "Are you sure about that?"

"No doubt in my mind. I felt hands on my back." I wince. The pain is no joke.

Shanelle rubs my good arm. "They shouldn't have that dang macaw free in the courtyard like that. It's a menace."

"Don't blame Cordelia," I say. "I provoked her

when I launched in her direction. She must've been petrified."

The examining room door opens and the doctor appears. I make that brilliant deduction from the young Asian woman's lab coat and stethoscope. Her smile fades fast when she sees my hand. "What in the world happened to you?"

"Cordelia. It's not her fault, though."

"This is a first," the doctor says. "I've never known her to bite anybody."

Minutes later, still in the waiting room, the doctor cleans my wound and teaches me a bit of bird lore. I learn there's only one poisonous bird in the world and it lives in New Guinea. I hope the hotels there have the good sense to keep it far from the tourists. Then I watch the doctor insert aloe vera gel into a short rubber thingie that looks like a condom. She slips it on my finger. "This will stop the pain," she tells me. "It's also good for helping to keep the bruising and swelling down." She instructs me how to take care of my finger. And she proves right about the pain receding. But as one woe recedes, another advances.

Who pushed me? Was it a warning? Is my investigating, such as it is, making somebody nervous enough to try to shake me off? If so, it means that Tiffany Amber's murderer truly does lurk among us. He or she must be one of the people I've talked to.

Mario sits beside me. He's as adorable as ever in twill cargo shorts and a navy slim-fit polo with white piping along the color, placket, and cuffs. I have to say, it's pretty fun being the object of his concern. "How are you feeling now?" he asks me.

"Better." I raise my condomed finger in the air. "The aloe vera is working."

"Do you really think somebody pushed you?"

"I'm positive."

"Who would do that? Has one of the girls been giving you grief since you won?"

Misty, I think. Magnolia. Or one of the others who hates me for winning but hasn't said anything to my face. And who else am I suspicious of? Sally Anne Gibbons. Keola. Dirk. Rex, though I don't have a motive for him. And Sebastian Cantwell, who's pretty mad at me at the moment. Though I have to think he would use more sophisticated techniques to make his point.

For that matter, I realize, looking into Mario's eyes, I should be suspicious of Mario. I don't want to be. Nor can I think of a good reason *to* be. But he's an important deity in the Ms. America pantheon and who knows what dealings he had with Tiffany? Or she with him, more to the point. Maybe she asked him to intercede with the judges, too, like she did Cantwell. He was obviously in the vicinity just now for the macaw incident. And even though I didn't see him backstage during the finale, I can't be certain he wasn't there. And I can't let his apparent niceness, not to mention supreme hotness, hamper my investigation.

"I don't know who would do it," I say. "I guess I'll just have to keep an eye out."

"You certainly do. And if anything else happens, you come tell me. Day or night. After all, I'm the emcee of this pageant. I can't let anything happen to our new title-holder."

I nod and watch him leave.

So does Shanelle, who winks at me the second he's out the door. Then, "Whoo-ee, girl!" she chortles. She bustles across the waiting room to sit next to me. "That man's loins are aflame for the new Ms. America."

"They are not."

"Yes, they are! No way you can dispute that obvious fact."

CHAPTER TWENTY-THREE

I don't try very hard to disabuse Shanelle of the notion that Mario Suave has a crush on me. Not while we're returning to our room so I can change out of my blood-soaked dress—because Shanelle determined we were still going to the luau, macaw bite or no macaw bite—nor while we make our return trip downstairs to join the festivities already in progress.

After all, there are sadder prospects to ponder than that of a gorgeous, successful, desirable man panting after your bones. And it's a nice change from imagining myself crownless and incarcerated for homicide.

There's a large gently sloping grassy area between the hotel and the beach and that's where the luau takes place. By now the sun is down and Party Central is illuminated by strings of white lights encircling the palm trees and the tiki torches Keola lit at sunset. The delectable aroma of roast pig fills the air. As Shanelle and I approach, we see long buffet tables covered with brightly colored sarongs and runners of fishing nets strewn with shells and sand. The tables are ready for the platters of food that will emerge soon from the kitchen. Tall baskets are scattered here and there, filled with stalks of brilliant red ginger. A band is playing Hawaiian music, complete with ukulele and slack key guitar. Slim young lovelies with wreaths of pink plumeria on their heads have begun to hula, their hips swaying under raffia grass skirts. Behind the music we hear the surf's timeworn rhythm.

If anything, the assembled multitude is more raucous than it was before. That's because the mai tais are flowing and everybody's been "lei'd." Ha ha. Shanelle and I order libations of our own and stand back to assess the crowd. "My mother and Jason are here somewhere," I tell her.

"I see Trixie," Shanelle says. "Look who she's talking to, over there by those two leaning palm trees. Misty Delgado's husband."

So she is. The husband—tall, buff, and blond—looks good dry as well as wet; the last time we saw him was poolside, when he reduced a *Ventura Aerial Tours* brochure to confetti.

"Maybe Trixie can pry some useful information out of him," I say.

"Maybe it's a good sign for Misty that he's still here in Hawaii," Shanelle adds. She starts laughing and pointing. "Look!"

"Oh God." One of the young hula women is trying to rope my mother into learning to hula. Hazel Przybyszewski is having none of it. She scowls and scuttles away, slapping the woman's outstretched hand when she persists. "She's going to slap that woman's face next if she doesn't give up," I say.

The woman soon finds a more willing pupil. Jason.

I watch as my husband, in white pants and the silk tropical print Tommy Bahama campshirt I bought him for the islands, winks at the woman and shimmies his hips. She giggles and gestures for him to mimic the hula's gentle sway. Which he does. Perfectly.

Shanelle lets loose an admiring whistle.

"He always could dance," I tell her. Jason may have put on a few pounds since his football days, but he can still shake it when he wants to.

The next man to grab our attention is His Highness Keola Kalakaua, clad in a sky-high headdress and Hawaiian loincloth. He positions himself next to the band and commandeers the microphone. *"Aloha, ahiahi,"* he croons. "That means good evening in my beloved language of Hawaiian."

"Oh, no," I whisper to Shanelle. "He's going native."

"Welcome to the Royal Hibiscus luau," he goes on. "I hope you are enjoying the *pupu* appetizers and getting ready for the main feast."

My mother sidles up next to me. "Did you see what your husband did?" she hisses.

"Hello to you, too, mom."

"If I were you, I'd tell that so-called hula teacher to keep her hands off what doesn't belong to her and never did."

"That's okay, mom." I eye Jason, who's been abandoned by the hula girl and is now standing next to Dirk Ventura. The chopper pilot is his usual dark and chiseled self. I'm more worried about *his* influence on my husband.

"That's another one." My mother cocks her chin at Keola. "Does he even own a pair of pants? I don't think

I've ever seen him anything but half naked."

Shanelle chuckles. "That may be how he looks best, Mrs. Przybyszewski."

By now Keola is regaling the crowd with tales of his royal lineage. "When my ancestor King Kalakaua had his fiftieth birthday luau, a long time ago, man, he had fifteen hundred guests to feast. We don't have so many tonight! I'm glad."

The crowd, pretty liquored up by this point, claps and whoops in agreement. I have a feeling it doesn't take much.

Keola goes on to describe the main attraction, the kalua roast pig, with whom I'm feeling a certain kinship tonight given my own prolonged bleeding episode. That poor beast has been roasting for hours in a pit dug in the sand, lying among wet banana leaves and burlap sacks. His day is not going to improve from here.

"We have a lot of entertainment for you later under the moon," Keola reassures us. "So relax and enjoy our native delicacies. Eat the pig, eat the *poi*, made from the root of the taro plant, and be sure to try the sweet potatoes, different from what you get back on the mainland, yeah."

My mother throws out her hands. "He can't even talk right! Why do they give him the microphone? Royalty, my you know what."

My mother recovers from her agitation sufficiently to dine, and Shanelle and I need no encouragement. We spy other revelers shamelessly loading their plates, including Magnolia Flatt and Sally Anne Gibbons.

"Sally Anne's in kind of a party muumuu tonight,"

Shanelle mutters.

Indeed she is. Navy blue with a ruffle not only at the shoulder but also at the hem.

"She doesn't look drunk yet," my mother says. "But I bet she'll be soused later."

Given that our figures are going to hell in a handcart, Shanelle and I don't even consider missing dessert. We dip into both the coconut cake and the pineapple pie. I'm licking the last of the cake frosting off my fork when a loud drumbeat amps up the excitement. A line of muscular Hawaiian men wearing loincloths, samurai-type headbands, and leis made of long grass run out near the band and strike fighting poses. Cheers and hollers rise from the crowd and get even more high-pitched when the posing men each brandish a baton that shoots out flames at both ends.

"This is what they call the flame dance," Shanelle shouts to my mom.

My mother shrugs. "They start knife throwing, they can call it a show."

The action gets more frenzied by the moment. Hula-dancing hotties shake their booty, baton-wielding macho men toss their flaming wands in the air, and the drummer pounds a beat so relentless I think I'll hear it in my head till dawn.

Then I notice a piece of drama the luau organizers could not have scripted. Standing near the front, facing each other and shouting, are Dirk Ventura and Misty's husband. I can't hear what they're saying but I can guess the topic is the hot tamale Misty Delgado. In short order the shouting match escalates. I watch as Misty's husband jabs a finger in Ventura's chest. Then Ventura goes one further and with both hands pushes Misty's husband in the chest. He stumbles backward a few feet but then recovers his footing and races forward to punch Dirk Ventura smack in the nose.

Ventura flies backward, tripping as he goes. He lands flat on his rump but he's not the only casualty of the punch. On his way down he topples one of the flame-throwing dancers in mid throw.

"Oh, no," I breathe.

Oh, yes. Because the flame dancer, eyes wide in panic, careens sideways and watches helplessly as his fiery baton goes seriously awry. There's no way he can catch it. Nobody can. It's loose and spinning and it will go where it may.

Which is right into Sally Anne Gibbons. Shanelle and I aren't the only ones screaming when the baton hits her corpulent self and sets her muumuu on fire. I watch in horror as Sally Anne staggers, her mouth open in a petrified yowl and her arms rising pitifully in the air. But who rushes to the rescue but Jason.

Quick as a flash he barrels into her and gets her horizontal on the grass. Then he whips his new Tommy Bahama campshirt up over his head and uses it to smother the flames.

It's over in seconds. I'm damn impressed. Everyone else seemed paralyzed—including me—but in the heat of the moment, literally, my husband had the wherewithal to leap to the rescue and save Sally Anne from what might have been a terrible burn. As it is, she has got to be suffering. This makes my macaw bite look like a paper cut.

I ram forward through the stunned crowd like a woman possessed. I get to the front just in time to see Sally Anne raise her head, stare into the eyes of my half-naked husband hovering above her, and faint dead away.

CHAPTER TWENTY-FOUR

Island time or no island time, it's only a few minutes before sirens announce the arrival of the ambulance come to transport Sally Anne Gibbons to the hospital. I watch as Jason, shirtless now, accepts praise and back slaps from all comers. He does it nicely, too, repeatedly declaring it was nothing and anybody would have done the same thing and he was only glad he could help.

It's clear, though, that nobody *did* do the same thing. It was Jason who came through.

I take my place in the Shake The Hero's Hand line and eventually work my way to the front. I hug my husband. "That was fabulous. You were really a hero tonight."

"Hero, huh?" He winks at me. "That should be good for something."

I give him a playful slap on his naked pecs.

"Sorry about ruining that shirt," he says. "You bought that special for this trip and it was expensive."

"Don't worry about it. We can always get another one."

"You saw that woman went and fainted when she saw me?"

"You're never going to let me forget that, are you?"

"Nope."

We get separated as a new gaggle of fans, female and tipsy, shoves closer to fawn over Jason. He grins at me as I step away.

I look around. It's pretty clear the party's over. Nothing like serious bodily injury to someone other than the kalua pig to bring a luau to a swift conclusion. By now the crowd has thinned to but a few.

My mom is one of the lingerers. I find her next to me. "So your husband is finally good for something," she says.

"Mom, that's not nice. He really helped Sally Anne."

Then she notices the mini condom on my finger. It takes a while to calm her down from the story of that incident. I don't tell her somebody pushed me. She'd freak out and decide I'm next to go the way of Tiffany Amber. It sure does seem as if somebody doesn't like my investigating, somebody besides Detective Momoa, and they are warning me. Okay, maybe threatening me. And it's probably the murderer doing it.

I'm full of secrets at the moment, I realize. It's a full-time job keeping track of who knows what about my life right now. Who knows Oahu PD has me under the microscope for Tiffany's murder? Who knows Sebastian Cantwell is threatening to rip the Ms. America crown off my head? Who knows I'm sort of blackmailing him to keep him from doing it? The only thing I'm clear on is that my mother and my husband don't know about any of the three.

Jason comes up to us a minute later and looks at my mom. "You ready to go back to the Lotus Blossom?"

She puts her hands on her hips. "About time you asked, Mr. Big Man. By the way, did you even notice that your wife has an injury, too?"

"Mom ..."

Jason may not have noticed my wounded finger before but I don't blame him for that. When I'm done giving him the same censored version of the tale I just gave my mom, he eyes me and says, "How about I drive your mother back to the hotel and then come back here and you and I have a nightcap?"

Somehow I have the idea he doesn't just want his heroism rewarded. I wait for him in the lobby, keeping a goodly distance from Cordelia. He returns in a new shirt and a serious mood. We settle in cozy upholstered chairs in the nearly deserted lobby lounge and order Irish Coffees.

"So tell me how you got that macaw bite," he says.

I feel his eyes on my face. I'm not quite sure what to say.

"You didn't just fall into that bird, Happy." His face assumes an even more worried expression. "Somebody pushed you, right?"

I won't lie to him. "Yes."

"Because you're trying to investigate how that California girl died?"

This is the problem with someone knowing you from when you're fifteen years old. They know you pretty darn well. I sigh. "Probably."

"You are, aren't you?" he presses. "Trying to find out who killed her?"

"I suppose. Maybe."

He shakes his head. "That's dangerous. You could get seriously hurt."

"I'm not seriously hurt."

"Not yet." He takes my hands. "Leave this to the cops."

"Because *they* know what they're doing."

"Exactly. And they have guns. And aren't working alone. And have been trained for this. And have done it before."

"You know, I'm not dumb—"

"No one's saying you're dumb!" He's getting exasperated. This is sort of an old argument we're having. He leans closer, still holding my hands. "I don't want you to get hurt. Or worse. Are you listening to me?"

"I'm listening." About as well as Rachel listens to me, though.

The thing is, I'm not really worried about getting hurt. Maybe I should be, but I'm not. And this whole macaw thing just goes to show that I'm getting closer to figuring out the truth. And if I do, not only is my tiara safe on my head, but people will recognize me for something other than my looks. They'll recognize me for my brain cells. For once.

Jason kisses the palm of one hand, then the other, then raises those big brown eyes of his to mine. "I don't want to go back to the Lotus Blossom," he whispers. His breath on my face is warm.

"We have a problem, though. Shanelle."

"I have this crazy idea that this hotel has other rooms. How about I go to the front desk and find out?"

We end up in a suite, not a swanky one on the penthouse floor like Sebastian Cantwell's but nevertheless one with an actual extra room. I've never stayed in a hotel suite before and I know Jason hasn't, either.

Jason pulls two beers from the mini bar and we go sit on the balcony. The suite has an ocean view. From far away, as the night lengthens, I hear the tinkle of glass against glass and snippets of laughter and conversation. And always the ocean. I even feel its salt kiss on my cheek.

You can guess how Jason and I end the evening. We're not exactly teenagers again, but for a few hours at least, we might as well be.

CHAPTER TWENTY-FIVE

In the morning, another first for this trip: room-service breakfast. Jason and I return to the balcony, both in the fuzzy hotel robes, and consume bacon, eggs, and sourdough toast with strawberry jam while watching far-away boats ply the ocean waters and nearby surfers ride the waves. We even catch sight of dolphins swimming, their smooth silvery bodies cresting the surface of the sea.

"Is it my imagination," I ask, "or is this the best coffee you've ever had in your life?"

He sips his. "What do they call it? Kona?"

"I think so." I set down my cup in its saucer. "So have you been thinking about the pit school thing at all?"

"Not really."

"So even though you could go now, you don't really want to?"

He looks at me. "Do you need a new project now that you've won the pageant? And that's getting me to go to pit school?"

I'm a little hurt. "That's not a very nice thing to say."

"I just know you, Happy." He laughs. "You always want something to work on." He spreads jam on a fresh piece of toast. "I don't mind, it's how you are, but you know, I'm happy now. I don't think I'll be any happier if I go to pit school."

I guess he and I are different that way. Once I get one thing accomplished, I'm ready to tackle another. "I guess you're right. I don't want to be a nag about it."

"Good. And so you know, it's not like I'm not thinking about it. I'm just not ready to pull the trigger." He finishes his toast, wipes his mouth, then bounds out of his chair. "I'm going to hop in the shower and then it's off to Best Buy."

"Flat-screens again?"

He nods. "I've almost decided which one I want."

An hour or so later, when Jason and I have left the fantasy of our Oahu suite behind, I dress, put a fresh bandage on my memento from Cordelia, and prepare to continue my investigation. After all, what did I tell Jason the night before? That I'd listen to him. I didn't say I'd do what he asked.

With that reasoning, the sort my teenager would be proud of, I go down to the front desk to ask them to put a call through to Sally Anne Gibbons' room.

The pretty young woman at Reception shakes her head. "She's not in her room, Ms. Pennington. We found out this morning that she hasn't been released yet from the hospital."

"Oh no! Is she all right?"

"We were told she's fine but to be on the safe side the doctors kept her overnight for observation."

I get the directions for the hospital and stop off at the hotel café first to pick up a coffee and a muffin for Sally Anne.

"You want me to make you your breakfast drink?" the girl at the counter asks me.

"I'll take it later, thanks." Maybe I'll have it for lunch. I've been eating so much high-fat food lately, it wouldn't hurt to make my midday meal fruit and wheat germ.

The hospital is cheerier than most, what with the abundance of tropical plants in the main reception area and the sunlight streaming in every window. Sally Anne's room is on the third floor. I find her not by inquiring at the nurse's station but by homing in on the bellowing female voice I hear the second I step out of the elevator.

She may be supine in a hospital bed with monitors attached to her body but Sally Anne is still Sally Anne. Maybe that's why she's in a private room. The staff couldn't bring themselves to foist her on another ailing individual.

"Happy Pennington," she declares when she sees me. She pretty much looks herself, just somehow deflated, as people often do in hospital beds. Her eyes narrow. "What do you want? You wouldn't be here without a reason."

I set the brown paper bag on the rolling food tray and get it within Sally Anne's reach. "Oh, I have a reason. I came to visit you."

"Fat chance."

I open the bag and extract the coffee and muffin. I see a flicker of interest in her eyes, which I couldn't raise but my food offering can. "Did anybody ever tell you that you have an attitude problem, Sally Anne? If not, let

189

me be the first."

"My problem isn't me. It's the rest of the world." Her eyes lower to the muffin.

"Lemon poppyseed. Trixie Barnett keeps telling me they're the best of the lot."

"How the hell would that string bean know? Unwrap it for me. And hand me that java before it gets cold."

I hold the cup back. "You're sure the doctors wouldn't object?" I've noticed what appear to be cardiac monitors attached to Sally Anne's copious bosom and don't really care to provoke a caffeine-induced heart attack.

"They gave me coffee with that sorry meal they call breakfast. I couldn't drink the crap. It tasted like well water."

I'm not sure I believe her but I hand the coffee over anyway. Even a laid-up Sally Anne is a commanding presence. "So how are you feeling? I'm surprised they kept you overnight."

"Racing heart beat." She downs a swig, then shrugs. "I don't mind. The bed at the hotel is just as empty as this one."

I claim the bedside chair. "Did you suffer a bad burn?"

"Barely second degree. Thanks to that hunka hunka burnin' love who doused the flames. Wouldn't mind giving him a thorough examination."

"It's been done. Most recently by me."

She almost chokes on the muffin. "He's your husband?"

I raise my left hand to show her the rings. "Seventeen years."

She looks chagrined, an expression I didn't think she could produce. "Guess I should apologize."

"No problem. I'm really glad he came through for you."

She eyes me. Then, "Thanks for the grub. And sorry if I came on a little strong. Habit, I guess. Anyway, I'd rather you come see me than the damn police."

Excitement pulses through me at the mention of the cops. "Have they been pestering you about Tiffany Amber?"

"That's putting it nicely. Guess they got wind of the fact that that bitch changed the evening-gown registry on me and I didn't exactly appreciate it."

"Maybe not, but people argue all the time and that doesn't mean they go around killing each other." I make that comment to lead her on. I'm hoping she forgets herself and says something useful.

"Suppose I can't blame the cops for asking questions. They've got to make a living, too. Believe me, that I understand."

"But are you sure it was Tiffany who changed the registry? Maybe—"

"Oh, it was her. She as much as said so."

"Really? When was that?"

"One time we were screaming at each other when nobody else was in earshot. Believe you me, that was no coincidence. So what if I did do it, she says to me. This is war! Talking about the pageant, of course." Sally Anne jabs her index finger in my direction. "She wanted any advantage she could get, that snot-nosed bitch. She wanted to win bad. Can't blame her for that, but who gave her the right to take me down so she could rise up?"

I notice a red light starting to beep on the monitor. I lean forward and lay what I hope is a calming hand on Sally Anne's arm. "Don't get riled up now."

Her face is flushing now. And her massive chest is rising and falling at a faster clip. "Besides all that, if there was anybody she shouldn't have messed with, it was me. I did that shrew a favor and what did it get me?"

"Sally Anne—" I rub her arm. The beeping's more frenzied now. I'm wondering if I should go get a nurse. But at the same time I am curious about the tidbit she just let fly. "What favor did you do her?"

"I invested in that damn currency scheme of hers. You know about that?"

I realize I've clutched Sally Anne's fleshy arm. "I do. You gave her money?"

"Twenty-five big ones. And do you think it worked out the way she promised me it would? With gains up the wazoo?"

"No?" I guess.

"No!" Sally Anne roars. "And after she screwed me on the registry, when I demand my money back, what's left of it, you know what she tells me? You get the money when I win the pageant. Until then, keep your trap shut."

On the monitor, a second light has gone on. To my credit, I stand up, preparing to run for a nurse. To my shame, I remain in place and ask a follow-up question.

"Why was she even doing that sort of thing? Her husband's a lawyer, right? He must make money."

"Not even Donald Trump could've supported that broad. Money flowed through her fingers like sand through an hourglass."

And with that timeless *Days of our Lives* reference, a siren blares from the monitor. That jumpstarts me into action. I head for the door but none too quickly, because Sally Anne's still talking. Shouting, really.

"Every single dime is precious to me!" she yells. "And no beauty queen with half a brain will trust me to register her pageant wear now! That describes most of you, am I right? So where does that leave Crowning Glory? Where does that leave me?"

Nurses and orderlies rush past me into Sally Anne's room. One of them glares at me. "What did you do to her?"

"Nothing. Just a little light conversation."

They swarm Sally Anne's bed. As for me, I skedaddle.

CHAPTER TWENTY-SIX

The second I get back to my room I boot up my laptop and create a spreadsheet. I label it: SUSPECTS IN TIFFANY AMBER'S MURDER. Then I start filling it in.

My fingers hover over the keyboard as I ponder whether Sally Anne's revelations make her more or less likely to have murdered Tiffany. On the *more* side, she had not one good reason but two to be irate with Ms. California: the gown registry and the loss of money in Tiffany's currency-trading scheme. But on the *less* side, wouldn't Sally Anne have a better chance of getting her money back if Tiffany won the pageant? That quarter-million dollar prize would go a long way toward allowing Tiffany to pay off her debts.

I'm leaning toward *less* until something else strikes me. Sally Anne had no guarantee that Tiffany would pay her back even if she did win. But Sally Anne could assure herself sweet revenge if she knocked Tiffany off. That outcome she could control.

That pushes me toward *more*. But none of this is conclusive. Why is it that the more I investigate, the more confused I get? Maybe that's how Momoa feels, too. I decide not to call and ask him.

I move on to Keola Kalakaua, he of the ever-present loincloth. He had money issues with Tiffany, too. He wanted a portion of her prize if she won. Keola said Tiffany told him no way and that I believe. That could be a motive for murder. But with him I have the opportunity issue. I find it highly unlikely that His Highness could have maneuvered around backstage during the finale with none of the queens noticing. Plus I think about him the same way so many people think about beauty queens: that he lacks sufficient brain cells to pull off a successful poisoning.

Then we have Rex Rexford, who had a financial arrangement with the victim. He stood to win 25 "big ones," as Sally Anne called them, if Tiffany grabbed the Ms. America title. Like Sally Anne, he was left empty-handed by Tiffany's death. But unlike Keola and Sally Anne, I have no reason to believe Rex was left with money troubles. In fact, given the likelihood he was the main heir to Sonny Roberts' gargantuan estate, quite the opposite. And I have discovered no reason why Rex would harbor any resentment toward Tiffany.

I sit back and think about Magnolia Flatt and Misty Delgado. To my knowledge, money played no role in either woman's relationship with Tiffany. But both of them had other motives to kill her, just as powerful. Rivalry, revenge, jealousy.

And Sebastian Cantwell? I know so little of his dealings with Tiffany. They might have involved money. Maybe she tried to blackmail him. He was richer than anybody else on my list and I certainly wouldn't put it past Tiffany to have dug up something juicy on him that she could use to further her own ends.

I type Tony Postagino's name into the spreadsheet

even though he had no opportunity to get backstage to slip the poison into Tiffany's lipstick. No doubt he would have been severely impacted by his wife's big spending, whether he knew about it or not. I saw on *Oprah* that some husbands are oblivious to that sort of thing, though Oprah pried it out of one guy that, in fact, yes, he sort of knew, he was just in denial. I wonder to what extent Tiffany's husband was aware of her financial machinations. Did he know about the currency trading? Maybe he was the one who came up with the idea. But somehow it seems more likely that Tiffany was doing it on the QT because she was trying to cover her spending.

I abandon the spreadsheet and go on-line. In short order I find myself at Tony Postagino's website. I scan it carefully, just like I did the first time I visited. There's nothing to suggest he's not a successful personal-injury lawyer. His home page sports a few fancy logos to highlight his credentials—one from the American Bar Association and another from the American Association of Justice. There's a section potential clients can fill in with their name and contact information and details of their situation. They are assured they will be rewarded with a *Free Case Analysis*. Sure, there are a few typos and grammatical errors in the encouraging text about how Tony P gets the most for his clients in the shortest possible timeframe. It's not *statue* of limitations, for example. But I doubt ambulance chasing puts a premium on excellent language skills.

I eye the Hawaiian shirt Tony Postagino is wearing in the website photo and decide that it's nicer than the campshirt I got Jason. It looks sleeker than most shirts of its type. It has white orchids on a red background but even with the bright color there's nothing kitschy about it.

I can't say the same about the photo's backdrop, though. Tiffany's husband is sitting in a room that screams *Hawaii!* in the cheesiest of all possible ways. There's a ton of Polynesian paraphernalia around him— lamps with pineapple bases, rugs that look like surfboards, sofa pillows embroidered with the phrase *Daddy's Little Surfer Girl.* Hanging on the wall is a big blue quilt with squares that tell the state's story. In one is a map depicting the seven main islands. In another, three women are caught in mid hula. One block shows Mount Haleakala erupting; in another dolphins are doing backflips.

In front of the quilt stands a tiki totem pole that must be a good five feet tall. It's carved out of wood, like they all are I guess, and shows two giant faces, one on top of the other, the top one grimacing fiercely, the lower laughing. I find the thing a little scary.

I'm staring at the totem when I get the funniest feeling I've seen it before. And the quilt. They're both unique, to put it nicely. But I can't for the life of me remember where. I haven't seen them in the flesh, if you get my meaning. I've never been in that particular room. But they're so dang familiar.

I work on the spreadsheet for a while longer, then flop onto the bed. On goes the TV. It's a little before noon and the early midday news is on. Both the male anchor and the weatherman are wearing Hawaiian shirts, just like Detective Momoa always does.

I've just watched the weather report—which broadcasts the shocking revelation that every day will be sunny with a high in the eighties—when on comes a commercial for Ventura Aerial Tours. After some beauty shots of Oahu taken from a thousand feet, Dirk appears in his chopper's pilot seat. He's wearing a sand-colored short-sleeved safari shirt, aviator sunglasses with reflective lenses, and headset. He looks dark, brooding, and mysterious. From what I've seen of him, that's his main mode. A second later he surprises me by cracking a smile, probably because the cameraman told him it would be better for business. Then the cameraman pulls back and we watch Dirk lift the chopper up, up, and away.

I wonder if Dirk and Misty ever did it in the chopper. That's not where they were, though, when Magnolia videotaped them for YouTube.

Or did she videotape them for Tiffany? You be the judge.

Half a minute later a synapse fires in my brain. I leap off the bed and race back to my laptop. In seconds I'm staring at YouTube's home page. The video of Misty and Dirk is still featured, though it's fallen quite a bit down the list. I click on it.

The video begins just as I remember. And then …

Oh … my … God. There they are, clear as day, behind Misty and Dirk, who are grabbing at each other like they're in a porn movie on its inexorable course to the main attraction.

But I'm not focused on the twosome. It's what's in the background that grabs my attention. The big blue

Hawaii quilt on the wall. And the two-faced tiki totem in front of it. Not to mention all the other stuff cluttering the place.

How bizarre is that? Tony Postagino's photo was taken in the same exact location as the Misty/Dirk video.

Where did Magnolia tell me she shot this? I wrack my brain. Then this, too, comes to me. At a B&B owned by Dirk's sister. I grab my cell and make a call. It's soon answered. "Trixie, where are you?"

"At the casual café in the lobby. Wanna join me?"

"Don't move. I'll be right there."

The place is jampacked. I run inside, slamming into bodies as I go. One of them is Rex Rexford, wearing dark plaid Bermuda shorts and a black tee shirt.

"Where's the fire?" he asks me.

"Sorry, Rex." I spy Trixie by the counter, where she's occupying one of the tall stools and eating a salad. She's in her bikini cover-up and her copper-colored hair is damp. I stand next to her—there are no open seats— and tell her what I just learned. She's as freaked as I am and nearly falls off her stool when I relay the good part.

"What is this telling us?" she squeals.

"I have no clue. I mean, it could just be a coincidence but don't you think it's really weird?"

"It's not a coincidence, Happy." She slaps the counter to emphasize her point. "There's no such thing as a coincidence, don't you know that?"

"Uh ... no."

"Deepak Chopra, you know, the spiritual guru? He says that everything that happens is related to something else, that maybe you know about or maybe you don't, or maybe you see it or maybe you don't, but it's there regardless, somewhere in the cosmos. So something that seems like a coincidence is really"—she grabs my arm—"a message."

"Well, if it is, it's in some dang code that I can't read! Because the only thing I'm picking up is that Tony Postagino had his website photo taken in the same location that Misty and Dirk used for their rendezvous."

Trixie nods. "Dirk's sister's B&B. What's its name?"

"I don't know. All I know is that Magnolia said it was about half an hour from here. And that it was funky."

Trixie frowns. "Tiffany's husband isn't the funky type. He's the regular businessman type."

"Tiffany wasn't the funky type, either."

The girl working the counter refills Trixie's lemonade and glances at me. "Can I get you anything?"

"Is it too late to get my breakfast drink?"

"Not at all," she says and bustles away.

This time it's me grabbing arms as a new idea occurs to me. I halt the progress of Trixie's lemonade halfway to her mouth. "I thought of something. Remember how Keola told me that Tiffany told him that she was having an affair to get even with her husband because he was having an affair? What if her husband went to that B&B not with Tiffany but with the woman he was having an affair with?"

Trixie gasps. "And maybe *she* was funky. Because you know it's always the woman who picks which B&B to go to. In fact, a man would never pick a B&B in the first place."

"No. They'd pick a hotel."

"Or a motel if it was" —Trixie wrinkles her nose— "you know, tacky, like an affair." Her eyes widen. "You need to find out who he went there with."

I feel something in my chest that might be what my mother calls palpitations. "Oh my God. Because maybe that's who murdered Tiffany."

"To get her out of the way. So she could be with her one true love. Tony Postagino." Trixie gets excited. "Maybe it's another contestant. Somebody we haven't even thought about."

"Or maybe a woman who wasn't in the pageant. Tiffany's husband wouldn't necessarily know any other beauty queens."

"True. Rhett doesn't know any except me." She looks worried all of a sudden. "At least I hope not."

"And," I go on, "it's completely possible that nobody noticed this woman backstage. She could have slipped in and out without anybody really seeing her."

Trixie's eyes are as big as oranges. "I cannot believe that you figured out that the photo and the video were shot at the same place. That's a perfect example of what Deepak Chopra is always talking about." She lowers her voice to a dramatic whisper. "Synchrodestiny."

The counter girl returns. "Sorry, but we ran out of wheat germ and I need to get more. Do you mind waiting a few minutes?"

"No, that's fine." I look at Trixie. "In the meanwhile I'll go find Magnolia and ask her where the B&B is."

"So you can go there and ask if they remember who

Tiffany's husband was there with." Her face falls. "That doesn't seem likely, though, does it? They must have a million people stay there."

"True. But who knows? Maybe it's really small with only a couple of rooms and they'll remember. I might luck out."

"You'll need to show them his photo."

"You're right. I'll have to print it off the computer."

"You can do that in the hotel business center." Trixie scribbles her signature and room number on her bill. "I'll come with you."

I call out to the counter girl. "Just leave my drink on the counter and put the bill on my tab, okay? I'll be back in a few to pick it up." Because I've got other business to attend to at the moment. This queen is on a mission.

CHAPTER TWENTY-SEVEN

Armed with the photo of Tony Postagino, I make a few phone calls and ascertain that Magnolia is in the hotel's babysitting center. Trixie and I head in that direction.

"What could she be doing there?" Trixie asks me.

"I don't know." I pull open the center's glass door and wave Trixie in ahead of me. "I just hope the kids survive her."

Truer words were never spoken, I realize, as Trixie and I stop dead in the foyer. In front of us stands Magnolia, dressed in her usual super-tight shorts and tee shirt, wearing a dazed expression and splotches of paint all up and down her arms and legs. Around her toddle about twenty kids, none of them older than three. Five of them are crying, at least that many are screaming, and some of them are taking a stab at finger-painting. One boy is standing by the floor-to-ceiling window swinging a toy truck in a wide arc. I suspect he's plotting to break the glass and escape.

I stop one little girl from shoving her paint brush up her nose while Trixie breaks up a fight between a couple of boys. The one who nearly got beat up sets up a wail even though he's just been rescued. Trixie scoops him up in her arms.

"Magnolia?" I move toward her. She doesn't even register me. "Magnolia!" This time I shout.

Slowly her head turns in my direction. "Yeah?"

I'm not even sure she recognizes me. "What are you doing here?"

She thinks a moment. Then, "Babysitting."

Out of the corner of my eye I see two little girls carefully upend a jar of water that had been holding used brushes. They giggle and watch with delight as the murky water puddles on the floor.

Trixie approaches, still holding the sobbing boy. "What's wrong with you, Magnolia?" She raises her voice and snaps her fingers in front of Magnolia's face. "Snap out of it!"

Magnolia yawns, not bothering to cover her mouth. "I'm exhausted."

"You're catatonic," I say. "Why are you even here?"

"Cantwell sent me. He's punishing me, obviously. He told the hotel I'd help out."

Trixie looks around her in shock. "Bad idea. These parents would sue in a heartbeat if they got a whiff of what was going on in here."

I sense activity at knee level and bend down just in time to remove a tray of paint colors from a little boy's hands. "We don't lick those, honey," I tell him. I straighten and face Magnolia. "So what happened to the regular babysitter?"

Her eyes, done up as usual with her Nefertiti-style eyeliner, drift toward the door. "Beats me. I lost track of her. I've been here since like six AM. I'm so zonked I can't see straight anymore."

Trixie shakes her head in disgust, then her eyes widen. She races toward the floor-to-ceiling window where the little boy is swinging a toy truck and grabs it just before it smashes into the glass.

"Okay, Magnolia," I say. "I'll see if I can get you some help in here, but before I do, I want you to answer me a question. Where is that B&B where you videotaped Misty and Dirk?"

"B&B?" she repeats.

"Yes. The one you said was half an hour from here. What's the name of it?"

She blinks. "I said there was a B&B?"

I take a deep breath. "Magnolia, you videotaped Misty and Dirk at a bed and breakfast that Dirk's sister owns. Remember?"

She shakes her head. "Damned if I can remember my own name right now," she says, then steps away from me.

I grab her arm but she pulls away. "Magnolia, come on," I call but am forced to watch as she droops to the side of the room and slumps into a tiny plastic chair. Her head lolls back against the wall and I swear in two seconds she's asleep.

"It's no use," Trixie calls to me from the window. She's made progress, I see. The sobbing and the swinging boys are now sitting calmly on the floor putting paint on paper. "You're not going to get anything out of her. You're going to have to ask Dirk."

I sigh. "You're right. He would certainly know." Though it may be challenging to pry the information out of him. He's not exactly Mr. Talkative.

"I'm staying here," Trixie says. "I can't leave these kids."

"You want me to stay with you?"

"No, you go. Hey!" she shouts at the bully boy who started the earlier fight and is about to incite another. "You lay one finger on that girl, you got me to answer to!"

The boy pulls his hands back from the little girl as if he's just been caught in the headlights of a cop car.

"I've got it under control here," Trixie says, which I can plainly see. "You go do what you have to do and then come tell me what you find out."

I cannot believe it given the racket but Magnolia is indeed sleeping when I turn to go. Maybe Deepak Chopra is right with his whole synchrodestiny thing, because otherwise I don't know what trick of fate sent Trixie and me to that babysitting center. All I know is I'm glad it did. For the kids' sake.

I grab my breakfast drink from the café and head for the hotel's courtesy shuttle, which zooms around Waikiki all day and all night dropping off and retrieving us Royal Hibiscans. This particular bus is standing room only. I drop my drink in my new white drawstring leather tote and clutch a pole for the ride's duration.

I note when I arrive at Ventura Aerial Tours' location that a chopper is returning to the helipad. I stand behind the Cyclone fence and watch it land. It's noisy and generates a lot of wind and blowing dirt. A minute after it touches down, a handful of tourists tumble from its open door and in various groupings pose for pictures below the slowing rotary blades. Dirk

Ventura himself emerges and is petitioned to pose as well. He doesn't look happy about it. His aviator sunglasses stay on and I don't see much of a smile on his lips.

I watch him. For all that I detest what I have learned about Dirk Ventura's behavior toward women—female tourists in particular—I do recognize he has a compelling aura. There's the tall, dark, handsome bit, sure; but there's also the man of few words, masterful-chopper-pilot thing going on. I can see why Misty found him attractive.

I find him a little scary, too. He seems mysterious, somehow, hard to read. None of this is inconsistent with how I think of murderers, I must say. But unless Dirk Ventura fell totally in love with Misty and so killed Tiffany in order to improve Misty's chances of taking the Ms. America title, I don't see a motive for murder. Plus there's no way he could have snuck around backstage and remained unseen.

Unless, of course, Dirk and Misty were in cahoots. He might have handled some phase of the operation—like getting the poison—while Misty laced Tiffany's lipstick while she was backstage. Again, that presupposes a serious love affair between the two, which had to have developed very quickly.

I wonder what's happened to it since?

Eventually the tourists file through the gate in the fence and return to their rental cars. Ventura perches half in and half out of the chopper scanning paperwork. I call him a few times from the gate but either he can't hear me or doesn't choose to, as he doesn't acknowledge me in the slightest. Eventually I ignore the DO NOT ENTER: AUTHORIZED PERSONNEL ONLY sign and approach the chopper.

He doesn't raise his head to look at me until I'm about ten yards away. Then, I note, his eyes travel nowhere else.

I do look kind of cute, I will tell you, in my True Religion stretch denim cuffed shorts—which I'm amazed I can still cram myself into given my dietary habits of late—and lapis-colored jersey halter top with beaded pintucks. The chunky stacked sandals don't hurt, either, I bet. They have four inch heels and a one-inch platform so I'm tall and leggy if nothing else.

"Hi, Dirk," I yell when I'm within earshot. Even with the chopper's blades no longer rotating, the wind in this area is so relentless it's impossible to hear.

He leans out of the chopper. "You're in the mood to break the rules today, I see."

"Oh." For a moment I'm flummoxed. Then, "Oh, you mean the sign?"

He nods. His eyes never leave my face.

"Sorry about that. I just wanted to ask you a question."

He cups his ear as if he can't hear me.

"I just wanted to ask you a question," I shout.

He gives me a once-over. From my long blown-dry brunette hair to my bright orange toenails and back again. "What'll you give me if I answer?" he asks.

I put my hand on my hip. "Dirk Ventura, are you flirting with me?"

I watch a smile form on his lips. That's an

achievement by itself. He exits the chopper, walks around to the other side, gets in there, and gestures to me to take the seat he's just cleared.

I stand there like a moron. "You want me to get in?"

"It'll be easier to talk," he tells me.

Probably so, but I'm not convinced that's the reason Dirk Ventura issued the invitation. I suspect he considers himself a more skilled practitioner of the seducer's art when he's in his chopper's pilot seat. I hoist myself up and assume the position Misty was in when it all began between her and Dirk. There I have an even stronger feeling that Misty's and mine are only two in a long line of female butts to have ridden shotgun with Dirk Ventura.

But I have to conclude this is a positive development. After all, I want information out of him. I'm more likely to get it if he's thinking he might get something out of me.

He shuts both chopper doors and immediately it gets quieter.

I scan his face, then bat my eyes. "You don't look any the worse for wear after that punch you took from Misty Delgado's husband," I tell him.

He shrugs and looks out the chopper's front window. "I guess he had to get it out of his system. Especially after—" He stops.

"After what?"

It takes him a while to answer. Then, "After he got wind of what I told the cops."

"You spoke with them?" I ask breathlessly. I'm embarrassingly good at Brunette Bimbo. "What did you tell them?"

He turns back to me. "That Misty Delgado isn't worth killing somebody over."

"Oh my God!" I give him my best Valley Girl. "Are you telling me the cops asked you flat out if you killed Tiffany Amber?"

"They did. And I told them they were out of their minds if they thought I'd commit homicide for Misty Delgado."

I slap him playfully on the arm. "That's not a very nice thing to say about the woman you're supposed to be in love with." I follow the line with a giggle.

He looks at me. Since he's still wearing his reflective aviator sunglasses I can't see his eyes. But again I have the funniest feeling that he's regarding me with, shall we say, heightened interest. "Let's just say that what I felt for Misty can be described with a different four-letter word than love."

I pretend to be shocked. "Do you mean ... lust?"

He gives me a piercing stare, as piercing as it can be through polycarbonate. "Over time, I've come to see that Misty isn't all I first thought her to be."

I guess his opinion was higher when all he knew of her was that she'd cheat on her husband in a heartbeat.

"For example," he goes on, "I don't like what she did to you last night."

CHAPTER TWENTY-EIGHT

The man speaks in riddles. "What Misty did to me?" I ask.

He reaches across my lap and very gently takes the hand with the condomed finger. "How's the bite today? Any better?"

"It's quite a bit better." Realization dawns. "Are you kidding me? Are you telling me that Misty—"

"She pushed you into the macaw."

"You saw her do it?"

"She told me she did it. At the barbecue, before I had my own"—he hesitates—"falling out."

My heart is dancing a mad jig. Does that mean it was Misty who killed Tiffany? And so tried to scare me out of asking any more questions? Maybe Shanelle's been right all along.

I look at my hand, lying in Dirk's. Was Misty in league with Dirk? Am I at this very moment holding hands with a murderer? "Why in the world would Misty push me into Cordelia?" My voice sounds high-pitched and squeaky.

"You have to ask?" He squeezes my fingers. "She hates you because you're the new Ms. America." Just like she hated Tiffany when she thought Tiffany would be Ms. America instead of her. "Is all this talk of murder frightening you?" he asks softly.

I guess my growing panic is telegraphing itself somehow. "Not at all," I lie.

"You shouldn't be," he says. "You're safe with me."

I highly doubt that, even though Dirk might not at this moment be plotting to slip poison into my system. I think of a pretext for extracting my hand from his and reach into my tote to pull out my breakfast drink. "I'm suddenly very thirsty," I declare. I try to pull back the opening tab on the lid but given the state I'm in, I can't manage it.

Dirk takes the drink from my hand. "Here." In one second it's open. He hands me back the drink. He's staring at me non-stop. "I'm making you nervous," he murmurs and chuckles.

I am nervous but not for the reason he thinks. I sip the drink and get another surprise. "Yuck."

"Is something wrong with it?"

"I'll say. It doesn't taste at all like normal."

He takes it from my hand and drinks some himself. "That is repulsive. But it's healthy, right?"

"Sure. But that's not the only reason I drink it. Usually it tastes good, too."

He holds it out toward me.

"No, thanks. The girl must've made it wrong today."

He shrugs, then throws back his head and pours the drink down his throat. I watch his Adam's apple work. He finishes the drink and smacks his lips. "See? You're already making a better man out of me. For you I'll eat healthy." He stashes the empty cup. "What did you want to ask me, anyway?"

"Oh." I almost forgot. The Misty macaw revelation pushed that right out of my mind. "I understand your sister owns a B&B here on Oahu."

"That's right."

"What's it called?"

He cocks his head. "You've had enough of the Royal Hibiscus?"

"No. I'm just planning for my next trip out here. When it's on my own dime and I won't be paying Royal Hibiscus prices."

He eyes me for a second longer, then straightens in his chair. "Buckle up."

"Why?"

He pushes a few buttons. I hear the rotary blades overhead start to spin. "I'll do better than tell you where it is," he says. "I'll show you."

"No, that's really not—"

But the chopper's engine is rumbling, the rotary blades are picking up speed, and the cabin is beginning to shudder. Dirk puts on his headset and hands me another. Either I fling myself out of the chopper this very second or I'm going for a ride. I feel the tail of the chopper rise. I guess I'm going for a ride.

It is fun, there's no doubt about that, and being in the front seat offers a different perspective. We nose along the ground briefly and then gain altitude. In front of us is Waikiki's skyline, one white skyscraper jostling with another for space in the wild blue yonder. A few cottonball clouds are gathering over the mountains. Dirk executes a slow 180 above a boat harbor and we hug the coast heading for Diamond Head. The ocean water is various gorgeous shades of blue and so transparent I see coral reefs in the shallower depths. I am awestruck when we fly over Diamond Head's massive crater, which dominates the south end of Waikiki Beach.

"Have you hiked to the top?" Dirk asks me over the headset.

"No, but I hear it's not that hard to do."

"Takes about an hour and a half. Misty liked the tunnel better than the hike. Especially at sunset."

I bet she did. After walking through a few hundred feet of pitch-black World War Two-era tunnel, you emerge to behold a drop-dead view of the west side of Oahu. That is, if you make it to the end. I imagine Dirk and Misty might have gotten waylaid, so to speak, before getting that far.

"I notice you talk about Misty in the past tense," I say. It's oddly intimate having a conversation over the headset, almost like the other person is whispering in your ear. "Are you trying to tell me that you and she are no longer an item?"

"And if we're not? Are you trying to tell me you're interested?"

I flash the rings on my left hand. "I'm not exactly available."

"For what I'm thinking of, you are."

One thing you have to say about Dirk Ventura: he's upfront about his intentions. I make my voice flirtatious. "So I could be your Ms. Right Now?"

"You sure could if I can get us to my sister's B&B fast enough." He kind of chokes out the last words.

I glance at him. "You okay?"

"Wow." He shakes his head once, then twice. The chopper dips a little to the left. Instantly he rights it.

I watch him rub his forehead. His chest begins to rise and fall quicker than usual. Suddenly he's panting. The chopper jerks to the right.

"Dirk!"

He straightens out the chopper, then raises his left hand to rub his forehead while the right remains on the joystick-like thingie he uses to fly the aircraft. "Sorry," he gasps. "It's just ... wow."

"You feeling okay?" I ask him again. In my opinion, at this moment there's only one right answer to that question. But Dirk doesn't deliver it. In fact, he doesn't say anything. Instead his breathing gets even more frenzied and his face grows more and more flushed.

I have the funniest feeling I'm getting my answer. But it's not the one I want to hear.

I can't believe it. For the second time today I've apparently pushed somebody into cardiac arrest, this time a 30-something fit male. And Dirk's attack is a lot worse than Sally Anne's because he's not in a hospital bed hooked up to heart monitors. In fact, he and I are in a tin can pitching through the air at a thousand feet above terra firma.

I'm getting a little panicky, as you might imagine. "What do you say we bring this baby down?" I try to keep my voice playful, as if there's nothing really wrong. "We can go up another time to get an aerial view of your sister's B&B. In the meanwhile—" I reach into the footwell for my tote. I have aspirin in my cosmetics bag.

My mind races. Isn't that what you're supposed to give somebody in the throes of a heart attack? It settles the old ticker right down. Or so I hope.

Next to me Dirk is wheezing. "Something ... something's wrong."

"Yeah, I got that part." I don't bother trying to sound calm this time. "I'm going to give you some ... Dirk!"

The chopper lurches downward this time. Dirk brings the nose back up. At least he can still manage that. I don't let myself think about what might happen if we get to the point where he can't.

"I'm giving you some aspirin," I say. "I think you're having a heart attack."

He shakes his head. "That drink—"

I find the mini aspirin bottle in my tote. My trembling hands attempt to shake out a pill or two. "Focus on the flying. Now is not the time to think about—"

My hands still. Oh, damn. Oh, no. It can't be. It absolutely cannot be ...

Did somebody put something in my drink? While it was sitting for who knows how long on the counter in the casual café? Something like ... poison?

I'm suddenly convinced that Misty decided the macaw attack didn't go far enough. *Enough with the warnings,* she's thinking. *Let's get cracking.*

And what did Jason tell me, just last night? That going after murderers is dangerous? And what did I do? Ignore him? Maybe people are right that beauty queens don't have two brain cells to rub together.

Dirk lolls back in the pilot seat. His hand releases from the joystick thing between us. The chopper takes a plunge and shudders to the left at the same time. I shriek. My insides take flight. I feel like I might throw up but I don't have time to because if I don't get Dirk to buck up, we'll both be food for the fishies. At least what's left of us.

I reach left across the cabin and punch his arm. "Don't you die on me! Wake the hell up! Pronto!"

He comes to, sort of. I grab his hand and return it to the joystick. We level out, sort of. I note with some consternation that we're not nearly as high now as we used to be. True, I want to be reunited with Mother Earth. But tenderly, on my terms.

"Do not take your hand off that thing again, do you hear me?" I scream at him. "I don't care how you feel!"

"Right," he chokes out. "Right."

"Just bring this thing down! No more discussion! Anywhere but in the water," I add as an afterthought, because that's what we're over now. It's safe to say we have not been following a straight line the last few minutes. "Go that way." I point helpfully at the coastline.

To his credit, he gets the chopper moving successfully in that direction. Until …

"Oh my God," he says, and starts to huff and puff like he's trying to blow the whole house down. The chopper jolts with every hectic breath he draws. Up, down, left, right … I feel like I'm riding a bucking bronco.

I hear wild screaming in my ears and realize that it's

coming from me. I try to shut up but can't until I hold both hands over my mouth. I never thought it would come to this. I never even took a helicopter ride until I came to this godforsaken island. And now I'm going to meet my Maker in this damn chopper, although the Almighty will barely recognize me because I'll be all smashed to pulp ... Of course, He's got to be used to meeting people at the pearly gates who aren't exactly looking their best.

"Can't I do something to help?" I shriek at him. "Like hold your hand on this joystick thingie?"

I do it even though I'm not sure whether it's helping or not. I'm waiting for my life to flash before my eyes when I realize that actually we're over land now, some grassy area or park or something, and we're not that high anymore, and even though we're still jerking around, we're also kind of circling like we're going to land, and ...

Ka-boom! We do land. It won't go in the record books as Dirk's best ever; in fact we kind of go down nose first, then tail, which I don't think is exactly textbook, but in my personal record book it's an all-time best because I'm not dead. Dirk's not dead and I'm not dead and we're both on the ground.

I hear sobbing and it takes me some time to realize it's coming from me. I manage to shut up and then I turn to look at Dirk.

Uh oh.

CHAPTER TWENTY-NINE

Maybe I concluded too quickly that Dirk's not dead. Because he's not looking too sprightly at the moment. His tongue is hanging out and I see no sign of breathing.

Oops, now I do see one. His chest just rose and fell. Then it repeats the performance. These signs of life snap me into action. I reach for my cell to call 911. I don't get far, though, because just as I clutch my phone in my trembling hands I hear a rap on the chopper's front window.

I look up to see a pudgy red-faced man with wispy white hair brandishing a golf club. "You ruined my tee shot!" he yells. "You got some nerve landing in the middle of the goddamn eighth fairway!"

"Listen, Buster!" I scream back. "This was an emergency landing! Look at this guy next to me! He could be dying! So get an effing grip!"

"I paid three hundred bucks for this round," he informs me, "and now I'll have to take a mulligan!"

I have no idea what that means. "Shove your golf ball where the sun don't shine!" I shout back. You will not be surprised to hear that suggestion falls on deaf ears. He goes on hollering but I ignore him, except for the time I scream that some people need to get a little perspective. Eventually he stomps away. His compadres, beefy bullies all, give me scornful looks, like Dirk and I planned this explicitly to ruin their round.

In the midst of all this I punch in 911. Matters do not improve when I attempt to relay my tale to the dispatcher. Yes, I think the chopper pilot was poisoned. No, I cannot tell her where we are, except that we're in the middle of the eighth fairway of a golf course south of Waikiki where rounds cost three hundred smackers. Yes, I'm the new Ms. America and yes, we had a previous poisoning and yes, this time I ingested some of the suspicious substance, too.

I am feeling a tad nauseous but that could just be from nearly snuffing it. That sort of thing has been known to cause stomach upset.

Despite my inability to pinpoint my location, in short order the paramedics find us and Dirk is transported to the hospital. So am I. I'm resting in the ER when who shows up to see me but your friend and mine, Detective Momoa.

He pulls shut the curtains that delineate my area. "Ms. Pennington. How surprising to find you mixed up in yet another calamity."

I sit up straighter. "Calamity? Are you saying that Dirk—"

"Mr. Ventura is in critical condition but he is expected to survive. No thanks to you."

"No thanks to me? I don't think so, Detective. You can't blame me for this one." I may be in a prostrate position but I have not lost my feistiness. "I'm pretty darn sure that somebody poisoned my breakfast drink. It's not my fault that Dirk drank it."

"How convenient that he ingested it and not you."

"What planet do you live on, Detective Momoa? How in the world is it convenient to have your chopper pilot poisoned right before he takes you up? I don't know how to fly that thing! I thought we were both going to die up there!"

He doesn't look convinced. "Why were you in his helicopter in the first place?"

"I wanted to ask him a question and it was easier to talk inside the chopper than outside. Because it was hard to hear over the wind."

He ponders a moment. Then, "So, Ms. Pennington, you're telling me that you didn't expect to go flying with Mr. Ventura when you went to see him, is that correct?"

"That's exactly correct," I say, before I realize where Momoa is going with this. His use of *Ms. Pennington*, which he trots out when he's most suspicious of me, should have tipped me off. "But that doesn't mean—"

"What it means is that you believed you ran no risk of being injured yourself if Mr. Ventura drank the poisoned beverage because you had no expectation of his flying you anywhere. It didn't matter to you how incapacitated he became."

I watch Momoa's features settle into a smug expression. It's pretty clear to me by now what Momoa thinks. He thinks I poisoned Dirk Ventura. That new conviction gives him even more reason to believe that I also poisoned Tiffany Amber.

This is not good.

"Tell me one thing," I say. "Do you know for sure that my drink was poisoned? Or did something else happen to Dirk, like he had a heart attack or something?"

"Oh, no," Momoa says. "We've already had it confirmed that Mr. Ventura ingested poison. Cyanide, to be precise."

Cyanide. In my breakfast drink. Kind of gets me in the gut, hearing that. I sound a little breathy when I next open my mouth. "Was it cyanide that killed Tiffany Amber?"

"The same."

In my mind's eye, I replay it all again. Tiffany in her silver gown writhing on the stage, gasping for breath. Finally breathing her last, in front of all of us. That could have been me. This morning, that could have been me.

I croak out another question. "Then how is it possible that Dirk will be okay?"

"Because the dosage wasn't large enough to kill him. This time"—he focuses his beady eyes on my face—"the killer miscalculated."

Maybe, maybe not, I'm thinking. Because I weigh considerably less than Dirk Ventura. The amount of cyanide might have been plenty enough to do me in.

"You needn't look so concerned," Momoa goes on. "After all, look at you. You emerged unscathed."

"I am hardly unscathed. I am a psychological wreck." I declare this before it occurs to me what hay Momoa might make of the remark. "I was beyond terrified in that chopper and now I am even more scared because it's crystal clear that somebody is trying to kill me. Someone tried to kill me today after someone tried to injure me yesterday."

I hold up my condomed finger and relay the tale of

my tangle with Cordelia. I finish with what Dirk told me. "He said that at last night's luau, Misty Delgado confessed to him that she pushed me into the macaw. So what do you make of that?"

Very little, from the look on Momoa's face.

"I am telling you," I go on, "that Tiffany Amber's murderer, quite possibly Misty Delgado, is trying to strike again. We'd both be better off if you focused on that."

"I promise you, Ms. Pennington, that all of my attention is directed at the behavior of the murderer." He gives me a pointed glare. "Now why don't *you* focus on explaining why Dirk Ventura drank your breakfast drink instead of you."

"I never had the chance to drink it! I picked it up right before I got on the Royal Hibiscus shuttle and it was standing room only and so I had to clutch the pole the entire ride. When I did finally taste the drink, it was awful. That's why I barely got any of it down."

"If it was so awful, why did Mr. Ventura drink it?"

"To impress me, I think. To show that he was willing to eat healthy for me despite how horrible the drink tasted."

The whole thing does sound pretty fishy when I say it out loud. I can see clearly that Momoa agrees with that assessment. *Likely story*, his eyes say. *Likely story*.

"You're wasting your time interrogating me," I pronounce. "You should be at the casual café at the Royal Hibiscus talking to everybody who was there a few hours ago to see if anybody happened to notice somebody tampering with my drink."

"I'll take that under advisement," he informs me. Then another cop pulls the curtains apart and pokes his head inside my area. He and Momoa step away and huddle. The new arrival, a young and short Hawaiian man, peeks at me from time to time as if I'm the topic of their whispered tete-a-tete.

I lay back against the pillows of my rolling bed. I've heard all my life, *Count your blessings*. It's good advice so I take it. I've got four blessings straight off. I'm not dead. Dirk's not dead. I'm back on solid ground. I'm still Ms. America.

Those are the good points and they're darn good. But the two bad points are kind of overwhelming. Someone's trying to kill me. And Detective Momoa, Oahu PD, is more sure than ever that I'm a murderer.

Momoa gives me one more meaningful glare before he and the other cop meander away. A minute or so later a nurse appears at my bedside.

She's fleshy and red-haired and cheerful-looking and somehow creates the comforting impression that she's been at this nursing thing a long while. Her name tag reads *Dorothy*. She smiles and pats my arm. "How are we feeling?"

"Fine. When are they going to let me out of here?"

She clucks her tongue and shakes her head. "I'm surprised you're in such a rush."

"Aren't most people? I mean, I know you work here but the rest of us don't really like being in the hospital."

Her face takes on a befuddled expression. "But you're safe here. After what's happened to you, I would think you'd never want to leave. At least not until they catch" —she hesitates—"you know."

"Until they catch who?"

She looks even more perplexed. "The person who's after you beauty queens. It's all over the news again, like it was after that poor woman got poisoned. Now, after what you've just been through, with the poison again and the helicopter accident ..." She sighs deeply, as if in amazement at the assaults humans perpetrate on one another. "It's terrifying. Just horrible. But here"—she glances behind her, where I see, positioned a few feet behind the open curtain, the squat cop—"you've got police protection."

It'd be nice if that's what it was. But I know something Dorothy doesn't.

It isn't.

CHAPTER THIRTY

Once Dorothy leaves and I am once again alone, I take stock of my situation. I am forced to admit that it is dire. Matters have indeed degenerated to a new low, so much so that I have the funniest feeling that if I stay put, I will be sprung from this rolling bed only to find myself on a like-sized cot in the Honolulu hoosegow, as my mother would call it.

There's only one thing to do. I must escape from this hospital.

Granted, I don't know what I'll do then. I've never been on the run before and I don't know that I'm really up to it, especially in my stacked sandals with their four-inch heels and one-inch platform. But a queen's got to do what a queen's got to do. I won't lie here like a ninny waiting for Momoa to arrest me on two felony counts: one successful murder and one botched attempt.

Now is not the time to thank Dirk for getting the chopper down safely, though I appreciate that big-time. Boy, was he heroic. Cyanide was coursing through his system but despite that he managed to save both our skins. He's still got a few big black marks against him in my book but I have to say he's gone up in my estimation.

I realize now that it couldn't have been Dirk who poisoned Tiffany Amber. After all, it must be the same person who poisoned her and tried to poison me. He never would have downed my breakfast drink if he'd known what was in it.

But Misty ... Misty's still high on my suspects list. I have to get out of here and return to my investigation, the next step of which is finding out the name of Dirk's sister's B&B so I can ask the staff if they remember who Tony Postagino stayed there with. Maybe it was Misty. Then the puzzle might be solved.

I look around me. One thing will make escape easier: I'm still in my clothes. No one forced me into a hospital gown. Dorothy pulled the curtain shut behind her but I can see in the one-foot space between the curtain and the linoleum floor the spit-and-polished black shoes worn by my supposed "police protector." I can't go out that way, clearly.

But one good thing about a curtained prison cell is that the potential escapee is presented with a full 360 degrees of escape route.

I twist around in my bed and listen for noise in the area behind me. I don't hear a thing. No conversation; no nothing. Very quietly I get out of bed and kneel on the floor, crouching down to peer in that direction. No feet are in evidence. There may be a patient in that area, lying in bed, but there's no nurse or ER tech.

That's as good as I'm going to get in these parts.

I grab my tote and turn off my cell phone so my Gloria Gaynor ring tone doesn't draw unwanted attention. I'm proud of thinking of that. It proves I learned something from my ill-advised mail-room escapade. Briefly I halt, wondering if this foray is as imprudent as that one was. I conclude I don't care. I'm blowing this pop stand.

I shimmy underneath the curtain, clutching my tote to my chest. I glance to my right as I go. Yes, there is a patient in this room, a wizened elderly man, lying in bed facing my direction with his eyes closed.

Not for long. They flutter open and fear crosses his face. I rise to my feet and hold my index finger to my lips. "Sshh." I point to the curtain that closes off his area and start tiptoeing in that direction. "I'll just be on my way," I whisper.

Immediately he does exactly what I don't want him to do. Pant. Then gasp. Gasp and pant, in relentless succession. I've seen a lot of that today, all of it caused by me. First with Sally Anne Gibbons, then with Dirk Ventura. Now with this poor fellow, who doesn't look like he can handle much of it. A little beep is emitted from the monitor at his bedside. I am toxic today, a true menace to society. Thank the heavens that when I locate the gap in his curtain and glance behind me, the man is still breathing. Fear remains on his face, though. I mouth a wish for his health and keep going.

What I want to do but can't is run, both because of my platform sandals and because I don't want anybody to notice me. Running is happening in the ER, but it's the nurses and techs doing it, not the plainclothes civilians.

I amble as casually as I can past what looks like the ER's intake area, a kind of reception desk, keeping my head averted. I walk as close to the opposite wall as possible. My body English says, *I'm not here. Don't bother looking at me because I'm not here.* Fortunately this place is such a beehive that nobody is looking at me.

At the glass exit doors, I halt all forward progress. Bad news: I face a new obstacle. Actually, a mob of them. Camera crews. Photographers. Reporters. Armed with microphones and smart phones and tape recorders.

I pull back from the glass doors and shrink against the wall of the foyer. Am I the story? Is this what Dorothy was talking about when she said that after the chopper incident, we beauty queens are all over the news again? Because now the going theory is that somebody's targeting us?

Jason will kill me when he hears about this. Because he'll know without anybody telling him exactly what I was up to that got me into trouble.

As I stand there, I realize there's someone besides Dirk I can cross off my suspects list. Sally Anne Gibbons. She was lying in this very hospital when my breakfast drink was spiked with cyanide. So she couldn't have done it.

I'm pondering that truth when opportunity presents itself in the form of a large Hawaiian family. They're on their way out of the ER, flanking what looks like the matriarch. She's wearing a bright pink and orange muumuu that might have been sewn by Omar the Tentmaker. The other family members are fairly imposing individuals as well, shall we say. And there are a lot of them.

I attach myself to their lee side, furthest from the reporters, and move with them outside. They don't advance as fast as I'd like but they provide excellent cover. As we skirt the reporters, who take no note of our lumbering posse, I hear snippets of live shots.

"—pageant be cursed? This is the second alarming—"

"—reigning Ms. America barely escaped with her life when well-known local helicopter pilot Dirk—"

"—confirm that poison was found in his system, the same fast-acting poison that caused the death less than a week ago of—"

When the family arrives at its vehicle, a Cutlass Cruiser station wagon that has seen better days, I dart away. In seconds I'm hightailing it from the hospital.

A cab ride later I'm back at the Royal Hibiscus. And what do I see massed on the wide sweeping driveway that fronts the hotel? The last thing in the world I expect. *Another* crush of reporters and news cameras and photographers and such like, as large and zealous as the horde I just avoided.

Boy, we queens have become a gigantic story. That, or it's a slow news day on Oahu.

I'm plotting how to evade this throng when I spy Misty Delgado holding court in front of a phalanx of TV cameras. J Lo, if you thought you were the Latina diva, prepare to meet Misty Delgado. Reporters are almost climbing over each other to get their microphones in front of her face. Misty flips her long dark hair over her shoulder. She flashes a smile before she remembers that murder and attempted murder are serious topics. She goes back to trying to look somber.

How fake! What a hypocrite! I want to barf. There she is, my number one suspect, preening like the Queen

Bee. No matter that Tiffany Amber is dead, that only a standing-room-only bus prevented me from joining Tiffany at the gateway to heaven, and that Misty's former lover—granted, she should never have had one, but still—is fighting for his life at this very moment. Ms. Arizona might be responsible for this macabre trifecta but clearly that won't stop her from trying to score some airtime. I half expect her to nail down a reality-show gig.

I tamp down my frustration. This is no time to let my emotions take over; I've got investigating to do.

Fortunately, by now I know the Royal Hibiscus like I know my Macy's back home. I could map every inch blindfolded. I retrace my steps to find the path that cuts down to the beach. That way I can access the hotel from the oceanfront side.

I'm just entering the lobby courtyard from the back when, to my right, the elevator doors to the penthouse level whoosh open. Quite a crowd emerges. Of cops, I soon see.

There's Sebastian Cantwell with them, too, I note. He seems his typical insouciant self, his ponytail as jaunty as ever. He's wearing his usual *I'm about to go yachting* blue blazer with the crest on the breast pocket. What makes me nearly fall off my platform shoes, though, is the next detail I spy.

Sebastian Cantwell is in handcuffs.

CHAPTER THIRTY-ONE

I'm spellbound as I watch the cops maneuver Cantwell across the lobby and out the hotel's main entry doors. I don't know if this is what the reporters here at the Royal Hibiscus were waiting for—maybe they got wind of an upcoming arrest—but they're sure getting some astonishing shots now. I get some idea what it must be like to be accosted by paparazzi. Even from this distance I'm almost blinded by the flashbulbs going off in Cantwell's face.

The cops hustle Cantwell into the back seat of a black-and-white. They slam the door and the sedan careens away, siren blaring. Other cop cars follow. The cameramen train their lenses on the disappearing vehicles until they're gone from sight. Then they swing back around and the reporters resume the live shot position.

The hotel staff appear shell-shocked. I see Neil, the sunburned surfer guy, standing next to the Reception Desk with his mouth literally hanging open.

As for me, I fall back against the wall behind me. Does this mean that Sebastian Cantwell is the murderer? Momoa got the proof he needed and so hauled the pageant owner in? On one count of murder and, gulp, one botched attempt?

That one was on me.

Oh my God.

I race across the lobby to get into the elevator and soon am whisked to my own ninth floor. Shanelle pulls the door open as I'm fumbling with my key card.

"Good Lord Almighty," she shouts and grabs me in a hug that's more like a wrestling takedown.

I'm able to resume breathing half a minute or so later. "I'm all right," I tell her, because she keeps on asking. "I'm all right."

"Here." She pulls her cell phone off the waistband of her shorts and shoves it in my hand. "Call your mama. She's frantic. You been all over the news, girl."

I see that our TV is on and tuned to a news program. On the screen, behind a pert blonde reporter, is the façade of the Royal Hibiscus. Along the bottom four words scream: PAGEANT TYCOON A KILLER?

"Once that chopper went down," Shanelle says, "and it came out that you and Dirk were both in it and that he was incapacitated somehow, you been on nonstop."

I give Shanelle back her cell phone and dig my own out of my tote bag. I turn it on to find scads of messages, from Jason, Rachel, my mom, my dad, and yes, Mario Suave. I raise my eyes to Shanelle. "You've been watching all along, right?"

"From time to time I pack a thing or two, because now this crime's been solved we're all gonna be forced off this island, but for the most part I can't tear my eyes off it."

"Have you seen Momoa at all? Making some

comment or saying he'd make a comment soon or anything like that?"

She frowns. "Not that I remember."

"So he didn't confirm that Cantwell's been charged with Tiffany's murder. Did any other official-type person?"

"Not that I've seen. But—"

"So maybe it's not official."

Shanelle throws her arms wide. "How much more official does it need to be? The man's in police custody! He's been arrested. Can't be no more clear than that."

I know Cantwell's been arrested. I comprehend that. And it's true he's been one of my suspects ever since I found out that Tiffany paid a surreptitious visit to his penthouse suite. It's also plausible that Cantwell tried to do me in today after I blackmailed him yesterday.

But still, something about this doesn't sit right with me. I never considered Cantwell the likely killer and there's a reason. Why would a man who's basically a master of the universe bother murdering a two-bit beauty queen like Tiffany Amber? He could eat her for lunch. She might have tried to blackmail him but why would he even care? He doesn't seem to give a fig what anybody thinks of him. And as for opportunity, he certainly wouldn't have gone unnoticed backstage.

Another thing strikes me as odd. Why wasn't Momoa here for the arrest? He's the lead investigator into Tiffany's murder. Wouldn't he want to take credit? Or at least be seen to be involved? And if he couldn't be here, why didn't he send his lackey, Jenkins? All my life

I've watched my dad's police department operate. Momoa being absent for a huge break like an arrest is not what I would expect of a homicide detective investigating the highest-profile case of his career.

Shanelle snaps her fingers in front of my face. "Don't you go daydreaming on me, girl. What's up with you? You're not acting like you should."

"You mean because I'm not jumping for joy? Because if Cantwell's been arrested for Tiffany's murder, I'm off the hook?"

"Maybe it's that post-traumatic stress thing that's got you tied up in knots. Wouldn't be surprising after what you just been through. Here, sit down."

She prods me toward my bed and sits me down. She makes me kick off my platform shoes and gives me a mini shoulder massage. Even after all that, I'm no less ill at ease than when she started. "You know why I went to find Dirk in the first place?" I ask her.

She doesn't so I tell her the whole story. About how hugely bizarre it is that Tony Postagino's website photo was taken in the same location as Misty and Dirk's steamy YouTube video. About how that location turns out to be the funky B&B owned by Dirk's sister. About how all day I've wanted to go visit that B&B to find out if anybody there remembered who Tony Postagino stayed there with.

"Because," I conclude, "Keola told me that Tiffany told him that her husband was having an affair. Maybe Tony was at that B&B with his fling, because neither Trixie nor I believe that Tiffany would be caught dead somewhere funky. And maybe—"

"It's the fling who killed Tiffany. I get it." Shanelle nods. "Nice theory but the problem is people have affairs all the time and don't kill each other over it. But why are we even talking about this now? Cantwell's been arrested."

"Maybe ..." My mind cranks. "Maybe they arrested Cantwell not because he's the murderer but because they think the murderer will relax now that someone else has been hauled in. And so he or she will reveal themselves. You know, a smokescreen. And Cantwell went along with it because he's so desperate to bring this whole thing to a close. And because he doesn't really care about his reputation anyway. Heck, for him, it's another story to burnish his legend."

Shanelle assumes a dubious expression. "You really think Momoa's smart enough to come up with a plan that savvy?"

"No. Not really." I sigh. Then I brighten. "There's something else, too. Dirk told me that Misty confessed to him that she pushed me into the macaw last night."

Shanelle's eyes widen. "Maybe Misty's the fling!" She jabs her fist in the air. "I always suspected that girl!"

Nothing like impugning Misty Delgado to get Shanelle Walker on board. "So you're willing to help me, right?"

Shanelle's hands settle on her hips. "You want more help? What now?"

"I want to go find Magnolia to get out of her once and for all the name of that dang B&B." I start snooping around for my beaded flip flops. My feet have had enough of those platform sandals for today.

"Okay." Shanelle starts nodding her head. "I get it now. I get it."

"What do you get?" I've just found my flip flops under the bed.

"All right, I'll 'fess up first. I'm not totally thrilled with this Sebastian Cantwell outcome. I'd prefer if it was Misty Delgado who got arrested for killing Tiffany, just because I would love and adore to see that girl go down. But you, you got a bigger problem. You got a deep-seated resistance to the idea that this murder's been solved at all. And I know why."

I go into the bathroom to check my face. As I suspected. All that hysterical sobbing in the chopper caused even my waterproof mascara to run.

"Do you hear me?" Shanelle trails me into the bathroom. "I know why."

I moisten a face cloth and go to work underneath my eyes. This'll take off my concealer, too, but I can reapply.

"Are you listening to me?" Shanelle's voice has gotten more demanding.

"All right, Dr. Philomena, I'm listening."

"You don't want Sebastian Cantwell to be the guilty party because you're not the one who figured out he did it. You want to get the props, yourself, for solving the crime. So you're going to keep investigating as though nothing happened. There's a name for that, girl." She comes to stand beside me, her eyes boring into mine in our shared reflection. "And it's not just a river in Egypt."

I toss the face cloth and snatch up my concealer. "I am not in denial."

"Do you not have one speck of self-awareness?"

"I am totally self-aware, Shanelle. Just like I am totally responsible. And that is why I am not comfortable abandoning my investigation prematurely."

Even as I say it, I wonder if Shanelle's right. I will admit to a smidgen of disappointment when I saw Sebastian Cantwell being hauled in no thanks to me.

I set down my concealer and turn to face her. "Look. What harm will it do? I go to the B&B, I ask a few questions. If I don't learn anything interesting, which I probably won't, I'll give up the investigation. I promise. This is the only lead I have left to pursue anyway."

She nods slowly.

"So you'll help me, right?"

She emits a dramatic sigh. "What do you need?"

"While I'm gone finding Magnolia, will you make a few phone calls for me to tell people I'm all right? Because if I get on the cell with Jason or my mom, I'll never get off." That's my story and I'm sticking to it. I know the real reason I don't want to call my husband is that he'll rake me over the coals for continuing my investigation, which this time nearly got me killed.

I dash out of the bathroom, grab the memo paper near the bedside phone and jot down a list of who I'd like Shanelle to call. I hand her the names then head for the door. "And then please come with me to the B&B. Please?"

She shakes her head. "If this isn't a wild goose chase, I don't know what is. And don't forget that now this murder's been solved, they'll want all of us out of this hotel and booked on flights home."

I pull open the door. "They can't make us leave if they can't find us. Maybe we'll score ourselves another day in paradise."

Shanelle seems to get a boost from that happy possibility. I watch her eyes drop to the jotted list of names as I disappear out the door.

A wee bit of investigating yields the tidbit that Magnolia Flatt is sunbathing by the pool. I gird myself for a viewing of Ms. Flatt in her swimwear.

To my amazement, I find her in a tasteful crimson-colored halter-style swimdress with shirring at the sides—quite slimming—and cute white embroidery along the hemline. She is, somewhat less graciously, noisily sucking down the dregs of a tiki-tiki drink. I claim the lounge next to her.

Her face assumes a sullen expression. "You again. I thought maybe you bit it when that chopper went down."

Same lousy 'tude as ever. "Sorry I failed to oblige."

"Just my luck you survived so you can ream me again about those brats Cantwell made me watch." She slams her empty glass onto the concrete pool deck.

I bite my tongue. "No," I respond sweetly. "I think we covered that pretty thoroughly before. I am a little surprised to see you here, though."

"Why? Don't I deserve time off?"

"I would think that with Mr. Cantwell being arrested, you'd have to man the phone lines or something. Lots of people must be calling in with questions."

"I won't do diddly now." She raises her finger to summon the male server working the pool area. "With Cantwell in the slammer, who knows if I'll get paid."

That makes me worry about getting my prize money, not a cent of which I've yet seen. I can't think about that now, though. "Do you know anything about Mr. Cantwell's arrest? Were you in his suite when it happened?"

"No. I was in that hellhole of a babysitting room. I don't know a damn thing about it." She looks up at the server. "I'll take one more of what I just had." She glances at me. "You want something? Better order now because the gravy train's about to dump us off."

"No, thank you," I tell the server. "Listen, Magnolia," I say once he's gone, "I'm hoping your memory's recovered because I would really like to know the name of the B&B that Dirk Ventura's sister owns."

"Oh, yeah, right." She squints her eyes. "Plum something. Like the flower."

"You mean plum blossom?"

"No. It's that Hawaiian flower that starts with plum."

The woman at the next lounger pipes up. "Plumeria?"

"That's it," Magnolia says. "Plumeria B&B."

I lean forward to thank our fellow sunbather. "And it's where?" I ask Magnolia. "Kailua Beach?"

"Yeah, it's about a half-hour drive from here."

"Great. Thanks." I stand up. "By the way, I like your swimsuit."

She swipes at it. "I hate it. My mother made me

buy it."

News flash. At least one female in the Flatt family tree has taste.

CHAPTER THIRTY-TWO

The Royal Hibiscus shuttle doesn't go as far as Kailua Beach so I pop for a cab and tell the driver to take the Pali Highway, which cuts across southeastern Oahu. We cross over the dramatic Koolau mountains, which run the whole length of the island's windward side. Shanelle and I find ourselves at the Plumeria Bed and Breakfast in 26 and a half minutes. But who's counting?

Shanelle steps out of the cab and hikes the spaghetti straps on her bright yellow patio dress. "We're a long way from Waikiki, girl."

"Not a skyscraper in sight." It's more of a residential neighborhood, with a mix of McMansions and older bungalow-style homes. The beach is gorgeous. We can spy it between the houses fronting the ocean. Beautiful white sand and turquoise water with more wind surfers than we're used to seeing on our side of Oahu.

The Plumeria Bed and Breakfast is a two-story board-and-batten cottage painted eggshell blue with white trim. Next to the front window on the first floor somebody painted a large bright pink plumeria, five oval petals springing from a darker-hued core. A plumeria tree with white blossoms dominates the small front lawn.

Shanelle leans close to me. "This place is *tiny*. How

many rooms could it have?"

"Probably no more than two."

"Isn't it a weird place for somebody from California to stay? I mean, it's cute and all, but of all the places to stay on Oahu, why would Tiffany's husband pick here?"

I was thinking the same thing. And I have the answer. "It's a perfect place to stay if you don't want to run into anybody you know, which you might at one of the big Waikiki hotels."

"For example, if you want to lie low because you're in Hawaii with somebody other than your wife."

"Precisely. And I think it's good luck for us that the place is so small because that makes it more likely that Dirk's sister, or somebody who works here, will remember who stayed here with Tony Postagino."

"He might have come here alone."

"Who would come here alone?"

Shanelle has to agree. It is very possible, though, that it was Tiffany who accompanied her husband. Then I've gone through all this to get nowhere.

We trod up the fieldstone walkway to the front door. It's one of those Dutch doors where the top and bottom halves move independently. The top half is open, probably to let in the breeze.

I lean inside and am about to call out when I behold before me the same tableau I've seen twice now, once on Tony Postagino's website photo and once in the infamous Misty and Dirk make-out video. There are all the Polynesian tchotchkes, the pineapple-base lamps and the surfboard-shaped throw rugs. There's the Hawaii quilt the same color as the deep blue sea. And in front of the hanging quilt is the totem pole with the two outsized faces, one grinning and one grimacing.

"We've come to the right place," I whisper to Shanelle, then I call out. "Hello! Anybody home?"

A woman about my age comes into view, wiping her hands on a dish towel. She's an attractive brunette wearing white shorts and a sleeveless print top. I detect a softer version of Dirk Ventura's features in her face. Clearly this is the inn's owner, his sister.

She doesn't smile when she sees us. First I think it's because she shares her brother's moody demeanor. Then I recall why she might not be at her most cheerful this afternoon: her sibling is in a hospital bed fighting for his life.

It occurs to me that she might blame me for that.

She stops a few feet from the door. On closer inspection I see that the skin around her brown eyes is puffy. "Please come in," she says. "It's open."

We enter. A small boy is splayed on one of the surfboard rugs playing with a huge collection of G.I. Joe figurines. He looks up at us and I see Dirk's Mini Me. But unlike Dirk, this little tyke's face cracks in a wide grin.

"That's Elijah," the woman says. She extends her hand to me, then Shanelle. "And I'm Deirdre. Are you interested in booking a room or two? We're full up right now but—"

I decide to plunge right in. "Deirdre, this is my friend Shanelle Walker. And I'm Happy Pennington." I watch recognition dawn on her face. "How is your brother doing?"

She answers in a rush. "I just got back from the hospital, as a matter of fact. My parents are still there. The doctors say he's out of the woods." Her face crumples. She twists away from us. "I'm sorry. It's just been such a terrible day."

"I understand. Please don't apologize." I struggle to think of something to add and decide I'll try to ingratiate myself. "Your brother was just amazing landing that chopper in the state he was in." That is no lie. "He saved both our lives. It really was an astounding feat."

That seems to calm her. She sniffles a few more times, then asks us to sit down. By the time she returns bearing iced tea, Shanelle and I have managed to seat ourselves without squishing any action figures.

Deirdre wants the whole story of what happened and I oblige, minus the details of her brother's attempt to seduce me, yet another married woman. Today at least the guy deserves a halo.

"The only thing that makes me feel better," she says when I finish, "is that I saw on TV that the cops found the maniac who did it. What is wrong with that sicko? He killed that contestant from California and then tried to kill you? He's so loaded, he probably thinks he can get away with it. They should strap him down and fire up the power, if you get my meaning."

Shanelle gives me a pointed look when Deirdre finishes her diatribe. Yes, here too is someone who's convinced Sebastian Cantwell is the killer. That leaves me as the lone delusional holdout.

I clear my throat. "Deirdre, I have a question to ask

you." I pull the computer printout of Tony Postagino's website photo from my tote. It's seriously dogeared from being carried around this long eventful day. I hold it out toward her. "This man came to your B&B at some point. You can tell from the background. Do you remember him?"

She squints at the picture. "Not offhand. Do you know how long ago he was here?"

"Not really. Probably not that long."

Clearly, Deirdre is not remembering Tony Postagino. She shakes her head and tries to hand me back the printout.

I'm not willing to take it. Not yet. "Do you think anybody who works here might remember him?"

She frowns at me. "Why do you want to know? Who is this person?"

Maybe she's thinking it's my husband. And I'm trying to catch him out in an affair. And maybe she wants no part of that. Bad for business.

Shanelle jumps in before I can decide how to answer. "He's the husband of the beauty queen who was murdered."

"The widower?" Deirdre gasps. "The poor man! He's a victim, too." She brings the printout up close to her face.

Shanelle and I are holding our breath—at least I am—when we hear a clattering on the stairs behind us. An older woman appears manhandling a vacuum cleaner. I take her to be Filipina and conclude she must be the housecleaner.

Deirdre stands up. "Luisa." She holds the printout

toward the woman. "Do you remember this man? Did he ever stay here?"

Luisa gazes at the picture only briefly. Then, "Yes, Missus. He was here with that other man. The one who was so blond."

CHAPTER THIRTY-THREE

Shanelle leaps to her feet so fast you'd think her thong caught on fire. "Are you telling me that Tiffany Amber's husband stayed here with a *dude*? Sleeping in the same dang room?"

Luisa looks taken aback. She glances nervously at Deirdre.

I intercede before Luisa clams up. "Are you sure, Luisa? This man could be involved in something big so it's really important."

Luisa keeps her gaze trained on her employer. "I am sure, Missus. Not so often we have two men together. You don't remember?"

Deirdre squints again at the photo. "He looks vaguely familiar, I suppose ..."

"Do you remember when it was?" I ask Luisa.

"Christmastime," she says immediately. "A little after. We still had the tree up. And the lights outside."

"New Year's," Shanelle mutters, as though the timing makes the stay especially naughty.

"And the man this man was with"—I cock my chin at the printout—"what did you say about him?"

"He had blond hair," Luisa says. "Not natural. Colored. And very ..." She runs out of words but raises her hands as if to indicate a bouffant style.

Shanelle and I stare at one another. My heart starts to thump. I can think of one man Tony Postagino knows who fits that description. And I'm sure so can she.

"Deirdre," I say, "will you look at your accounts for late December and early January and see if you have both these men listed as guests?" I'm having crazy thoughts of going to Momoa with this. And if I do, I'll need more than Luisa's say. And more than the photo of Tony Postagino in this B&B's living room.

But Deirdre is balking. She's shaking her head and backing away. "No. I'm not comfortable doing that. Live and let live, is my philosophy. I'm not going to give out information about who stays here, and with who."

"I understand. And believe me, I'm not making any moral judgments here." Although truthfully I am. Tony Postagino was married at that time, after all. And it wasn't his wife he stayed with at this B&B. That doesn't sit right with me. "But this man's wife was murdered in cold blood. And the fact that this man was here, with another man, only months before …" My words trail off.

Deirdre is obviously shocked by the implication. "You think he had something to do with killing his wife? But that doesn't make any sense! The police already arrested the killer!"

"I don't know if this man had anything to do with the murder or not. And they did arrest someone, true. But I think the situation is more complicated than we know."

Deirdre still doesn't look convinced.

"Look," I say. "Somebody tried to kill me today. And you know who else got hurt. And might've died."

She stares down at the picture of Tony Postagino. "Dirk," she breathes. She crushes the printout into Luisa's hand and races out of the room. "I'll be right back," she calls over her shoulder.

Seconds later I hear the click of keys on a computer keyboard from somewhere deep inside the B&B. Luisa makes noise of her own by shoving the vacuum cleaner into a hall closet. Elijah has all his G.I. Joes shooting at each other with automatic weapons and moaning in agony as they drop dead. But Shanelle and I are as silent as corpses. My mind is cranking at warp speed. Probably hers is, too.

Deirdre returns with a sheet of paper in her hand. "This is what you want, I think." She hands it to me. "It's a copy of the guest record."

The paper bears the Plumeria Bed and Breakfast letterhead. On it is a detailing of the expenses of a two-night stay ending January 5th. It specifies that the number of guests was two and that they stayed in room B. The amount billed was slightly more than three hundred dollars. And the guest name in the upper left hand corner, the person who paid the bill, is Rex Rexford, complete with his Beverly Hills address.

As soon as I heard Luisa's description of the blond helmet hair, I knew it had to be Rex. He's a one and only.

"I don't know what that'll be good for," Deirdre says, "but you can take it with you."

"I really appreciate it," I say. "You've been tremendously helpful."

Shanelle and I make ourselves scarce. We're barely

out of the house and onto the walkway when she hisses into my ear. "What the hell do you make of that?"

"Is there any chance Rex and Tony could have stayed at this B&B for a reason other than an affair? Like they were strategizing how Tiffany could win the Ms. America pageant?"

"They could do that in California! And if they did do it here, where was Tiffany?"

"It is very hard to imagine two men would stay in the same room in this B&B, or any other, and not be … you know."

"It's impossible!" Shanelle pronounces, and I have to agree.

We get to the street and realize we need a cab. Once I place that call, I look again at Shanelle. "So Tiffany was right when she told Keola that her husband was having an affair. But I doubt she knew it was with Rex."

"She never would've kept working with him."

"I wonder if the affair was over by the time the pageant started."

"Who knows? And there's still the matter of Sebastian Cantwell getting arrested today. How do you explain that?"

I can't. We mull the various possibilities until the cab arrives and after we're inside. We're only about a five-minute drive from the Royal Hibiscus when a flash of memory illuminates my mind. I grab Shanelle's arm. "Oh … my … God."

"What?"

"I remember who I bumped into today, literally, when I went to the casual café to tell Trixie about the photo of Tony Postagino."

"Who?"

"Rex Rexford."

"*What*?"

"Yes! Right at the entry. I crashed into him, no kidding, because I wasn't watching where I was going because I was so anxious to talk to Trixie."

"Did you talk to him?"

"Yes. He said ..." I try to remember. "He said something like what's your hurry? I don't remember exactly."

Shanelle scrunches her face. "I wonder if he eavesdropped on your conversation with Trixie. Because he could see you were agitated. And he probably knew you were investigating. Could he have overheard you?"

"Yes." I feel like an idiot. "Because I didn't really try to keep quiet. And neither did Trixie."

"Maybe he's the one who poisoned your drink," Shanelle says.

That had occurred to me.

When the cab halts at the Royal Hibiscus, Shanelle gets out but I stay put. She frowns at me through my open window. "What are you up to now, may I ask?"

"I have another stop to make."

"Should I be worried about that?"

"No. But answer your cell if it rings. You may be my one phone call." I realize as the cab screeches away that that probably wasn't the thing to say to keep Shanelle from worrying.

We have to wend a circuitous route through Waikiki as some beachfront blocks are being closed off for the night's weekly street fair. I soon discover that the Honolulu Police Department is in a neighborhood with which I'm somewhat familiar. It's close to the hospital I visited twice today, once as a patient and once as a cardiac-arrest inducer. Actually, I realize, remembering the old man whose ER area I invaded on my hands and knees, I sort of did that on my second stop-by, too.

It's getting on toward twilight as I enter the reception area. The fluorescent lights are so bright the cops could perform surgery. There's a big sign on the wall that says: SERVING AND PROTECTING WITH ALOHA. There's also a small sign that says: SAFETY IS NO ACCIDENT. PLEASE DRIVE WITH ALOHA.

Maybe that's my problem. I'm not doing enough things with aloha.

I find out from the cop manning the front desk that indeed Detective Momoa is in. And yes, he will see me. I pace, because I'm too amped up to sit while I wait.

Finally, Momoa emerges from the sanctum sanctorum. "Ms. Pennington," he says.

"Detective Momoa. You look surprised to see me."

"I am. I heard from the hospital earlier that you disappeared before you were released."

I just bet that's how he found out I was no longer in the ER. "I felt fine and I've never been one for a lot of rules about where I can and can't go," I tell him, though he might already have figured that out about me.

"Then what brings you to my little neck of the woods this evening?"

"Information that might crack the Tiffany Amber murder case wide open."

CHAPTER THIRTY-FOUR

He eyes me. "You may not be one for rules, Ms. Pennington, but you do not shy away from hyperbole."

"Do we have to talk out here, Detective?" Somebody else in street clothes just entered the reception area. "I'd be more comfortable discussing this somewhere more private."

I know. This might seem risky behavior for a woman who mere hours ago took extraordinary measures to avoid being incarcerated. But I'm less freaked about that possibility now. Armed with my incendiary new information, not to mention the fact that Sebastian Cantwell was arrested today, I feel able to, as Trixie would say, *deflect suspicion*.

Momoa ushers me into his lair, one of numerous nondescript offices along the perimeter of a large open room crammed with desks for the smaller fry, many of whom appear to work the night shift. His desk and credenza are piled high with manila folders, a testament to his workload. His walls are loaded with framed citations and photos of his unsmiling self shaking hands with various luminaries, almost all of whom are unknown to me but who together create the impression that Momoa has enjoyed a lot of success as a cop. Also as captain of the Honolulu PD's baseball team, I see. He has a few trophies from trouncing teams from the Big Island and Kauai.

I settle into the chair in front of his desk. I've always been comfortable in police stations, truth be told. Must be because I've been visiting them since I was knee-high, proudly striding their dingy halls as the daughter of a veteran cop.

"I just saw Dirk Ventura's sister," I say. "She tells me he's out of danger."

Momoa nods and says nothing. He's got to be curious what the heck I'm here for. Maybe he's hoping I'll confess.

In that case I'm going to disappoint him. "She told me something else, too." I relate what I've learned about Rex Rexford staying with Tony Postagino at the Plumeria Bed and Breakfast just after New Year's.

Momoa leans forward. "Ms. Pennington, you are jumping to a conclusion for which you have no evidence."

"What do you mean?"

"You have no evidence that the two men stayed there together."

"What are you talking about? I have—"

"You have the website photo which proves that Mr. Postagino at some point visited that inn, and you have the guest record which proves that in early January Mr. Rexford stayed there for two nights with a second individual. That's all you have and it proves nothing."

"I also have Luisa the housekeeper who says that they stayed there together. Besides, it's a tiny little B&B and it's totally inconceivable that these two different men would choose at two different times to stay there above all the other amazing places they could stay on this island."

"What if one of them recommended it to the other? Mr. Postagino stayed there at some point, when he had his photo taken, and suggested it to Mr. Rexford when the latter was planning a trip to Oahu."

I hadn't thought of that and it sounds plausible. Suddenly I feel sort of deflated. "But what about Luisa? She remembers them being together."

"The human element is often the weakest link. The housekeeper's memory does not constitute proof."

"But I mean—" I throw up my hands. "What are the odds?"

"In this business we don't deal in odds, Ms. Pennington. We deal in evidence."

He's trying to put me in my place with that comment, which I think is somewhat snarky. "That's not all I have. I know you interviewed Keola Kalakaua, and you and I both know that he and Tiffany Amber were having an affair. Do you know that she told him that she thought her husband was, too?"

Momoa shakes his head. "That's hearsay. That's not admissible in court."

"But it adds weight to the idea that Tony Postagino and Rex Rexford were involved. And another thing." I describe how I ran into Rex at the casual café, and how he might have overheard my conversation with Trixie, and how he had the opportunity to spike my breakfast drink with poison.

"He, and, from what I understand, dozens of other

people," Momoa says.

"Like Sebastian Cantwell? Are you dismissing this line of reasoning because you've already charged Cantwell with Tiffany Amber's murder and my attempted murder?"

Momoa leans back in his chair and folds his arms over his chest. "I am not at liberty to discuss that matter."

"Detective Momoa, I have a right to know what's going on here! After all, somebody tried to kill me today. Don't I deserve to know if the person who did that is behind bars? Because if the perp is still out there roaming free, I am in serious danger, because he or she may make a second attempt."

"Remember, Ms. Pennington, I have reason to believe that you yourself spiked that beverage with poison. And that you yourself are behind Ms. Amber's murder."

"I'm not! I know that even if you don't." I stand up. "Coming here was a waste of my time."

He remains seated. "Why did you come here?"

"Because I believed, and I still do, that there is or was some extramarital entanglement between Tony Postagino and Rex Rexford. And given that Tony Postagino's wife is now dead, and that Rex Rexford had the motive and opportunity and maybe the means to kill her, that that was something you should know about. But apparently you could care less."

"Were you hoping to get my help?"

"Yes. Because obviously you have more resources to pursue this than I do. I also don't have it in my power to keep all the people who might have had a hand in Tiffany Amber's murder on this island. You do. And I would think you'd want them here until such time as you can announce you've nabbed the killer. Maybe you have, and it's Sebastian Cantwell, and for some bizarre reason you just can't disclose that yet. I don't know. But it all seems kind of fishy to me."

Momoa rises to his feet. "I'll walk you out."

So I guess he's not going to arrest me. I suppose that's good news. Nevertheless, I retrace my steps toward the reception area feeling, more than anything else, disappointed. That this visit was a bust. That Momoa poked so many holes in my theory, it's now as solid as a Whiffle ball. That I'm a lousy crime-solver.

Back where we started the evening, Momoa has one more salvo to fire. "Ms. Pennington, I suggest that you steer clear of Mr. Postagino and Mr. Rexford and that you leave the investigating to the police. That is the best thing you could do. And it would probably go a long way toward helping you calm down."

It drives me crazy. That's pretty much exactly what Jason said.

"If I'm too fired up for your taste, I apologize, Detective." I pull open the glass door. "Somebody trying to kill you does that to a person."

CHAPTER THIRTY-FIVE

Minutes later I find myself taking my third taxi ride of the day. This cabbie has even more trouble than the earlier two wending his way through Waikiki. We often slow to a crawl, or get stopped altogether, because so many beachfront streets are being blockaded for the fair. Tents and booths are going up left, right, and center. In the distance I hear a live band testing its sound system.

The cab lurches to another stop. I grit my teeth. But it's too far to walk to the Royal Hibiscus, at least for this dragged-out beauty queen, so I force myself to settle back against the cracked Naugahyde seat. The sun is setting; I think I've decided once and for all that's my favorite time of day here on Oahu. The sky is exploding in stripes of pink and purple as the sun's great orange ball of fire disappears inch by glowing inch into the sea.

I didn't get anywhere with Detective Momoa; that much is clear. And yes, it is true that even if Tony Postagino and Rex Rexford were or are having an affair, that doesn't mean either of them offed Tiffany Amber. After all, as Shanelle pointed out, people have extramarital flings all the time and no one ends up tumbling dead out of an isolation booth.

Something else occurs to me. Maybe my exciting new tidbit was exciting and new only to me. Maybe

Momoa's known about it for days and already explored it and dismissed it. I have to allow the possibility that I'm behind the curve investigation-wise.

Or ... maybe this revelation was new to Momoa but he dismissed it because it came from me. He listened politely enough but inside he was chuckling all the while. *What an imbecile*, he was thinking. *How could I have thought for a moment that this woman killed Tiffany Amber? It should have become apparent in the first minute of talking to her that she's too stupid to have pulled that off ...*

It's very dispiriting, because I expected Momoa to give this information more consideration. I carried it to him like a found treasure that only I was cunning enough to uncover. I see now that I wanted props from him, a pat on the back, maybe a compliment or two. *Good work, Ms. Pennington*, would've been nice. *I'll take it from here.*

Who am I kidding? I'm not a cop. I'm just a beauty queen with delusions of investigative grandeur.

What with Cantwell now in jail, I need to accept the fact that my instincts about who killed Tiffany, and tried to kill me, were flat out wrong. I should be glad of what I was able to accomplish here on Oahu, winning the Ms. America title and the prize money to put Rachel through college.

Not that I've gotten the check yet, or that my daughter wants to go to college.

I sigh. Soon I spy the Royal Hibiscus in the distance and decide to walk the rest of the way.

The sidewalks are crowded with revelers en route to the fair. As usual, I'm going against the flow. At one point I pass Top Fiver Sherry Phillips and a bunch of other queens among the fair-bound throng. With every long-legged stride, Sherry's red hair bounces on her shoulders like she's in one of those slo-mo shampoo commercials.

I don't know why I ask her this, but I do. "Hey, Sherry, you know where Rex is?" I figure she might, since I remember Shanelle telling me that Rex is her consultant, too.

"Uh ..." Her green eyes open wide. Any and all questions, even the most elementary, seem to test Sherry's reserves. I know I'm judging her in the same harsh way that Momoa's probably judging me, yet I can't help but think that Ms. Wyoming isn't the brightest pixel on the computer screen. "Not really," she comes up with. "Maybe he's at the fair?"

"Maybe he is," I agree, and move on.

When I get back to my room, where Shanelle is nowhere in evidence, I use the hotel phone to call Rex's room number. He doesn't pick up. I don't leave a voicemail.

I lope out to the balcony. From here I cannot see the fair but I can hear it. I can also smell it. I know from previous visits that one of its main attractions is the international food tent. I swear that I'm picking up the aroma of teriyaki chicken, which is reminding me that I haven't eaten since breakfast. A few skewers of grilled chicken, a handful of salted edamame, a cold beer—that would make me feel better.

I realize I really should call Jason or my mom—or both—to go with me but I just don't have the energy. I'd have to justify all my actions, and relive the chopper incident in all its petrifying detail

I make another decision. Since all I want to do is dash out for some quick grub, I'd rather not be recognized as Ms. America and have to deal with questions about what went down today with Dirk Ventura or with Sebastian Cantwell. So I simple down. I slip into my Juicy Couture sweat pants and a tank top and slide my feet into my floral Keds. I slick my hair back into a braid and clamp on the baseball cap I wear when I run. Off goes all makeup save for a neutral lip gloss.

I am a beauty queen after all; I can't go out completely clean-faced.

This street fair boasts the usual vendors and a few unique to Hawaii, like a guy selling surfboards and another hawking totem poles similar to the one gracing the Plumeria B&B. There are the craft booths, with paintings and wood carvings and blown glass and ceramics; a ton of tents with artsy jewelry of all description; florists selling exotic orchids and plants I can't begin to name; a woman peddling antique dolls; another with an astonishing assortment of beeswax candles. The band I heard tuning up is now deep into a set of traditional island music. The kids who aren't in the bounce house are getting their faces painted; a few are riding donkeys being led among the fair-goers. A Scientology booth is offering free stress tests, and I slow as I walk by because I know I'm the perfect candidate.

My disguise must be working pretty well because I make my way to the food tents unmolested. There's all kinds of Hawaiian and Asian fare, plus the cotton candy, candied apples, and corn dogs you'd find on the mainland. My stomach's set on teriyaki chicken, though, and I scarf it.

I take a slightly different route back, focusing on the oceanside rather than the inland booths, when I am stopped short by a vendor offering holistic massage. Three mobile massage units are set up, the kind where you sit down and lean forward to lay your head on a leather-covered rest. There's no question I could use several of the benefits the massage claims to offer. *Release unexpressed emotions. Relieve stress and anxiety. Increase mental clarity.* All that for two dollars a minute!

I am about to claim the one unoccupied chair when I find myself mesmerized by the hair of the man in the middle chair. Dyed blond. Bouffant. Sprayed to within an inch of its life.

I draw a mental picture of Rex Rexford's hair. Dyed blond. Bouffant. Sprayed to within an inch of its life.

Coincidence? I think not.

A few seconds' further inspection yields the certainty that indeed this is Rex Rexford, in plaid board shorts and a loose-fitting polo, currently undergoing an oil-free, shoulders-only, holistic massage. Since I am the sort of girl who seizes opportunity when it presents itself, I approach Rex's masseuse, whisper in her ear, "May I? He's my boyfriend," and gesture that I'd like to take over. She apparently possesses a romantic streak but exceedingly weak Gaydar, because she giggles, shrugs, and allows me to switch my hands for hers, as seamlessly as if we've been doing this all our young lives.

I've never had any massage training but Jason has

always told me I'm pretty good at this, so I just do to Rex what I usually do to Jason. It seems to go over pretty well, though this time it won't end the way it usually does with Jason. At the moment, I must say, it's much the same. Rex emits a soft moan.

So far, so good. But what the heck do I do now? Engage him in light, unthreatening conversation? *Do you perchance have any unexpressed emotion you'd like to release, Rex? Like regret over lacing Tiffany Amber's lipstick with cyanide? Or maybe spiking my breakfast drink with the leftovers?*

"You have quite a knot here," I murmur, kneading an area high on his right trapezius muscle. "Have you been under a lot of stress lately?"

"I'll say. But most of it went away earlier today." He chuckles.

I have to force myself not to clamp down as I process that response. Why would Rex's high stress be reduced today? Because somebody else got arrested for the murder he committed? Somebody like Sebastian Cantwell, in whose innocence—sort of—I've long trusted?

"Ooh, tell me," I breathe. "I love stories about negativity flowing away from troubled souls."

"Well ..." He readjusts his head slightly. "Let's just say that I've been worried about something. But you know the saying that it's always darkest before the dawn? That was true for me. I was at my lowest point when something totally unexpected happened. And all of a sudden the burden I've been carrying was lifted clean away."

That was pretty vague but I can translate it in my own mind. I have no difficulty guessing what the absolute lowest point was: Rex overhearing me tell Trixie in the café that I was going to Dirk's sister's B&B to find out who stayed there with Tony Postagino. At that moment Rex thought he was going to get caught out, so in desperation he decided that he had to risk a second murder by poisoning me, too. The something totally unexpected? Sebastian Cantwell's arrest. See above.

"So the way is clear for you now?" I say. "No encumbrances or impediments? Your personal cosmos is in balance?"

"Never more so." He releases a sigh of deep contentment. "I am about to be blissfully happy. Like I haven't been for years."

Since Sonny Roberts died, I surmise. *Sonny would be ashamed of you!* —I want to shout. It's not okay to murder people even if you're doing it in the name of love. Nor is it okay to amble merrily away while somebody else takes the tumble for what you did.

It takes some doing to keep my hands from pummeling Rex, or settling around his throat in a chokehold. I struggle not to gag as I say, "I'm only guessing but it sounds like romance has blossomed anew for you."

"I never thought it would a second time. I don't know what I did to deserve it but I've been blessed." He resettles himself a bit. "You've gotten very chatty all of a sudden." Then he tilts his head up and looks right at me.

I think I'll remember his expression until the day I die. His eyes fly open so fast you'd think Tiffany Amber just popped out of her grave to goose him. I smile sweetly. "What's the matter, Rex? You look like you just saw a ghost."

He scrambles out of the massage chair. "You! You!"

"Me. Me." I approach him. I'm feeling cocky because there are a million people around us. Nothing bad can happen to me here, in plain sight. "You had to know I wasn't dead, right? You must've found out that I made it out of that chopper alive. No thanks to you," I add, quoting Detective Momoa from earlier today.

"What're you talking about?" He continues to back away. "Of course you're not dead. I'm just surprised you're the one giving me the massage, that's all." He lets out a laugh that sounds pretty darn nervous to me. "You're playing a joke on me, right? That's what you're doing. Playing a joke on your old friend Rex."

"We've never been friends, Rex," I inform him. "And I'm feeling less friendly toward you now than I ever did."

He bolts. He turns and bolts. The masseuse starts screaming after him to pay up but he's gone.

And I'm gone after him.

CHAPTER THIRTY-SIX

I don't work out just to look good in a swimsuit under the klieg lights. So while beauty queens who achieve their figures through starvation alone might find themselves left in the dust by Rex Rexford at a dead run, your plucky heroine can keep up.

It helps that Rex is the one clearing a path for us. It's him who's slamming into bodies left and right, him who's sideswiping little kids, him who's forcing dog owners to drag their leashed poodles and Labradors out of the way.

"Somebody stop that man!" I scream, dodging an elderly couple toting a painting of a sailing ship on a black velvet background. "He's a menace!" I get no takers.

Rex caroms into a table loaded with seashell jewelry, staggers briefly, but keeps going. I just avoid a slow-moving Asian woman carrying a peach-colored cymbidium.

"Watch it, you bimbo!" she screams after me.

Ooh, them's fightin' words! I so want to stop and give her a piece of my mind—and yes, I would have enough left—but I don't dare. I'm in hot pursuit of the murderer in front of me—and if he's not a murderer, why the heck is he running?—so I can't waste my breath on educating the yahoos in the crowd.

Something besides sheer adrenaline is pushing me forward. Pride. *Take that, Detective Momoa! Let's see who's right about this murder thing now …*

Ahead I spy trouble. The walkway for pedestrians gets narrow and one of the *TAKE A RIDE!* donkeys is blocking the way. It's a mild-looking gray and white beast being led by a brunette in jeans and a gingham shirt who appears to be doing her best Mary Ann from *Gilligan's Island* imitation. To make matters even more exciting, the burro has a toddler on its back.

Uh oh.

When Rex gets close to the donkey, he tries to push its rump aside so he can squeeze past. The burro's having none of it. It starts braying. The toddler starts shrieking. The brunette's sweet-as-can-be expression disappears in a nanosecond. "Get your hands off my ass!" she hollers.

Rex is unfazed. He leaps over the donkey like he's a gymnast competing in the pommel horse. The beast must have a healthy fear of dotty women, though, because it sees me coming and moves just enough out of the way.

I am impressed by Rex's speed, I must say. The man has to be pushing fifty but he is booking.

We come to an intersection, all four ways closed to traffic, and Rex surprises me by veering to the left to head off into side streets and leave the street fair behind. I watch him cut between a booth selling hip hop tee shirts and another whose sign says it offers paperweights made with real insect specimens.

Ewww!

Another block and we've left the fair well behind. We're into a residential neighborhood now, and not the nicest one I've ever seen. This must be Waikiki's seamy underbelly, full of three and four-story apartment buildings that look like they might never have seen better days. Peeling paint, bars on the windows, browned-out lawns or just dirt where browned-out lawns used to be. A few unsavory characters are roaming around and they're giving me the eye. These aren't the tourist types or cheerful locals that are still enjoying themselves at the fair. Speaking of which, its raucous noise sounds pretty distant now. And did I mention that it's dark out? It's dark out. And many of the street lights here aren't working.

It's hard to see but I can make out Rex veering right at the intersection ahead. I'm about half a block behind, slightly further back than I used to be.

I glance back over my shoulder. Is that somebody behind me? I can't tell. Just what I need.

The part of me that's rational is starting to wonder if I should call this chase thing off. Especially since it's not going so well anymore. And what do I really expect to get out of it?

I arrive at the intersection where Rex turned and I stop, panting. I look in the direction he went and I don't see him. I look in all four directions. I don't see him. Shoot. I guess I lost—

Slam! I find myself grabbed from behind and picked up and carried to the sidewalk, where I'm pitched forward onto the pavement like a sack of garbage. My hands scrape, my elbows, I'm just glad my head doesn't crash into the concrete. I twist around and who do I see looming over me but Rex Rexford, hands on hips, chest heaving, shaking his head back and forth, back and forth.

"You made me do that, Happy," he says. He's sucking wind as hard as I am. "It's your fault. So don't you blame me."

"What in the world are you talking about? Rex—" I try to get to my feet. He lurches forward and pushes me back down. I scream. He gets around behind me again, fast as can be, and slaps his hand over my mouth. "Shut … up," he says. "Now."

I shut up. I really, truly shut up because now I am really, truly scared. Rex is quite a bit bigger than me, which I've always known but which is only coming home to me now, and besides that I have just learned that he is both damn buff and damn strong. His hair may be mired in the past but Rex is totally up-to-date when it comes to fitness level.

I nod my head to reassure him that I do not intend to scream again. Truth be told I don't, because I'm petrified what he'll do to me if I do. And also because I have the funniest feeling that other people in this neighborhood have screamed and it hasn't done them much good.

Half a minute later his hand relaxes. "You're going to be quiet now?"

I nod again.

He moves his hand away.

"I'll be quiet," I whisper. We sit for a while, me splayed on the sidewalk, him crouching next to me.

"What now?" I ask him.

He lets out a breath. "I'm trying to figure that out. Darn it!" He slaps his forehead. "Why'd you do it, Happy? Why? You couldn't leave well enough alone, could you?"

"You are talking gibberish, Rex Rexford!" I hiss. "I should just ignore the fact that Tiffany Amber is dead? That Dirk Ventura and I almost snuffed today? That Sebastian Cantwell is in the slammer for things he didn't do? That I've come under suspicion for things *I* didn't do? Is that what you mean?"

He frowns. "You came under suspicion? Why?"

"Because I was the last one in the isolation booth with Tiffany! And because I got awarded the title afterward."

"Oh." His face sort of crumples. "I'm sorry you had to go through that." Then he seems to remember himself and jabs his finger at my face. "But you've got nothing on me, Happy Pennington!"

"Rex, just be honest with me. Why did you kill Tiffany? So you could be with Tony Postagino? I know you two stayed together at the Plumeria B&B."

I don't know whether or not to be amazed when he doesn't immediately dispute my statement. We're in an odd limbo now, he and I, squatting together in this insalubrious neighborhood. It's dark. It's late. Maybe he feels the same way I do, that something in the atmosphere is confessional.

He hangs his head. For a long while he says nothing. Then, "You're a married woman, Happy. I assume you've been in love?"

"Yes, I have. And I love my daughter in a way I can't even describe. I'd do absolutely anything for her."

"Well, see? That's what I'm talking about."

"Did Tony put you up to it? To killing Tiffany?"

"No. Absolutely not." He shakes his head vigorously. "He had nothing to do with it."

"So you did it on your own? You killed Tiffany on your own?"

He looks away. I was raised Catholic, and I know from my own time in the confessional that even when a wall with a latticed window separates you and the priest, it's easier to look away from his profile when you 'fess up.

"It was that or lose him forever," Rex says.

CHAPTER THIRTY-SEVEN

I let out a breath. There it is. I was right that the killer isn't Sebastian Cantwell. Of course at various times I thought it was Misty or Sally Anne or Magnolia or Keola or Dirk. But still. My instincts may not have been spot on but they weren't awful.

Take that, Detective Momoa!

Fat lot of good Rex's confession is going to do me, though. I, who am under suspicion, am the only person to have heard it. And I might end up dead.

"With Tiffany in the picture, we could never really be together," he goes on. "We could never have the lives we wanted. A home together. Serenity. Happiness." He looks at me. "Isn't that everybody's right?"

"Maybe. But why didn't Tony just divorce Tiffany?"

"He talked about it all the time. But there were huge risks in a divorce. She would've taken half of what was left of his money, after already spending most of it. And with our being, you know, gay, she would have gotten custody of his daughters. And ruined his reputation."

"So she spent a lot of money?"

"She spent like crazy! She was totally out of control. And then to try to make up for it she hatched this

273

psychotic foreign-exchange trading scheme, which went to hell, which made everything even worse. She tried to get me to invest in it but I told her thanks but no thanks."

"She got Sally Anne to invest in it."

"Huge mistake on her part."

This time I jab my finger at him. "You told me, when I sat down with you when you were having dinner at the hotel, that you thought Sally Anne killed Tiffany."

"What did you expect me to say? That I did it?"

"What about messing around with Sally Anne's gown registry? Did Tiffany do that?"

"Of course. She told me all about it." Rex shakes his head. "Tiffany Amber was not a nice person."

There is a certain irony here. Rex Rexford, nearly a double murderer himself, casting aspersions on one of his victims.

Suddenly in the distance I hear a succession of sharp cracking sounds. I grab Rex. "My God, what was that? Gunshots?"

"Geez Louise, I don't know." He's holding on to me, too. I have the fleeting thought that he's as scared as I am. "In this neighborhood it could be."

A few seconds later, when it's all quiet again, I release him. He stands up. I do, too. He looks at me. "I can't let you, you know, just *go*."

"Of course you can." I try to sound as matter-of-fact as possible. I brush the dirt off my sweatpants and straighten my baseball cap.

"You're not going to tell anybody what I told you?"

It takes me a beat too long to open my mouth to say, *No, of course not!*—and in that nanosecond he says, "I guess I'm going to have to finish what I started."

I take a stab at running away but in like two steps he's got me by the arm. I try to shake him off but he holds on. "You can't kill me, Rex!" I shriek. "How stupid would that be? A zillion people just saw me chasing you through the street fair! Think of the lady with the ass. You don't think she'd remember your face? Or the masseuse? She'd recognize you in a heartbeat. No, it's beyond stupid to murder me."

He manhandles me closer. "I can't think about that now. I'm a desperate man."

"*You're* desperate?" I try to wriggle out of his grasp before he can get his hands around my throat, which is what I think he's angling to do. "You're going to kill me with your bare hands, Rex? I don't think so! That is so not your style."

I hear another popping sound and this time it's incredibly close. I scream. Then I hear a male voice shout.

"Get your hands off her, Rexford! And put 'em up!"

I look to my right. Who's standing there in one of those wide-legged shoot-'em-up poses but Mario Suave. Wielding a gun. Which I believe he just fired. And now he's pointing it straight at Rex and me. "I heard what you said, Rexford! Every word! So let her go!" With his free hand Mario pulls a wallet type thingie out of the pocket of his cargo shorts and lets it drop open. I see that it contains a badge. "Now, Rexford! FBI!"

Rex doesn't budge. But I see my opportunity. I twist in Rex's grasp and jerk my knee up into his groin.

"Uggg," he grunts and lets me go. I scamper away

but don't get far because I trip—how embarrassing—and before long am back on my hands and knees on the sidewalk.

By the time I look up, Mario is standing between me and Rex, his gun aimed at Rex's chest. I scramble to my feet. Mario is shouting things at Rex and now Rex is obeying, kneeling down, holding his hands behind him, getting them cuffed with the handcuffs Mario apparently had on his person. His body is shaking, Rex's that is. I think he's sobbing.

How can I possibly feel bad for him? He killed one person. He tried to kill me. He almost killed Dirk Ventura because Dirk got in the way. But still I have a warm spot in my heart for him. I must be a sentimental fool.

Or maybe I'm all warm and fuzzy because once again I'm not dead. And at long last, the perpetrator has been caught. By me.

Well, sort of by me. Mario Suave certainly played a role.

The police come and take Rex in. He doesn't even look at me as he's led past. I'll have to grow a thicker skin because part of me actually feels guilty that because of me he's on his way to the pokey. And he won't be out any time soon.

This doesn't make any sense either, but once Rex is gone I start trembling again.

"It's all right," Mario says. He leans down and looks into my eyes. "You're all right now."

I know that, I know it, but I can't stop shaking.

Mario gets one of the cops to take us back to the

Royal Hibiscus. The fair is still going on, which kind of stuns me. How can something so ordinary be continuing as normal when I just survived whatever the heck I just survived? Mario insists I get checked out at the hotel clinic, even though I tell him repeatedly there's nothing wrong with me apart from the twitching, and wouldn't you know it, it's the same doctor on duty who treated me after the macaw bite.

"You're having an eventful stay," she says to me, dabbing antiseptic on my scrapes, but she doesn't make any further pithy observations. I think that's because Mario pulls her aside at one point and whispers something in her ear. Her eyes grow wide at whatever he tells her. I think in that second her respect for me grows. I become more than just an unusually incident-prone hotel guest.

When the doctor lets me go, Mario leads me to the lobby lounge. We sit in two overstuffed chairs and he orders two brandies. Even though I'm almost too jittery to hold my snifter, I manage. And that first sip goes down way easy.

"What in the world happened back there?" I ask Mario.

He leans forward, his snifter resting in his cupped hands. "Thanks to you, Rex Rexford was arrested for the murder of Tiffany Amber."

"Not that part. The part where you suddenly appeared and saved the day."

"Let's get something straight, Happy." His tone is very earnest. "I'm not the one who saved the day. You did that. All I did was help out."

"Well, at kind of a crucial moment. Like when Rex was about to kill me."

He nods his head as if to acquiesce. "I was following you. I saw you running through the fair after Rex and I followed you. It was clear that something was going down."

"You took me by surprise. First with the gun. Then with the badge."

"Yeah. That." He hangs his head.

"I don't think most pageant emcees have one of those."

He raises his eyes to meet mine. He actually looks sheepish. "I'm hoping we can keep that our little secret."

"What, that you're a spook?"

He glances around us and leans closer. He speaks very softly. "Happy, the FBI recruited me years ago to help ferret out illegal accounting practices in the entertainment industry. I'm in a unique position where I can find certain things out."

This man has secret talents even my mother didn't guess at. "You know accounting? I thought you started your career in Spanish soaps!"

He smiles. "I did. But my mother wanted me to have a fallback. And it's led to this." His smile fades. "But Happy, my show business career would come to a screeching halt if my sideline became known. You understand why."

Sure. Who would hire a spook who wants to spend his break time analyzing the books? Where pretty often in showbiz the numbers don't add up? "I'm happy to keep this to myself," I say.

"I'd appreciate it. I really would."

He stares at me. I stare at him. Then I look down into my brandy snifter, where I see my pensive reflection in the amber liquid.

How different this day is ending from the way it began. And not just for me. For Rex Rexford. For Tony Postagino, if he knows what just happened. For Dirk Ventura. And for Sebastian Cantwell.

I raise my eyes to Mario. "I wonder if Mr. Cantwell's already been released. Any second now we might see him walk across this lobby." Boy, is he going to love me after this. Not only did his new Ms. America not kill his almost Ms. America, she figured out who did! And got him sprung from the big house.

Mario cocks his head. "I wouldn't hold my breath."

"Why not? If Rex Rexford—"

"Cantwell wasn't arrested for Tiffany Amber's murder. Or for the attempt on you."

"Then what was he arrested for?"

"Tax fraud. He created false losses in the pageant to dodge taxes on his other businesses."

"That's bad enough to get arrested for?"

"Sure is. It's a felony."

This is amazing information. "No wonder he kept telling Momoa to look for Tiffany's killer outside the pageant! He didn't want the organization scrutinized. Did he have any idea what you were up to?"

"I don't think he knows my role even now."

"Damn!" I just thought of something. "Does this mean I'll never see my prize money?" The second the words leave my mouth, I wish I could haul them back in.

I am such a dunce! What a self-absorbed thing to say! And to Mario Suave, too.

I realize a second later that my husband overheard it, too.

CHAPTER THIRTY-EIGHT

This situation may not look quite right to Jason.

Although it is totally innocent. Totally.

"Jason," I say. I gesture to the other overstuffed chair in our little grouping. "Sit down and join us. This is Mario Suave." That is a needless introduction. It's obvious Jason knows who Mario Suave is, given that he's such a celebrity and the pageant emcee to boot. Introducing Mario to Jason is, however, necessary.

Jason shakes Mario's hand but doesn't really smile at him. He gives him more of an assessing look.

Mario stands up. "I'll leave you two alone." He sets down his snifter. "Happy, just so you know, what we talked about is not yet public information. But don't worry, you don't have anything to worry about. Everything will work out just fine for you."

I think he is telling me in coded language that I will get my prize money. That is a giant relief. We exchange good nights, then Mario nods at Jason and heads off.

Now Jason gives *me* an assessing look. He claims the chair Mario just vacated. "So you're okay, then."

I remember I haven't talked to him all day. "Oh Jason, I am so sorry. I—"

"I was really worried about you. By the time I got to the hospital, you were gone. Then I called your cell a bunch of times."

"I know, I—" How do I explain? "I got caught up in a bunch of stuff and—"

"I can guess what that bunch of stuff was."

I don't know what to say. The truth is that I didn't call him because I knew he'd object to my investigating. Because he knew it was dangerous. And he was right.

What makes it even worse is that all he knows about is the chopper crash. He doesn't know a thing about what happened later with Rex Rexford, when my life was once again on the line. And I really don't feel like explaining that now, too.

"Happy," he says, and he sounds just so tired, "I don't like having to find out what's up with my wife from TV news. I find out from TV news that she's hurt in a chopper crash. Then I find out from TV news that she's gone AWOL from the hospital. The only thing TV news won't tell me is where she is after that. Because all I know is she's not with me."

I take a deep breath. "I don't know what to say except I'm sorry. Please don't be mad at me."

"It's not so much that I'm mad, Happy. It's that I'm hurt."

We look at one another. His eyes are so sad.

He shakes his head. "This probably isn't the best time to tell you this but I got to thinking about what you said this morning and so I signed up for pit school. I ended up getting a slot in the course that starts in two weeks."

"Oh. Wow."

"Since I knew that getting me to go was kind of your

new project, I thought it would make you happy."

It's funny. Now that it's happened, I'm not sure whether it makes me happy or not. All I know is that in two weeks, he'll be gone to North Carolina for three months. Wow. It occurs to me that today he was missing me. But soon it will be me missing him.

"I can tell you're exhausted," he goes on. "I know I am. What do you say we both get a good night's sleep." He doesn't wait for me to agree. He gets up, kisses me softly on the cheek, says, "I'm glad you're all right," and walks away.

I watch him go, wishing I could rewind the tape and do today over. I can't. All I can do is better tomorrow.

When I get to our room, Shanelle still isn't back. I kick off my Keds and drop into bed.

The next morning Shanelle is snoring quietly when I wake up. The digital clock informs me it's 9:23. With the blackout drapes pulled shut, the room is as dark as it was at 2 AM. But I can see that she scrawled a note to me on the memo pad that sits on our shared nightstand. *You didn't get arrested, girl! Or if you did, you didn't call me ;-)*

I guess I can finally put those fears to bed. Funny, though, I still don't feel at ease. Maybe it's the fact that Jason's going away to pit school. Or that everything having to do with Tiffany's murder happened so fast, I'm having trouble adjusting.

The one thing I know for sure is that I'm starving. I shower and dress and hustle down to the casual café.

I've barely walked into the place when the girl working the counter runs up to me and grabs my hands. "I am so sorry," she says. "I am so, so sorry."

I think she's about to burst into tears. "That's okay. It was totally not your fault."

"When the cops came in here yesterday to talk to me, and I started to understand what happened with your breakfast drink, I freaked. I totally freaked. If you or ... or if that helicopter pilot—"

She's losing it. I hug her. "It's okay. Really. He's going to be fine and I'm fine, as you can see."

"Really? I am going to be so freaking careful from now on."

"Don't worry about it. I am really okay. I don't think I want one of those drinks this morning, though. You have any of that coffee cake?"

"I'll get you a piece. On the house."

She makes me a cappuccino, too, and throws in a side dish of pineapple and blueberries. But it takes me forever to get any of it down because suddenly I am the most popular girl in the room. My fellow contestants come up in droves to find out what's been going on with me the last 24 hours. Other guests from the hotel crowd around my table. Finally somebody says, "Let the poor woman eat!"—and people drift away, contenting themselves with stealing glances at me from adjoining tables.

One thing emerges from all the brouhaha. It is clear that people know about the helicopter accident, and Dirk Ventura downing my drink, which was spiked with the same poison that killed Tiffany Amber.

But people don't know that Rex Rexford was arrested last night for both those crimes. They still think Sebastian Cantwell is the culprit. None of that information has yet been released by the Oahu PD.

I want to know why.

But first things first. I learned a lesson last night.

I call Jason's cell, which goes immediately to voicemail. It must be turned off. I hope that means he's still sleeping and not that he doesn't want to speak to me.

Call number two. My mother.

I call her in her room at the Lotus Blossom because she always keeps her cell phone turned off. If by some act of God she decides to use it, she turns it on, places a call, and then turns it off. Nor does she know how to retrieve her voicemail. Not even Rachel, who is endlessly patient when it comes to her grandmother, can train her to use the thing properly.

"Mom, this is Happy," I say.

Silence. Then, "Are you sure this isn't her roommate Shanelle? Who has the kindness in her heart to make time for people's mothers?"

"I am sorry about that, Mom. But I had a very good reason for not wanting to get into an involved phone conversation yesterday."

"You don't say."

"It's true. I was solving Tiffany Amber's murder."

I know I have to tell this story now; I can't keep putting it off. And as you might imagine, it takes a while, even leaving out the most gnarly details, like how the killer was gearing up to strangle me. By the time I get to her room to pick her up, because I promised we would spend some time together, she's moderately calmer. Moderately.

We get in one of the cabs queued up in front of the

hotel. "I warn you, you will be a little taken aback by where I want to go first." I then address the driver. "The police station on Beretania, please."

She looks aghast. "Why in the world would you want to go there?" Then her face softens. "Unless they're giving you a medal. They certainly should." She calls out to the driver. "I'll have you know, young man, that my daughter here solved a murder. This one right here." She motions to me. "Yes sirree. Just last night. And for your information, she's also the winner of the Ms. America beauty pageant."

He glances at me in the rearview mirror, then at my mother. I half expect him to drop us off at a psychiatric hospital but indeed he does roll to a stop in front of Detective Momoa's place of employment. I find out once we're inside that Momoa is in.

He appears less surprised to see me than he did last night, but he does a double take at my mother.

I make the introductions. Momoa does a fine job of pronouncing Mrs. Przybyszewski, which has undone lesser men. He invites us into his office and has to scuttle away briefly to import a second chair. He offers us coffee. I decline.

"Yes, please," my mother says. She sits and primly crosses her legs at the ankle. "Cream and sugar. And I would appreciate real sugar, not that fake stuff that gets passed off as sugar."

He glances at me on his way out. I am experiencing a first. I have never before felt that Detective Momoa and I were on the same team. But at this moment I do.

He returns with my mother's java and assumes the

position behind his desk. "What can I do for you, Ms. Pennington?"

I see we're still on a surname basis. I also note he does not congratulate me on solving the crime he's been investigating for a week. "I'm curious to find out why Rex Rexford's arrest hasn't been made public yet."

He steeples his fingers. "We have been conducting further investigation into the role Tony Postagino might have played in the murder."

I lean forward. "And?"

"And we have been unable to find a single piece of evidence to link him to"—he glances at my mother—"either incident."

"Does Rexford still claim that he acted alone?"

"He does."

"Do you believe him?" Momoa says nothing. I fill the silence. "I have to say, I find it very hard to believe that Postagino wasn't involved. Rex Rexford does not strike me as the type to have pulled this off alone. Conceived the plan, obtained the cyanide, laced the lipstick—" I glance at my mom. "The other thing I think he did do by himself, because he got desperate. But otherwise I don't believe he was a lone operator. He's just too soft-hearted. Postagino seems the more conniving of the two."

My mother pipes up. "You should listen to my daughter. After all, she's been doing your work for you."

"Mom—"

"If you had listened to her sooner, this whole mess might have been cleared up sooner. She's got a good head on her shoulders. Straight A's from kindergarten on."

"Mom—"

"And when the time comes, she better get credit for this. I want her name, not yours, all over the news."

"Mom, really." I reach over and grab her hand. "You've got to stop."

She harrumphs. "What's right is right."

"Mrs. Przybyszewski," Detective Momoa says, "you should know that I have been listening to your daughter."

My head snaps in his direction.

He keeps his gaze on my mother. Maybe he can't bear to look at me as he says these words. "When she came to me yesterday with information about these two men, I dispatched investigators to look into it."

I almost fall out of my chair.

"They confirmed what she told me." His eyes move to mine. "I must commend her for her fine work, and apologize for not making immediately clear that I intended to pursue the lead she gave me. Not to mention that I heartily applaud her efforts last night, which were truly remarkable."

Oh God, I'm tearing up.

CHAPTER THIRTY-NINE

"Look what you did now!" My mother's out of her chair, hurling accusations at Detective Momoa while digging frantically in her purse for a Kleenex.

I'm sniffling and waving my hand rapidly in front of my face, as if somehow that will prevent me from bursting into tears. "I'm okay," I keep repeating. "I'm okay."

Finally I am. Until I think about why Momoa's praise means so much to me. He's not praising me for being pretty. He's praising me for being smart. Why can't my father ever do that? That age-old question makes me choke up all over again.

Momoa, like many men, seems confounded by female tears. He remains seated, looking terribly uncomfortable, during my prolonged fit. Finally I recover, for good this time, and he clears his throat. "We all understand that it's been a very stressful time for you, Ms. Pennington."

"You can say that again."

"Perhaps the best course of action would be for you to relax today." He gestures to my mom. "You and your mother could do some souvenir shopping, relax at the beach, maybe indulge yourselves and go to the Halekulani for lunch."

My mother is nodding emphatically. Until I hear myself say, "Detective, what I would really like to do is talk to Rex Rexford." I didn't come here with that goal in mind, but now that it's come out of me, it seems a tremendously obvious next step.

"What?" My mother nearly drops her coffee. "The killer? I should say not!"

Momoa frowns. "And what would you hope to achieve in that conversation?"

"You would allow it?" my mother shrieks. "Over my dead body!"

"Mom, please." I look at Momoa. "He ended up being pretty forthcoming with me last night. We have a lot of history together in the pageant world. He knew me as a competitor fifteen years ago. I think he might tell me something he wouldn't tell one of your investigators."

"I gather you're hoping you could persuade Rexford to implicate Postagino. I consider that outcome highly unlikely."

"Probably so, but I'd still like to try. What do we have to lose? And I have an idea how I might go about it."

I can tell from Momoa's expression that he's considering it. So can my mother.

"Are you insane?" she asks him. My mother is not cowed by a badge, as maybe you can tell. "My daughter has had enough of killers, enough to last her three lifetimes."

"Mom, I wouldn't be alone in a dark alley with the guy." Like I was last night, but she doesn't know that. "There'd be absolutely zero danger to me. He's in jail.

There would be an armed guard right outside the door. And he's probably in manacles, too, right, Detective?" I shoot Momoa a pleading look.

"He may well be," Momoa says. He keeps his eyes on my face. "I will allow this on one condition, Ms. Pennington."

My mother emits a snort of disgust.

"What's that?" I ask.

"That you refrain from any further investigating on your own. I applaud you for what you have achieved so far but this is a dangerous matter. I do not want you confronting Mr. Postagino. I do not want you approaching him in any way. None of us wants a repeat of last night."

My mother scowls at me. "What happened last night?"

"I agree," I tell Momoa. I look at my mother. "Mom, do you want me to get you a cab to take you back to the Lotus Blossom? Or is there somewhere else you'd like to spend a few hours?"

"There are some shops that my wife enjoys in this neighborhood," Momoa suggests. "Perhaps—"

She rises. "I can entertain myself perfectly well with no help from you," she informs him. Then she focuses on me. "I never thought you'd take after your father like this." She shakes her head as if in deep regret. "All this fascination with sickos."

"Oh, mom." I stand up and hug her. "I take after you, too. Remember what got me here. My fascination with beauty pageants. And that's been true all my life." That's a bit of a fib. The fascination was hers; the desire to please, mine. But it all worked out in the end.

She waves her hand dismissively and stomps out the door.

Momoa pipes up. "Do I take it that your father has an interest in criminal matters?"

"He's a cop. Like you." Sort of like Momoa. My father wishes he'd done Homicide. But he never made it to that level. He retired pretty frustrated about that.

"Very interesting." Momoa taps his pen on his desk. "So you're a chip off the old block."

I rise. "May I go see Rex now?"

Momoa makes it happen. He's like my new best friend.

Rex Rexford doesn't look like himself in his bright orange jail jumpsuit, though I suppose neither its cut nor color—not to mention its symbolism—is flattering to anyone. He shuffles into the windowless jailhouse meeting room Momoa made available. He looks like a defeated man. His skin is mottled and puffy and his hair is flat and pressed up against his head on one side, as if he rose from his cot just moments before. My mother would be screaming bloody murder because he's not constrained by manacles or handcuffs or anything. At this point, though, I find him about as threatening as a kitten.

He slumps into a chair. A desk separates us. He doesn't meet my eyes.

"How are you doing?" I ask him.

"Not great."

It's hard to respond to that. I can't exactly reassure him that things will get better. It's all so dire and grim in here it's almost impossible to believe cheerful Hawaiian life is going on just outside these walls.

He pipes up again. "They're not respecting my rights."

"Why do you say that?"

"They haven't let me make a phone call."

I wonder if that's because Momoa doesn't want Rex to call Postagino, who'd thereby be alerted that his lover was arrested. That might alter his behavior. "I don't really know how it works. I'm sure they'll let you make a call soon."

"It's my right."

I can't believe Momoa would risk doing anything that's not exactly by the book. "You'll probably find this hard to believe, under the circumstances. But you and I have known each other a long time, Rex, and I do care about you. I have your best interests at heart."

He meets my gaze. "I've always thought you were a nice girl, Happy. Not like certain beauty queens who shall remain nameless."

I nod.

"I also know what I did was wrong. I'm not one of those people who thinks it was justified or anything. I'm not deranged," he adds, with some vigor.

"I never thought you were."

"None of this means I'm not going to fight these charges tooth and nail. I will."

"That's your right, too. Absolutely."

"Whatever I did, I did for love." He juts his chin. I watch his eyes fill with tears. "Maybe in a court of law that counts for something."

I take a deep breath. To steel myself, I suppose. I hope on some cosmic moral level what I'm about to do can be justified. "Rex, I believe you when you say you acted out of love. I totally do. And that's why I'm here. Because I'm concerned you're doing the same thing again."

His eyes grow wary. "What are you talking about?"

"You know I visited the Plumeria Bed and Breakfast, right? I went there yesterday. That's how I found out that you and Tony Postagino stayed there together."

"Okay."

"Well, when I was there, I found out that Tony Postagino stayed there more than once." *Liar, liar, house on fire.*

"You mean—" Rex frowns. "What do you mean?"

"He stayed there another time." I say it with as much portent as I can manage.

"You mean ... alone?"

I sigh. "Rex, I don't think he stayed there alone."

"With Tiffany, then."

"Not with Tiffany." I shake my head. "No."

"Goddammit!" He slaps the table and looks away. "I bet he went with that dog, Robert. That so-called real estate broker." I watch emotions, one after the next, cross his lined face. Anger. Shock. Hurt.

As for me, at the same time that I'm applauding my instinct that Tony Postagino might well be a player, I'm an emotional basketcase, too. Am I wrong to tarnish Rex's love affair with information that is a total fabrication on my part? Information he'll believe because it comes from me, whom he trusts? I was careful to remind him of our years of acquaintance, because those are the basis of that trust.

I'm not even sure I'm right that Tony Postagino was involved in Tiffany's murder. But if it turns out he was, I don't want Rex to be the only one paying the price. That doesn't square with my notion of justice.

And less noble than that, I wonder how much of me just wants to be the Super Duper Number One investigator. I don't uncover just one killer. No, Happy Pennington nabs two!

Well, the truth is, if there are two, I do want to nab both.

"Rex," I say gently. "Are you sure, totally, absolutely sure that you're the only one who should be facing the music here?"

He hangs his head.

"I mean, you're in here. He's out there. Living his life."

Rex remains silent. Then, "I want him to live his life." The words choke on a sob. "If I can't, at least he can."

"But is that fair? To you?"

Rex looks at me. A tear streams down his cheek. "Tell me what's fair. What's fair for his daughters? They're such little girls, such adorable little girls. They've lost their mother. Because of me. How can I take their father away from them, too?"

"It's not you taking their father away. It's their father taking himself away. Because of things he never should have done." I can tell I'm making Rex think. "If he did the same wrong things you did, Rex, he should not allow you to take all the blame. That's not fair to you. You're very concerned about how fair you're being to him. How about how fair he's being to you?"

He shakes his head. "I can't help you get him."

Much as I cajole, plead, and beg, Rex refuses to say another word.

CHAPTER FORTY

I have this thing about beating my head against a wall. I don't like it. So eventually, I leave Rex Rexford to his own devices.

It's no fun admitting defeat to Momoa.

"You did your best," he tells me. He's all warm and fuzzy with me now. It's kind of amazing.

It's when I'm back at the Royal Hibiscus scanning the overpriced gum at the sundries shop when who do I see purchasing a six-pack of chilled Longboard Island Lager but Tony Postagino. It's clear from his trunks, T shirt, and sunburned nose that he's just come from a long basking session at the beach or pool. He looks way too relaxed and happy for my taste.

I force myself not to stare at him as he completes his transaction but I let my gaze trail him as he departs the shop. He's just exited when I watch him cock his head at another man who's lounging against the wall across the lobby, wearing a similar trunks and tee shirt get-up. He's blond, like Rex, and about Rex's age, and looks like he's spent the better part of the day outside, too. The man waits ten seconds or so, then looks around him and follows Postagino to the elevator bank. Postagino's already gone up.

No, this isn't proof of anything. But it prompts me

to call Momoa, who gets Rex on the jailhouse phone to talk to me. I relate what I just witnessed. And I add, "Look, I know you said you want Tony to live his life. But is this really what you meant?"

He says nothing for a long while. Then, "Maybe you've got a point."

"You know I do. Now tell me. Was he involved in Tiffany's murder?"

He hesitates for a few seconds but then it all comes spilling out. "Yes and no. He came up with the plan. And he got the cyanide. But I'm the one who actually did it. And he had nothing to do with that breakfast drink of yours. That was all me. And I'm so sorry. I can never apologize enough for that."

"That's okay." I can't believe I'm saying that. "I survived and Dirk survived and I'll have a heck of a story to tell my grandchildren."

He sniffles but says nothing. I may be crazy but I get the sense that on some level he feels better.

"Rex," I go on, "make up for what you did to me by helping me out now. Please. I have an idea but I need your help."

CHAPTER FORTY-ONE

"Okay," Shanelle says. "You got to run this whole thing past me one more time."

"I need to hear it again, too," Trixie says.

My mother is silent. But you could see the confusion in her eyes from Molokai.

We're in the room Shanelle and I share. Trixie is splayed on the floor by my bed, my mom is in the desk chair, Shanelle is perched on her bed, and I'm standing in front of the French doors that open to the balcony. The room still smells of papaya shrimp and chicken satay because we just finished the room-service lunch I popped for. I insisted that no one order a tiki tiki drink, not to save money but because we all need clear heads. People with nothing on their minds but fun are nine floors below frolicking in the pool. It's a little irritating that we can hear them so clearly, but oh well. When we finish our assignment, and only when we finish it, may we join them.

"What we're going to do," I say, "is write an email to Tony Postagino as if it were coming from Rex Rexford."

"And we have to write it in code," Shanelle says.

"Yes. Rex explained the code to me this morning." I pace as if I were on the stage of a lecture hall.

"Obviously, since he and Postagino were planning a murder, they couldn't communicate with one another in straightforward language because that would leave a trail of evidence. So they devised a code."

Trixie shakes her head. She appears awestruck. "I never would have thought Rex had such a big brain. So big that he could write in code."

"Well, it's not a very complicated code," I say, "which is good for us."

"Didn't the cops find it suspicious that they were in touch at all?" Shanelle asks. "I mean, I had a pageant consultant in the past and Lamar barely knew his name."

"But it is plausible," I say, "that a contestant's husband and a consultant would know one another, and strategize together. Some husbands get very involved in their wives' pageant careers."

"Like Colleen Novotny's husband," Trixie offers.

"That one from Vermont?" Shanelle asks. "You're right. Her husband's always butting into her business."

"Anyway," I say, "Rex and Postagino were careful to establish a pattern of email traffic between them long before Tiffany came to Oahu. They traded emails about all sorts of Ms. America-related business. And they created an email account for Tiffany so that it would look like she was involved in the communication, too."

"Because it would seem extremely weird if she weren't," Trixie points out.

"Exactly," I say. "They cc'ed her and they wrote responses as if they were her. But she never even knew that account existed."

"Slimeballs," Shanelle says, as if that were the worst

thing they did.

"Perverts," my mother adds.

"Moving right along. They had a system for signaling whether an email was a normal communication or in code."

"That's where the commas and dashes come in," my mother says.

"Precisely." I am glad my mom is taking this seriously. She groused at first, but once she saw Shanelle and Trixie were enthusiastic, she got into it. Anything that has to do with beauty queens—she's in. "For a normal communication, in the greeting line they'd type the person's name and follow it with a comma. Tony, comma. Rex, comma. But if it were in code—"

"They'd follow the name with a dash!" Trixie yelps.

"Yes. And to understand the coded message, they would read only the first letter of each word." I hold up a sheet of the nightstand memo paper. "Here's an example I came up with so everybody would understand. On the surface it reads: *Try helping each contestant out. Perhaps she'll* ... blah blah blah. But what," I ask my three charges, "is the coded message?"

I watch them all squint at the words and move their lips.

Shanelle gets it first. "The cops!" she shouts.

"Correct, Ms. Walker. So our mission—"

"If we choose to accept it—" Trixie interrupts, and giggles.

"—is to craft a coded message to Tony Postagino in the hope that he will respond in such a way that he incriminates himself. If that happens, Momoa will have a basis for arresting him."

"Because at this point in time, Momoa's got nothin'," Shanelle says.

"Exactly right."

"It doesn't count," Trixie says, "that Rex told you Tiffany's husband was as involved as he was?"

"That wouldn't hold up in a court of law. It's hearsay."

Trixie's eyes widen. "You sound like a lawyer, Happy."

I have no ambition in that direction. But this investigating thing, at least when it works, and when you're not about to get killed, is fun.

"And tell us again," Shanelle says, "what Momoa's agreed to do?"

"He has agreed that his guys from the police department will send the email to Postagino so that it looks like it came from Rex's email account."

"That's called spoofing," Shanelle says.

"He also agreed that, for the time being, Oahu PD will not make public two pieces of information. That Rex Rexford was arrested for Tiffany Amber's murder—"

"Or for the attempt on you," Trixie says, then she winces. "Sorry, Mrs. P. I know you hate when anybody brings that up."

My mother does assume a sickly expression when that matter is raised, it's true. "And," I continue, "they will not release any information about why Sebastian Cantwell is being held."

"Because," Trixie says, "everybody thinks it's because he's the murderer."

"Which is crucial to our plan. Because we want Tony Postagino, in particular, to think he and Rex are off the hook."

"We know better, though," Shanelle says. "In particular, *you* know better, when it comes to Sebastian Cantwell. Am I right, Ms. Pennington?"

"I am not at liberty to say," I respond primly.

"She's on the inside now," Trixie declares.

Of course, Trixie and Shanelle and my mom think that my source for Sebastian Cantwell information is Detective Momoa. Only I know it's Mario Suave. Because, I think with some gratification, only *I* know *his* secret.

"Okay, ladies." I begin handing out sheets of memo paper. "These are the four coded messages."

My mother frowns at hers. " *'I'm worried the cops are onto us,'* this says."

" *'We had a bad plan,'* " says Trixie.

I made sure to give myself a long one. I read it aloud. " *'I should have known we'd never get away with killing Tiffany.'* "

"Yours is too long for me, girl," Shanelle says, then reads hers aloud. " *'Now I'm sick to death we'll both get caught.'* "

"Yours is bad enough," Trixie informs Shanelle.

Shanelle lets fly an exaggerated sigh, then flops onto her stomach on the bed. "Girls, prepare yourselves. We gonna be here allllllllll night."

Actually, we're sprung by the cocktail hour. I proudly call our coded message in to Momoa.

Now we sit and wait.

303

CHAPTER FORTY-TWO

Hours later, Shanelle and I are both asleep when the phone in our room rings.

She sputters awake. I bolt upright in bed. "I'll get it," I tell her. The red numbers on the digital clock read 2:06. "Hello?" I say.

"Ms. Pennington."

"Detective Momoa." I told Momoa to call anytime so I've been expecting this call. Or should I say, hoping for it. If it is what I think it is.

"About an hour ago we received an email response from Tony Postagino," he tells me.

I know what he means. 'Rex Rexford' received an email response. I cross my fingers in the air. "Did he bite?"

"In coded language Postagino wrote: '*Don't worry. Haven't you heard? Cantwell's been arrested. We're in the clear now.*'"

I don't think I've ever heard sweeter words in my life. "Will that do it, Detective? Is that enough to get Postagino arrested for his wife's murder?"

"He's in custody now. Investigators in California will be helping us out from that end."

I give Shanelle a thumbs-up and she raises her arm in a silent cheer.

"So what does all this mean, Detective?" My voice is teasing. "Now that you've brought in the real fish, am I off the hook?"

"That is correct, Ms. Pennington," Momoa says.

Other people might say he sounds exactly like normal. But I can tell he's smiling.

CHAPTER FORTY-THREE

I am such a ham. I do so love being the center of attention.

When I hear my name called, and it's my moment to enter the Royal Hibiscus banquet hall where my fellow Ms. America contenders and their husbands and children are sitting at long tables, I get such a kick out of the raucous applause that rises to the beamed ceiling above. I wave gleefully, my grin stretching my mouth so wide I think my lips might split from the effort.

"Thank you!" I cry. "Thank you so much!"

Flashbulbs blind my eyes, not to mention the lights on the TV cameras just inches in front of my face. Cameramen are falling all over each other trying to get their shots but not get in my way—heaven forbid!—as I stride to the front of the hall. In short order I'll be taking the place of honor at the front and center of the table elevated on the dais.

Beneath my Ms. America sash I'm wearing a sleeveless black and white dress, very fitted and chic, black Gucci pumps with bamboo detail on the sky-high heels, and a stunning turquoise necklace. Shanelle, Trixie, and my mom helped me pick everything out this morning. For once I let loose and spent a fortune. Now all three are enjoying the benefits of nepotism and are seated at the table of honor, too, along with Jason and Mario Suave and my runner-up Sherry Philips and the outgoing Ms. America and the vice chairman of the Board of Directors of the pageant, who just flew in.

I arrive at the front and take hold of the microphone the vice chairman passes to me. He's already addressed the crowd, explaining what's up with Sebastian Cantwell and that he'll be running the organization until Mr. Cantwell can resume his duties, yada yada. From the corridor outside, I heard him put the best possible spin on the pageant owner's alleged felonies. None of us knows how bad this really is for Cantwell. All we know is that he's about to be released on some giant amount of bail.

The applause lessens in intensity. That's my cue. "Mr. Vice Chairman, Mario Suave," I nod in their direction, "my fellow contestants, ladies and gentlemen, thank you so much. I am tremendously honored."

The applause crescendos again. I bow my head, wait a beat, and go on. "I don't need to tell any of you that the Ms. America pageant has suffered terrible shocks over the last week. But I am confident that with the organization's steady and committed leadership, the pageant will emerge stronger than ever from these challenging times."

I pause. More clapping. I glance at the vice chairman, who's portly, red-faced, and beaming. I figure the more he likes me, the faster I get my prize money.

"We will never forget our fellow contender, Ms. Tiffany Amber of Riverside, California." Applause again, more tepid this time. "We offer our thoughts and our prayers to her two young daughters, her parents, and her sister."

You'll note I omitted a notable family member from that roster.

"I am very proud of the role I was able to play in assisting the Oahu police in their investigation." Boy, am I being humble. "I hope the criminal case finds a swift resolution and justice is served."

Hearty applause that time, and Mario lets rip a *hear, hear!*

"I look forward with great anticipation to my year of service, and to seeing many of you as I travel this great country of ours promoting Ms. America and all the wonderful causes it supports. And, don't forget, be sure to set your DVRs to eight PM on Tuesday, September 23rd, to catch the first episode of the new season of *America's Scariest Ghost Stories*, hosted by our own Mario Suave!"

Mario rises, waves at the crowd, blows me a kiss, and sits back down. Jason, who's next to him, gives him a weak smile. I think he could have done without the blown kiss.

"I know we all have planes to catch this afternoon, so let's enjoy this terrific lunch prepared by the fabulous staff here at the Royal Hibiscus, which has been our home away from home these last several weeks. Safe travels, everyone, and see you all soon!"

Now I clap, too, in acknowledgment of the servers moving swiftly among us bearing plates of food. I turn off the mike, hand it to the vice chairman, chat with him a bit, give Jason a kiss, sit down, and am about to catch my breath when my mother leans into me.

"Do you know what that husband of yours is up to?"

"Mom, keep your voice down."

"Moving to another state to go to NASCAR school. Yes!" She slaps the table. Her silverware rattles.

From down the table, I see Jason and Mario both glancing our way. "Sshhh."

"He can't wait to spend your prize money!" she hisses.

"For your information, mom," I whisper, "I encouraged him to go to pit school. In fact, I practically pushed him into it."

She harrumphs. "Well, let him go, that's all I have to say."

Trixie pats my mother's arm, doing her best to quiet the woman down.

I smile at Jason, who's clearly trying to figure out the cause of the ruckus at my end of the table. He and I had a good chat this morning, before the shopping expedition, and things are more normal between us. It's ironic that I pushed him into pit school, all in the name of "betterment," because it's coming home to me now just how much I'm going to miss him.

Shanelle pipes up. "You did good, girl. And I don't just mean in the crime-solving department. You been the best roommate a beauty queen could ever have. I don't know how I'm going to sleep tonight without you there."

"Oh God, no." The tears are coming. Not a good time. I start waving my hand rapidly in front of my face.

"Oh Lord, me, too," Shanelle says.

Trixie sees us and her eyes fill. "I'm going to miss you both so much!"

"Stop!" I say. "Just stop." We all manage to control ourselves, with some effort. The waterworks threaten to resume, though, when I again open my mouth. "I hope you both know that I could never have done my investigating without you."

"I was happy to help," Shanelle says.

"I didn't do much," Trixie demurs.

"Yes, you did. You both did. And we're just going to have to make a vow to see each other at least once a year, regardless how much plane tickets cost."

"I can't wait a year!" Trixie yelps. "Maybe I'll come see you sometimes when you're traveling for Ms. America. Like if you're in the south or something."

"That's not a bad idea," Shanelle agrees.

A server sets a plate of food down in front of me. Grilled mahi mahi with some sort of delicious-looking salsa, exotic vegetables, cous cous with pine nuts...

Shanelle peers down at her identical plate. "You're not all I'm gonna miss, girl. How am I ever gonna get used to my own food again?"

We all dig in. A few minutes later I look around the banquet hall. "You know who I don't see here? Misty Delgado."

"Oh—" Shanelle jabs her fork in the air. "She's gone. I saw her check out this morning, her and her husband. She was loaded down but he wouldn't carry a single one of her bags. Did you hear Ventura's supposed to get out of the hospital this afternoon?"

"I did hear that," I say. From Momoa, who seems

relieved I don't intend to hog the crime-solving spotlight. "But apparently he won't be able to fly for several days at least, until all the poison's worked its way out of his system."

Magnolia, decked out in a supertight hot pink sundress that matches the eye shadow she's plastered on her lids, approaches the dais. "So you're flying back home this afternoon, right?" she says to me.

"Yes."

"Since my last check from Cantwell cleared, I decided to start working again. So you're gonna get an email from me."

"Okay. Glad to hear you're back on the job." I think.

"It's about scheduling your appearances."

"Ooh, that's exciting!" Trixie claps her hands. "You're going to be in such demand, Happy. You're a total celebrity now because of this whole murder-solving thing. A beauty queen and a sleuth to boot! She's getting tons of requests, right, Magnolia?"

Magnolia looks away. "Maybe."

"That's a yes," Shanelle mutters.

"Oh, and I'm supposed to give you this." Magnolia hands me an envelope and waddles away.

"What is it?" my mother wants to know.

Maybe it's my prize money! But no. I pull a handwritten letter out of a heavily-scented envelope. "It's from Sally Anne Gibbons." It turns out Sally Anne has a beautiful hand and a nice way with the written word. Who would've thunk it?

"What does she say?" Trixie asks.

I return the letter to the envelope. "She had to fly out this morning but she wanted to thank me for helping to clear her name. You know, over the gown-registry snafu?"

I asked Detective Momoa if one of his minions would write a blurb to post on the Crowning Glory web site, with the official Oahu PD seal, noting that a "third party," who would remain nameless, was responsible for inputting incorrect data into her registry. It makes clear that no blame should be assigned to Sally Anne or to her shop, so pageant contenders should have every confidence about making their purchases there.

"Sally Anne asks if I'll put my picture and an endorsement on her site, too," I say. "I'm happy to do that." Maybe I'll shop at Crowning Glory for pageant wear for Ms. World. Now that I've won Ms. America, I'll compete, representing the US of A. How exciting is that!

The luncheon winds to a close. People empty the banquet hall, eager now to catch their flights home. I have only the tiniest goodbye moment with Mario, what with him sitting next to the vice chairman. Probably that's best.

While my mom is in the ladies room and Jason snaps a few last pictures, I amble to the lobby lounge, filling now with travelers who are just arriving on the island. They're suntan-free and boasting fresh leis around their necks. I watch Keola wander in from the beach, wearing his loincloth and floral wreath. Unaware of me, he stands barefoot in the corner assessing the newcomers. I watch his eyes alight on a pair of attractive young women who appear to have traveled to Oahu on their own.

Good luck, ladies.

Cordelia squawks once in my direction. I look at her and swear she's staring straight at me. Maybe she senses I'm going and is giving me a macaw goodbye.

It's nice to hear. But I much prefer hello.

Diana loves to hear from readers! E-mail her at **www.DianaDempsey.com** *and sign up for her mailing list while you're there to hear first about her new releases. Also join her on* **Facebook** *at* **DianaDempseyBooks** *and follow her on* **Twitter** *at* **Diana_Dempsey**.

Diana Dempsey traded in an Emmy-winning career in TV news to write fast, fun romantic fiction. Her debut novel, *Falling Star*, was nominated for a RITA award for Best First Book by the members of Romance Writers of America. Other of her novels have been Top Picks of *Romantic Times* or selections of the Doubleday Book Club.

In her dozen years in TV news, the former Diana Koricke played every on-air role from network correspondent to local news anchor. She reported for NBC News from New York, Tokyo, and Burbank, and substitute anchored such broadcasts as *Sunrise*, *Today*, and *NBC Nightly News*. In addition, she was a morning anchor for KTTV Fox 11 News in Los Angeles. She began her broadcast career with the Financial News Network.

Born and raised in Buffalo, New York—Go, Bills!— Diana is a graduate of Harvard University and the winner of a Rotary International Foundation Scholarship.

She enjoyed stints overseas in Belgium, the U.K., and Japan, and now resides in Los Angeles with her husband and a West Highland White Terrier, not necessarily in that order.

Diana loves to hear from readers! Visit her website at **www.DianaDempsey.com** and while you're there sign up to her mailing list to receive her newsletter. Join her on **Facebook** at **Diana Dempsey Books**, and follow her on **Twitter** at **Diana_Dempsey**.

MS AMERICA
AND THE
VILLAINY IN VEGAS

(Beauty Queen Mysteries, No. 2)

Beauty queen and budding sleuth Happy Pennington returns, this time to gaudy, garish Las Vegas ...

When Happy pulls bridesmaid duty for pageant-wear purveyor Sally Anne Gibbons, the last thing she expects to find at the altar is a corpse. But at these over-the-top nuptials that's what she gets: a dead best man and a groom who just might be the killer.

Sometimes it seems everybody in Sin City has a secret, from the cocktail waitress trying to land a reality-show gig to the silver-haired cougar with a penchant for blackjack dealers. Maybe hunky pageant emcee Mario Suave is hiding something, too: like the hots for everybody's favorite beauty queen ...

Chapter One

Never in my life have I seen a bridesmaid dressed as a showgirl. Until I turn and look at myself in the mirror.

"Sally Anne Gibbons." I tug my rhinestone-encrusted push-up bra a tad higher. "I cannot believe you're making us wear this to your wedding."

"This is Vegas, baby." Sally Anne lifts her double chin and glowers at me. "Roll with it."

My fellow bridesmaid Shanelle is attempting to pry her thong out of the nether regions into which it has largely disappeared. "I haven't flashed this much skin since I gave birth. Are you sure you don't want, I don't know, a classier look?"

"It's a little late for that now, don't you think? I'm getting hitched in fifteen minutes." Sally Anne's inch-long red fingernails flip a coppery curl behind her ear. "Besides, if I wanted classy, would I be getting married on the Strip?"

Shanelle and I glance at one another. Perhaps a more rhetorical question has never been posed.

"What's your problem, anyhow?" Sally Anne smooths her sequin-studded sateen. "You two prance around onstage wearing nothing more than a few inches of Lycra."

True. That's what beauty queens do. "But that's in the name of pageant competition," I remind her.

"This is in the name of wedded bliss," Sally Anne

shoots back. "Which I am due for, big time."

As for myself, I've enjoyed wedded bliss for seventeen years now, half my life. Safe to say I married young. But I can understand what Sally Anne's driving at.

"I'm fifty-four years old!" By now she's shouting. "I'm a bride for the very first time!" She throws her arms wide. "I want a big fat shindig that nobody will ever forget!"

Shanelle straps on a spangled choker and hands me its evil twin. "Well, if you have to wait that long, I guess you can do whatever the hell you please."

"You got that right, sister. Now let's get this show on the road. I don't want to give Frank time to think twice." Sally Anne points across the bridal dressing lounge at two rather frothy items calling our names. "Put on your headdresses and let's skedaddle."

Flowers in the hair? Lovely. A small veil? A nice touch. But Shanelle and I are called upon to sport two feet of ostrich plumes atop a spangled crown.

Shanelle sidles closer. "How many ostriches gave their lives for these things?"

"Whole flocks of them." I settle it on my head. "It doesn't sit nearly as well as my tiara."

Yes, I am the proud owner of a tiara. From when I, Happy Pennington, representing the Great State of Ohio, won the title of Ms. America in the nation's foremost beauty pageant for married women. I've just begun my reign and so far it's everything I ever dreamed it would be. I didn't win in quite the usual way but we don't have time to get into that now.

Shanelle Walker, otherwise known as Ms. Mississippi, roomed with me on Oahu during the pageant. Now she's one of my best friends.

Sally Anne, not so much. Because she's the founder of Crowning Glory Pageant Shoppe here in Las Vegas, the largest full-service pageant-wear purveyor west of the Mississippi, I've known her for years. And once you help somebody dodge a murder rap—another aspect of the long story to which I referred earlier—I guess they feel closer to you than they did before.

By the way, she asked me to stand up for her just last week, which is why Shanelle and I are only now getting wind of what we're required to wear. Sally Anne knew our sizes from Crowning Glory's database, not that those are so hard to guess for our ilk. Shanelle and I may illustrate that we beauty queens come in a variety of colors—me a pale-skinned brunette and Shanelle more a darkish toffee—but take any two of us and you'll find that we're pretty much all the same size: skinny and tall.

"One more thing," Sally Anne says behind me. I turn to see her holding out two, shall we say, *unique* bouquets.

"Are those … spray painted, Sally Anne?"

"You bet they are. I got the brainstorm to spray gold metallic paint on white roses. You've never seen anything like 'em, I bet."

It is safe to say that I have not.

Shanelle and I do one last check in the mirror as Sally Anne sashays out of the room. We are also sporting white gloves that extend above the elbow and are ornamented by rhinestone bracelets. "Is nothing real here?" Shanelle mutters.

"Let's hope this romance is real," I whisper back. "I get the impression Sally Anne didn't know Frank very long before he popped the question." And given what she told us, she probably said yes before Frank got all four words of the proposal out of his mouth.

Shanelle straightens her choker. "Too bad you didn't bulldoze Sally Anne into letting Trixie be a bridesmaid, too."

"I should have." Trixie Barnett is our other best friend from the pageant. She's from North Carolina and is the reigning Ms. Congeniality. "I miss her."

"I do, too." Shanelle heaves a sigh. "We can't keep putting it off, girl. We best get out there."

"I suppose so." I feel unbelievably naked. As the foremost representative of the Ms. America pageant, I am called upon to maintain a dignified appearance at all times. That's no easy trick in this getup but how can I not hew to the bride's wishes? The last time I was a bridesmaid I had to wear yards of iridescent blue satin fashioned into huge poufs. At the time I thought it was hideous but now I miss all that fabric. "Do you think maybe Sally Anne forgot to hire a photographer?"

Apparently she hears me from the hallway. "Fat chance. In fact, the whole shebang is gonna be streamed live over the Web. There are hidden cameras all over the chapel."

"Fabulous." I hope none of the cameras zero in on my thong. I wish Sally Anne had popped for the fantail she reported having considered. I force myself to step outside the dressing room into a sort of holding area behind the chapel. We're not in a church, mind you. We're in the Cosmos Hotel, one of the big hotels on the Vegas Strip. And when I say big, do I mean big. Of course, everything in Vegas is humungous. They don't do anything on a modest scale here.

Shanelle is peering into the chapel through a door left partly open. I sidle next to her, righting my plumage as I walk. Apparently these ostrich feathers do not care to point heavenward even on approach to a chapel. "How many guests are there?"

"Seventy or so. Hey, I see your mom. It was nice of you to bring her to Vegas. How's she doing?"

"Only mediocre."

"Still bummed about the divorce?"

"It's not really that surprising. They were married almost fifty years. I asked Pop to come on this trip since he couldn't go to Oahu but he didn't want to." I don't say why. It bothers me, though since the divorce he has every right. "Jason would've come but he couldn't get off pit school this weekend," I add.

She chuckles. "Your husband, the NASCAR stud. When he finishes his training, he's gonna get hired on some pit crew, girl. I just feel it. You best prepare yourself."

"I know. I'm trying." I had to push Jason into pit school, even though he's wanted to go forever, but now that he's there he's really getting into it. I'm kind of taken aback by how much.

"And Rachel's a senior now, right? How goes the whole applying-to-college thing?"

"She's studying for the SATs. Which is why she's

not here this weekend." I don't mention that Rachel has proposed a course of action other than college next year. I cannot dwell on that possibility or I'll get too upset. Just so you know, I was Rachel's age when I got pregnant. I don't let myself think about that much, either, but when I do I understand my mom a whole lot better. "What's the latest with Lamar and Devon?"

We're just getting started on Shanelle's husband and son when Sally Anne appears behind us. "Follow me," she instructs.

We wend our way to the wide corridor outside the chapel's entrance. It's teeming with the usual Vegas horde, people on their way to or from the gigantic lobby-level casino, a midday show, a restaurant, or the Olympic-size pool beyond a glass panel. And before us, behind wide double doors, is the *Forever Yours* chapel, which according to its signage offers nuptial services of the quickie or planned variety.

That's not all that's in front of us.

Shanelle sets her hands on her hips. "Whoa! Is that a Rolls Royce or is that a Rolls Royce?"

I've never seen one like it. Convertible. Mirrored exterior. Hot pink leather interior. Uniformed chauffeur behind the wheel.

"Of course it's a Rolls." Sally Anne hoists herself atop the rear bench seat. "This is Vegas, baby!" she chortles.

"Why does she keep saying that?" I mutter to Shanelle. I attempt to follow Sally Anne into the Rolls but she leans forward and slaps my fishnet-stockinged leg.

"Are you crazy?" she demands. "You think I'm gonna make my entrance with you two in the car? Nobody'll give me so much as a glance! You walk behind."

"No way!" Shanelle says. "The bridesmaids always go first up the aisle."

"Not this time, sister. I want all eyes on me."

I gesture to Shanelle to retreat. It is Sally Anne's Big Day, after all.

We get into position behind the Rolls. A middle-aged woman in a pastel suit emerges from the chapel to huddle with Sally Anne. I'm guessing she's the wedding planner.

A few minutes later she gives Shanelle and me the high sign. Apparently all systems are go. The chapel's double doors swing slowly open.

By this point I wouldn't expect anything traditional out of this wedding, but to my amazement I hear the opening strains of Wagner's "Bridal Chorus" pipe from the music system. On a more unconventional note, pink smoke billows from a fog machine, providing rather a contrast with the dignity of the processional music. Of course, neither the Rolls nor the showgirl costumes are exactly elegant touches.

The Rolls moves forward. Shanelle and I follow clutching our sprayed rose bouquets. On both sides of the aisle guests stand and crane their necks in our direction. Ahead at the altar I spy the tuxedoed groom and best man.

Frank Richter, Sally Anne's intended, can best be described as burly. He's not the tallest of individuals, nor has he been gifted with a full head of hair. Most of what remains has faded from brown to gray. But I am happy to see that his eyes positively glow as they fix on his bride.

Frank's best man is his nephew Danny. He's good-looking in a bad-boy way. He sports stubble along his chiseled jaw line and clearly puts in the hours in the gym. He has kind of a cocky attitude, too, I can tell, even though he's just standing there.

"Are my eyes playing tricks," Shanelle whispers, "or does the best man have a black eye?"

"He does. That's weird."

Even stranger, though, is that by this point I am having trouble seeing what's ahead of me. The rose-colored smoke is doing a bang-up job of filling the chapel.

Beside me Shanelle coughs. "Dang, I hope my asthma doesn't act up."

"What's going on with this smoke?" a man bellows from the east forty.

Soon all I can see is the rear of the Rolls and Sally Anne's hulking outline up top. I note that Shanelle is no longer the only person coughing. As we creep up the aisle, I hear hacking from every quarter. An older woman stumbles past me making for the exit, her hand over her mouth. It's not my mom, though I can hardly imagine she's sitting still through this. Then I hear a few popping sounds.

"Now the damn Rolls is backfiring," I manage to spit out. I'm close to wheezing. Poor Sally Anne. She may have a hard edge but I want her to be happy. I don't think that'll be the case if her wedding guests get asphyxiated. I clutch Shanelle's arm. "Is it just me or are you feeling dizzy, too?"

"I'm way past dizzy," Shanelle gasps. "I can barely get air in my lungs. I can't take much more of this."

"Then get out, Shanelle. If you can't breathe, get out."

She needs no more encouragement to bolt. And she has lots of company. This chapel is emptying faster than a beach after a shark sighting.

I'm trying to decide whether I, as an official personage in this event, should take action to prevent Sally Anne's wedding guests from suffocating when the bride herself rears up from the Rolls.

"Stop the music!" she yowls. "And stop the goddamn fog machine!"

Good!—I think. Sally Anne's taking charge. I'm surprised Frank isn't.

I toss aside my bouquet and help Sally Anne eject herself from the Rolls, no easy task given her heft, her bridal gown's voluminous sateen, and the fact that neither one of us can see more than two inches in front of her face.

But lack of visibility doesn't prevent Sally Anne from stomping up the aisle once she's cleared the vehicle. "Where the hell is my wedding consultant?" she hollers. "And what's she using for brains? We could all choke to death in here!"

I watch Frank emerge from the fog, waving his arms in front of him as if he's cutting a swath through the stuff. He tries to calm Sally Anne by taking hold of her arms but she'll have none of it.

"I was promised perfection and this sure as shootin' isn't it!" Sally Anne pushes past Frank to go further up the aisle. I'm right behind her. I am her bridesmaid after all, and my duty is to serve.

I would say that the main goal has been achieved. Someone did turn off the fog machine and the air is starting to clear. I can—sort of—see again.

Sally Anne is about to accost the reverend when she trips over something on the carpet. I squint a few seconds and then realize that a man—in fact, the *best* man—is sprawled there, face down.

"Just what I need!" Sally Anne yells down at him. "What did you do last night, Danny, go on a bender?"

"Sally Anne!" I grab her arm to pull her back. "Maybe he fainted because he couldn't breathe."

I kneel down and gently roll Danny over. It rapidly becomes clear that he may not be breathing but it's not because he fainted. The bloodstain blooming on his chest is my first clue that it wasn't pink smoke that did in Danny Richter.

Made in the USA
Las Vegas, NV
11 April 2023

70471104R00198